HARD ROAD

J. B. TURNER
HARD ROAD

THOMAS & MERCER

Text copyright © 2016 J. B. Turner
All rights reserved.

Published by Thomas & Mercer, Seattle

www.apub.com

Amazon, the Amazon logo, and Thomas & Mercer are trademarks of Amazon.com, Inc., or its affiliates.

ISBN-13: 9781503936560
ISBN-10: 1503936562

Cover design by Stuart Bache

Printed in the United States of America

For my late father

One

The call came from a man he knew only as Maddox.

Jon Reznick was sitting on his freezing deck as darkness fell over Maine, nursing a bottle of beer, staring out over the ocean. He let his cell phone ring a few times, knowing what lay ahead.

It had been ten long weeks. He pulled his jacket tight and watched his breath turn to vapor. He sighed long and hard before he picked up the phone.

"We got a delivery problem in Washington," Maddox said.

Down below in the cove, the Atlantic breakers crashed with a deafening roar, sending salt water into the winter air. The silhouettes of the tall oaks and maples shorn of their leaves—trees his late father had planted in the garden when he was a boy—bent and creaked in the wind. Away in the distance, out in Penobscot Bay, Reznick could see the lights of the lobster boats as they headed back to Rockland with the day's catch.

Maddox finally broke the silence. "They want to know if you can ensure the safe transfer of a consignment."

"When?"

"You must leave tonight."

Reznick said nothing.

"Is this inconvenient for you?"

"Kinda short notice."

"Are you available?"

"Tell me, how's the weather where you are?"

A long pause. "It's wet."

The word "wet" said it all.

"Someone must want this delivery real bad."

"Will you do it?"

Reznick was silent again.

"This has got to happen. This is an important customer."

He let out a long sigh. "Tell them I'm in."

"Smart move, Reznick. Pick up your tickets at the airport."

"Where am I going?"

"You'll see."

The line went dead.

Reznick's plane landed at Dulles just before midnight. He wore a black leather jacket, a gray T-shirt, dark blue Levi jeans, and scuffed cowboy boots. He slung his overnight bag over his shoulder and headed over to the Avis lot. There he picked up a black Chevy Camaro. In the trunk was an envelope with a fake credit card and two thousand dollars in cash alongside a reservation receipt for three nights at the Omni Shoreham Hotel in northwest Washington.

Reznick knew the city well. He headed onto the airport toll road and drove due east on Interstate 66, over the Roosevelt Bridge, then exited onto Constitution Avenue. The traffic was still heavy, despite the late hour. His mind flashed back to the time he first visited the city with his father. It had been the winter of 1982, the first of many trips to see the Vietnam Veterans Memorial. He remembered his father in the rental car, cursing the snarled-up traffic. But most of all he remembered what his father wore: a dark suit, white shirt, Marine Corps tie, and black shoes polished to a glassy shine. On every visit, without fail, his father had touched the names of the young men carved into the black granite wall the moment he arrived. Reznick would stand in silence, arms by his side, as his father fought back the tears.

The blaring siren of a fire truck in the distance snapped him out of his reverie as he drove over the historic Taft Bridge, past the imposing concrete lions guarding each side. He took a left onto Calvert Street, the hotel up ahead. He pulled up outside the traditional, eight-story building and tipped the valet ten dollars.

Reznick walked through the grand, sprawling lobby. Marble floor, ornate columns, chandeliers. A young man at the front desk took his details as he signed in under a false name: Ron Dixon.

"Three nights. Good to have you with us, Mr. Dixon. Do you mind me asking if you're in town for business or pleasure, sir?"

Reznick managed a smile. "A bit of both."

"Excellent. Can we help you with any bags?"

"No, you're OK, thanks."

His fake credit card was swiped and he took the elevator to the sixth floor.

Reznick used the keycard to open his door and flicked on the lights. He hung a "Do Not Disturb" sign outside before locking the room.

It was too warm, but it was spacious. A huge TV was on one wall, a welcome message on the screen. The decor was the "classic" look—green, floral-patterned carpet, and a king-size bed with a couple of rosewood dressers. The drapes matched the carpet.

Reznick peered out the window over the upscale Woodley Park neighborhood: a good base, well away from downtown. He turned down the climate control switch to "Cool," showered, and wrapped himself in a white terry bathrobe. Then he lay down on the bed and stared at the ceiling, waiting for the phone to ring.

———⌣———

The next morning, Reznick ordered a freshly squeezed orange juice and a black coffee from room service, before getting changed into his jogging gear—navy T-shirt and sweatpants with well-worn Nike running shoes. He walked over to Rock Creek Park under the flawless winter sky for his daily run. When he arrived at the water-powered Peirce Mill near the entrance, he did some stretching and warm-up moves, the temperature in the low thirties. A handful of runners were already pounding the snowy trails.

He switched on his iPod, blocking out the outside world, helping him focus on the task at hand. The thunderous riffs and beats of a Led Zeppelin song got his blood flowing. Reznick checked his watch: 8:48 a.m. precisely. He headed north on the Western Ridge Trail, a smell of pine trees in the mid-December air.

After about a mile, he passed a young woman sitting on the curb of a parking lot near Broad Branch Road. She grimaced as she rubbed her knee.

Reznick ran on by. No need to engage in unnecessary conversation with a stranger. Being anonymous was best. He knew the rules—the list was endless. Do not wear loud clothes, talk too much, appear distracted or lost; in fact anything that meant you were no longer blending in. Appearance is crucial: grays, navy tracksuits, and business suits are good; black shoes, also. But you have to fit in to the surrounding environment.

The way you speak, the way you carry yourself, your accent, dialect—they all give off signals. The moment a concierge thinks your luggage looks too flashy or too beaten-up, it all paints a picture. If you're in a top-end hotel, wear top-end clothes and carry smart cases.

The small things matter. Be attentive. Logos are easy to remember—better without them. The trick is to be anonymous. But don't try too hard. Don't shun eye contact. That in itself will attract attention. *What has he got to hide?*

The senses have to work overtime. And tactics have to be changed, depending on the circumstances. Move to another hotel, change into new clothes, ditch the car and get a different model.

He headed along Beach Drive as he ran through the park. Heart rate steady. Deeper and deeper into this verdant urban sanctuary in America's capital city.

Reznick's mind began to feel clearer. Slowly, he felt his senses sharpen as the sun flickered through the branches of the leafless trees. On and on he ran.

Up a hill and down a ravine, and back onto the main trail, passing a small stone police substation in the center of the park, two officers leaning against a cruiser, drinking coffee. He gave a polite nod and they nodded back.

Heart pumping harder as his head cleared. This was his routine ahead of every job and it passed the time. Kept him focused.

Up in the northern section of the park, he passed Rolling Meadow Bridge and doubled back along a trail by the public golf course. On past the amphitheater and across Bluff Bridge to where he'd started.

He checked his pulse. Only slightly raised.

Ten minutes later, Reznick was doing some cool-down stretching exercises against a park bench when the cell phone in his pocket vibrated. He switched off his iPod and saw the familiar caller ID.

"How you feeling today?" It was Maddox.

"I'm fine."

"So, any questions?"

Reznick wiped some sweat off his brow with the back of his hand. "You got a name?"

A beat. "All I know is that he's an American. OK?"

"On home soil? How come?"

A long pause. "Look, they wanted to keep it in-house. That's all I can say. This is a sensitive one."

"Tell me, where's the subject now?"

"Walking the National Mall with his son."

"What kind of monitoring?"

"Electronic. Far safer."

Reznick stayed quiet, knowing Maddox was right.

"How about we speak later today?"

"When?"

"I don't know. But stay close to your hotel."

Reznick shielded his eyes against the sun. "Why?"

"Why what?"

"Why stay close to the hotel?"

Maddox sighed. "Look, I've not had any confirmation, but I've heard from someone higher up the chain that we might have to move very quickly on this particular delivery."

"Timescale?"

"Sooner rather than later. Bear that in mind."

The rest of the morning dragged as Reznick waited for Maddox to call.

It could be a matter of hours. He dialed "12" and ordered a brunch of scrambled eggs, black coffee, buttered toast, and more freshly squeezed orange juice. After a warm shower, he channel hopped between CNN, Fox News, and the Weather Channel. Bombings across Kabul and Helmand province, as the Taliban launched a coordinated series of attacks to destabilize the Afghan government and instill fear in the population. He could see the way the wind was blowing there and it was all bad.

Early evening, he ordered a club sandwich and a Coke from room service. Afterward, he went for a walk, keeping within six blocks of the hotel. He returned to his room, lay down on the bed, and fell into a fitful sleep.

When he woke, he checked the time. It was 8:09 p.m., and still Maddox hadn't called. Had there been a delay? Perhaps a last-minute change of plan?

The thought of delays depressed him. He'd been asked to do a job; he wanted to get it over with. Then move on. He couldn't abide the drawn-out ones.

Feeling groggy, Reznick headed down to reception, bought a pair of swimming shorts, and swam forty lengths of the empty pool, leaving his phone on his towel on top of a lounger.

He headed back upstairs and changed into a fresh T-shirt and jeans. He paced the room, stopping occasionally to do push-ups and sit-ups, trying to keep sharp, not knowing when the call would come—if it would come at any moment.

Eventually, he slumped in the room's easy chair and turned on an old black-and-white Jimmy Cagney film with the sound down.

His cell phone vibrated in the chest pocket of his T-shirt.

"You're on the move." The voice of Maddox.

"Where?"

"Go to the Park America garage, one three zero one K Street Northwest, and leave your car on Level Two."

Reznick made a mental note.

"Proceed to Level Five, where you'll find a black BMW convertible. Your key fob can electronically open it. Proceed to the St. Regis hotel, and book in under the name Lionel Fairchild. New ID and documents are in the glove compartment, and a brown Louis Vuitton travel bag with overnight essentials is in the trunk."

"What's in the bag?"

"The usual kit. Laptop, delivery equipment—it's all there. After you check in, head straight to your room, which has already been allocated, and await final instructions."

Reznick did exactly as he was told.

First, he checked out of the Omni, taking time to thank them for such a pleasant stay but he was sorry, he had to cut short his visit for family reasons. He picked up his car from the valet and drove to the nearby parking garage as instructed. He left the vehicle on Level 2 and climbed the stairs. A rather smart BMW with tinted windows was parked at the far end of Level 5. He popped open the trunk—the monogrammed men's travel bag was inside. He picked it up, got into the car, and clicked the fob to centrally lock the doors before he unzipped the bag.

Inside was a thirteen-inch metallic MacBook Pro, a specially modified cell phone, a pair of night-vision binoculars, a 9mm Beretta handgun and sufficient ammo to kill a small town, a high-tech fob that opened all cars and jammed any surveillance, a sleeping drug in a nasal spray, a military-issue Taser, a powerful muscle relaxant in a syringe disguised as a ballpoint pen, and five thousand dollars in cash.

Reznick zipped up the bag and slid it under the passenger seat. Then he drove straight to the deluxe hotel in downtown Washington to await final instructions.

Two

The St. Regis on 16th Street was known as one of Washington's smartest hotels. Two blocks north of the White House, its impressive limestone facade was festooned with Christmas lights, only hinting at the grandeur inside.

Reznick pulled up shortly after 10 p.m. and handed his keys over to the valet, careful to take the Louis Vuitton bag.

A concierge opened the door and he strode into the lobby. It was like some Italian Renaissance dream—chandeliers hanging from coffered ceilings, gilt-framed paintings, oriental rugs on the marble floor, dark wood furniture.

Reznick handed over the new fake driver's license and credit card to a young woman behind the desk. "Good evening," she said. "Nice to have you at the St. Regis, sir." She brought up his details on the computer. "Is this your first time with us?"

"Yeah."

"Well, we hope you enjoy your stay." She handed over a swipe card as a smiling, uniformed bellhop approached. "This is Andy. You need anything, don't hesitate to ask."

Reznick smiled and was escorted to the sixth floor by Andy, tipping him twenty dollars. "I'll get it from here."

"Are you sure, sir?"

"Absolutely."

The bellhop gave a polite nod and headed back to the elevator. Reznick waited until the guy was out of sight before he carefully swiped the keycard. Inside, the large room was decidedly upscale. A king-size bed, large flat-screen TV, an antique-style writing desk, chair and sofa, and a minibar stuffed with Krug and Rolling Rock beer. Original artwork on the walls and chandeliers set the scene. The bathroom featured brass fittings and earth-toned mosaic tiles, a large mirror that doubled as a fifteen-inch "intelligent" TV, two marble sinks, and a fluffy white St. Regis bathrobe hanging behind the door.

The first thing he did after looking around was hang a "Do Not Disturb" sign outside his room and lock the door. Satisfied he wasn't going to be interrupted, he unzipped the Louis Vuitton bag and placed the pre-configured MacBook on the desk. He opened it, and within a matter of seconds it was up and running.

Reznick sat down, punched in his allotted password—*coldbracelet1*—and brought up his inbox. A soft beep, and there was one encrypted message with an attachment.

He clicked on "Decrypt Message" to view the file and was prompted to confirm two unique passwords. He keyed in *OfwaihhbTn,* initials from the first line of the Lord's Prayer, followed by *DNalKcOr,* his hometown spelled backward. Then three personal questions: his grandmother on his father's side's maiden name—Levitz; his father's birthplace—Bangor; his blood group— Rh negative.

He typed in the answers and the email displayed on the screen. He clicked on the "Reply" button and the attachment was downloaded securely.

A two-page dossier and six black-and-white photos appeared before his eyes. The man he'd been sent to kill.

Reznick's stomach knotted as he scanned the screen. Tom Powell, aged fifty-nine, described as an "imminent security risk." Powell lived with his second wife and their two school-age children in a quiet cul-de-sac in Frederick, Maryland; his oldest son was away at university. According to the file, he had checked into the St. Regis the previous evening—room 674, three doors down. It didn't say exactly why he should be neutralized.

Reznick pondered on that. Usually when he did a hit, the reason was made quite clear. It could be spying, terrorism, or one of a whole host of threats to the country. Invariably, they had an explanation.

So why not now?

Reznick read on. The file said Powell had to be a "suicide." No other options.

This was the first time that Reznick had been asked to kill an American citizen on American soil. He knew that it would have been impossible if he were still a part of Delta Force because of the Posse Comitatus Act, which under federal law prohibited the military being used in operations within the United States. But he was no longer constrained.

In the past he'd taken out a Saudi military attaché in New York, a billionaire banker in London who was funding Hezbollah, a Russian spy in Vienna, a host of jihadists across the Middle East, and a smattering of Islamic fundamentalists living and working in America.

It was business. Realpolitik. The stone-cold reality of politics based on facts and material needs.

He studied the pictures of the man—including one of him playing football in a local park in Frederick with his eldest son, John, a law student at George Washington University. The son was a good-looking kid: clean-cut, short hair, preppy clothes.

He looked at the photos of Powell until he could remember the smallest details. The dime-sized mole on his left cheek, the graying sideburns, the bushy eyebrows, and the small scar above his right eyebrow caused, according to the file, by a schoolyard fight.

Reznick's training at "The Farm" in Virginia, all those years ago, had stressed the importance of knowing the subject inside out. This enabled an appropriate plan to be drawn up and executed.

Maddox and his team would have explored Powell's lifestyle and habits. His sleeping patterns and any health problems. The file noted that he was a keen golfer, not on prescription medication, and led a clean life—a glass or two of expensive French red wine at dinner on a Friday or Saturday evening was his only vice.

Reznick finished reading the dossier, shut down the computer, and waited for Maddox to call. The waiting was always the worst part of the job. Endless hours spent hanging around motels, hotels, safe houses, halfway houses, flophouses, apartments—a myriad of places—before the final phase.

The endgame.

Reznick was not the judge. Nor the jury. He was the executioner. Except he didn't sit in on the trial, because there was no trial. This was summary justice, as practiced by every government in the world. Sometimes the dirty work was subcontracted to a foreign intelligence agency or their associates. But this was in-house.

Just after midnight, Reznick's cell phone vibrated in his pocket. He switched on the TV, which was showing highlights of a Redskins game, to drown out his voice.

"Are you in place?" Maddox asked.

"Yes."

"This is a wet delivery. Do you understand?"

"Absolutely."

"OK, run-through time. Our guy is a creature of habit. He's in his room, fast asleep."

"How do you know?"

"GPS on his BlackBerry and a bug in his room's smoke detector. Hold back until five minutes *after* zero two hundred hours, when the video camera in the corridor will be remotely switched off until zero three hundred and the lights dimmed. You have a copy of his swipe card. Assume you have fifty-five minutes to make this delivery."

It was enough time.

"Do good," Maddox said.

"Count on it."

"Your room will be cleaned as soon as this delivery has been made. A maintenance uniform is hanging in your closet." A long pause elapsed. "Sit tight. Then it's just you and him."

With less than one hour to go, Reznick was sitting in his darkened hotel room, primed to carry out the delivery. He had changed into a pale blue, short-sleeved work shirt and black pants, gold wire-rimmed glasses, and shiny black shoes. There was a metallic nametag on his lapel—*Alex Goddard, Service Engineer*—and a bag at his feet. He pushed a tiny audio device into his right ear for communication; the nametag concealed a hidden microphone.

Everything in place. No diversions. No TV, radio, music, magazines, or newspapers to sidetrack him. The way he always worked during the crucial last hour.

The LCD display on his digital watch showed 01:21. *Not long now.*

Reznick's earpiece buzzed and he tensed up.

"Reznick, do you copy?" Maddox's voice was a whisper. "Reznick?"

"What?"

A small sigh. "OK, we have two room-service types—a guy and a woman—one dropping newspapers outside doors, the other pushing a trolley with food and drinks. They're in the elevator, and they're heading your way."

Reznick could hear his heart beating.

"OK," Maddox whispered, "now they're on the sixth."

On cue, the ding of the elevator doors opening and dull footsteps padding down the carpeted corridor. The faint tinkling of metal against glass, accompanied by a low male voice. Thuds as the papers were left outside each room. The sound of a door opening.

Three long minutes later, they were gone.

"OK, buddy, sorry about that. You all set?"

"How's our guy?"

"Sleeping like a baby. Slam dunk, Reznick. You've got a clear run."

The line went dead at 1:23 a.m.

——— ———

When it hit 02:05, he peered out of the peephole. No movement or sound. He lay flat down on the floor and pressed his left ear—the one without the earpiece—to the carpet, listening for elevator vibrations, footsteps, sudden noises . . . anything.

He heard the faint sound of water pipes creaking. Perhaps the merest hint of laughter somewhere below.

Apart from that, all quiet.

Reznick got up and stood, picking up the bag. He took half a dozen slow, deep breaths.

Just breathe.

His breathing even, he was ready.

Slowly he turned the handle, stuck his head out of the door, and peered down the dimly lit hallway.

Not a soul.

Slow is smooth, smooth is fast.

The military dictum of the Marines kicked in. It meant moving fast or rushing in was reckless, and could get you killed. If you move slowly, you are less likely to put yourself at risk.

He edged out and closed the door as softly as he could. The metallic locking system sounded to him like a rifle reloading.

Reznick looked around and took the short walk to Powell's door. Carefully, he swiped the card, the metallic clicking noticeably softer. He cracked the door. The sound of deep snoring.

He kept the door ajar for a few moments as his eyes adjusted to the semi-darkness. The room smelled of stale sweat and old shoes. Underneath the window, the crumpled silhouette of the man lying in bed, facing the wall, duvet on. Reznick shut the door softly, and it barely made a noise as it clicked into place.

He crept toward the sleeping man. Closer and closer, careful not to trip on any objects lying around.

Standing over him, Reznick saw the dime-sized mole on his left cheek. Suddenly the man groaned and turned over onto his back. The springs of the bed creaked.

Reznick froze, not daring to breathe. A deep silence opened up for a few moments as he wondered if the man was really awake. He stood still and waited.

One beat. Two beats. Three beats.

Eventually, on the fourth beat, the snoring continued as before, rhythmic and deep. Reznick exhaled slowly. Then he reached into his pants pocket and pulled out a lipstick-sized Taser. He leaned over and pressed the metal device hard against the man's temple. Electric currents provoked convulsions for three long seconds. Powell's eyes rolled back in his head. The sound of gurgling and groaning. Then nothing.

Unconscious.

A standard first-step procedure. Eight minutes, maybe ten, before the man came to.

Reznick rummaged in the bag and produced the auto-injecting syringe disguised as a ballpoint pen, containing succinylcholine chloride, which he knew as "Sux." The drug was a skeletal-muscle relaxant used as an adjunct to surgical anesthesia and had been employed as a paralyzing agent for executions by lethal injection. A twist of the nib and a quick stab into the man's skin would deliver seven milligrams of the drug. But only five milligrams was necessary for death.

The victim would be paralyzed within thirty seconds. The muscles, including the diaphragm, would shut down, with the exception of the heart. He would be unable to speak or move, although his brain would still be working. Then he had three minutes until his breathing ceased, unable to scream out for help.

The beauty of the drug for assassinations was that enzymes in the body begin to break down the drug almost immediately, making it virtually impossible to detect.

Powell was to be injected in the buttocks, as—in the absence of evidence of foul play—most medical examiners would suspect a heart attack as the natural cause of death.

Reznick pulled back the duvet and switched on his penlight, examining the paunchy, unconscious man lying before him. He wore pale blue pajamas with a white tank top underneath. He had on a cheap watch with a frayed, brown leather strap. The last moments in his life, and the poor bastard didn't know anything about it. Reznick never usually felt anything when he had to kill a foreign terrorist or one of the billionaires who bankrolled them. But in this case it did feel strange, knowing that this was an American.

The penlight picked out something around the man's neck, tucked inside his tank. Reznick looked closer, and thought it looked like an aluminum dog tag. He held it in his hand, turned it over, and saw an inscription in Hebrew—the name Benjamin Luntz—and a seven-digit identification number.

Israeli Defense Forces.

He stared at the dog tag for a few moments.

Why the fuck had Tom Powell got the dog tag of an Israeli soldier around his neck? It didn't make any sense.

The doubts began to set in. He needed certainty.

He had to wait more than eight minutes before Powell came to with a low groan. Reznick pressed the Beretta to the guy's forehead. Powell gazed up, confused and scared.

"Shut up and listen," Reznick snarled, hand covering his mouth.

The man nodded.

"Any sound, and you die. Got it?"

He nodded again.

Reznick removed his hand. "All right," he said in a low voice. "Gimme your name, and date and place of birth. Right now."

The man gulped hard. "Please, take whatever you want."

Reznick pressed the gun tighter to his skin, making a small indentation as the guy began to tremble. "This is the second time I'll ask. I don't ask a third time. Now, give me your name, date and place of birth. Failure to comply will result in the maids cleaning your brains off this wall in six hours' time. Got it?"

"My name is Frank Luntz, born New York City, October twelve, 1953."

Reznick's mind went into free fall for a split second. The target's name was Powell. Something was badly wrong.

"Tell me about the dog tag around your neck."

"It's my son's."

"What's his name?"

"Benjamin Luntz."

Reznick wondered whether to believe the man or not. Something wasn't adding up. Was he being played?

"Are you Israeli?"

"No. My son emigrated. He had joint citizenship."

"What do you mean *had*?"

"He was . . . he was blown up by a suicide bomber at a check-point in the West Bank three years ago."

The man made a sudden movement and Reznick pushed him back down into the pillow. "Don't even think about it."

"I want to prove it to you."

He reached under his pillow and pulled out a silver photo pendant. A faded color picture of a young man in combat fatigues, rifle slung over his shoulder, sitting atop a Merkava tank.

The man pointed to the bedside cabinet. "The top drawer. Check my wallet if you don't believe me."

Reznick reached over and opened the top drawer. Empty. No driver's license or credit cards to establish the man's true identity. "There's nothing there, you lying bastard."

"That's impossible. Perhaps Connelly has it next door."

Reznick was tempted to kill the fucker there and then. "Who's Connelly?"

The man began to cry.

"Answer me. Who's Connelly?"

"He's a Fed. He's in the adjoining room. He's looking after me."

Reznick's stomach knotted. "What the hell are you talking about?"

"He has the adjoining room to this." The guy pointed a shaking finger in the direction of a door next to the dresser.

"Are you lying to me—because if you are, you die, here and now."

He began sobbing. Reznick placed a huge hand over his mouth to muffle the sound.

"One more peep out of you and I'll rip out your wiring. Do you understand?"

The man nodded, tears spilling down his cheeks.

"Hands on your head."

He complied. Reznick pulled a sock out of the dresser and stuffed it into his mouth, before tearing up strips of the bedsheet and tying it around his head to secure the sock. Then he tied the man's wrists and ankles to the four corners of the wooden bed, crucifixion style.

Reznick shone the penlight directly into his eyes. "Don't even think about fucking moving."

He nodded quickly. Reznick walked across to the door and pressed his ear up against it, listening for several seconds for any sounds. Creaks. Groans. But he heard nothing.

Slowly, he turned the handle and opened the door. His eyes scanned the room. The bed was made, the wooden blinds and curtains shut, as if awaiting the next hotel guest. Perfect order. Empty.

Or so it seemed. The hint of sandalwood in the air told another story. The room had been occupied.

Reznick sensed something was wrong. He shone the penlight toward the bathroom and opened the door. Opulent white marble sinks, bath, and floor. White towels neatly stacked on a metal rack above the bath. A slight smell of damp pervaded the air, as if from a recent shower.

Again, that didn't add up to an unoccupied room.

Reznick went back into the bedroom as the penlight raked the high-quality carpet beside the huge closet. His gaze wandered around the room, past a small flaxen sofa, until he fixed on a white louver door. He saw it wasn't shut properly. Perhaps half an inch ajar.

He moved closer. Kneeling down, he shone the light through the slatted openings. Inside, he saw what looked like tousled blond hair.

He held his breath. Then he reached out and felt the wooden handle, before yanking open the door.

Reznick's heart jolted as the penlight picked out the crumpled, semi-naked body of a blond-haired man. Telltale purple bruises around the neck and throat, hemorrhaging around the dead eyes. Reznick had seen this sort of thing before. Many times. The man had been manually strangled.

This was so fucked up it wasn't real.

His mind was racing when he returned to the first room. He leaned down beside the man strapped and gagged to the bed. The guy stared up at Reznick like a terrified child, afraid of his fate.

Reznick untied the strips of bedsheet around the man's mouth and pulled out the sock. Then he pressed his face right up against the other man's, smelling the sweat and fear. "Who the fuck are you?"

"I already told you."

"Why do people want you dead? Who do you work for?"

"I work for the government. Look, please tell me who you are. What've you done to Connelly?"

"Forget about him. Forget about me. What about you? What exactly do you do?"

"I told you, I work for the government."

"Doing what?"

The man closed his eyes and shook his head.

"Answer me."

"I'm a government scientist."

Reznick stuffed the sock back into the guy's mouth. He walked over to the window and buzzed Maddox on his lapel microphone, giving him the lowdown. The discovery of the murdered man's body—perhaps a Fed—and the possibility that they had the wrong guy.

Maddox listened in silence before he said, "Gimme two minutes and I'll get back to you."

In less than a minute, the earpiece buzzed into life.

"The subject is to be protected and brought in. Make your way with the subject to a motel, the Clarence Suites, six blocks away on N Street Northwest, due northeast, and sit tight. Room seven eight seven. You're booked in under Ronald D Withers. He's your brother, Simon Withers. Clear?"

"Then what?"

"We're sending two of our guys, Bowman and Price. They'll take him off your hands."

Three

"Get dressed," Reznick snapped as he untied Luntz.

He needed to get them both out of the hotel. And fast. But he couldn't just walk out of the lobby as he was, dressed as a fucking maintenance man.

He rifled through the dresser and found a navy cashmere sweater. He pulled it on but the sleeves were too long, so he rolled them up a couple of inches.

"One word out of line, and you and your family will die," he said, picking up his bag. "Do you understand what I'm saying?"

Luntz nodded and licked his lower lip.

Reznick shoved the gun into the back of his waistband. The cold metal felt reassuring against his warm skin. He cracked the door, saw the coast was clear, and grabbed the man's arm and marched him down the corridor toward the stairs. They passed a fire alarm. He punched the glass with his knuckles and pressed the red button.

An ear-splitting noise shattered the calm.

Got to keep moving.

He hustled Luntz through the fire-exit doors and down the stairwell. Luntz appeared bewildered and groggy, eyes heavy. Behind them, some shouts and instructions to "Get a move on."

Luntz asked, "Please, where are you taking me?"

"Shut up and do as I say."

Reznick pushed through the doors at the bottom of the stairwell and emerged into the huge lobby. Scores of frightened guests in nightgowns and pajamas were filing out of the main doors. He found it easy to blend in and leave the hotel.

They emerged into the cold night air as doormen and valets handed out blankets. In the distance was the sound of fire truck sirens.

His mind replayed the grid of streets he'd walked the previous night as he got his bearings. They headed along a still-busy K Street—the main east–west artery through Washington's business district—past anonymous redbrick and concrete office blocks. These buildings were home to powerful lobbying firms, think tanks, and numerous advocacy groups, all wanting to be close to the levers of power. But at that ungodly hour, the street was busy with groups of young revelers and professionals heading to hip lounges and clubs nearby.

Reznick was glad to cross the road and go up 17th Street NW, away from the main drag. Past the Pot Belly sandwich shop and the YMCA.

He took off his earpiece, lapel microphone, and nametag, dropping them down a storm drain. He hurried on along the sidewalk and across the street, squeezing between two huge SUVs parked next to each other.

"Quicker!" he said.

Luntz nodded furiously.

Reznick hustled him as they turned left and headed west along N Street NW—a broad, tree-lined street full of elegant row houses—past the Hotel Tabard Inn, until they came to the redbrick Clarence Suites. He took a few moments to gather his thoughts.

His mind flashed to the dog tag. Was it genuine? Was it a ruse?

He turned to the man. "Not a word."

Luntz nodded, fear in his eyes.

Reznick held his arm as they climbed the stone steps and walked through the motel's doors. The night-desk guy looked very young, but was clean-shaven and sported a maroon vest and matching tie.

"Good evening," the kid said. "You guys booked a room?"

Reznick forced a smile. "Sorry we're so late. We got delayed with a connecting flight. My name's Withers and this is my brother. We've booked a room."

The kid smiled back. "Not a problem." He checked the computer in front of him, going down a list of names with a pencil. "OK—room seven eight seven." He handed over the swipe card. "You guys in town for a convention or something?"

"Yeah, something like that," Reznick said.

"Any luggage?"

"Got lost at the airport, I'm afraid."

"Oh, I'm sorry. Do you want me to try and contact your airline?"

"Don't worry, we've already been onto them. Should arrive later today. But thanks anyway. Appreciate your help."

The night-desk guy smiled. "Anytime."

Reznick looked at the kid's badge, which read *Steve Murphy, Night Desk.* He was clean-cut, polite, and doing a thankless job for what probably amounted to minimum wage. He looked sixteen, if that. The kid reminded Reznick of himself when he was that age. Having to work shitty jobs on weekends and during vacations to help his dad make ends meet. "Hey, Steve, tell me—have you got a room nearby which is free?"

The kid shrugged and checked the register. "Room seven eight eight is vacant. Across the hall. You want to change rooms?"

"No, I'd like to book room seven eight eight as well, if that's OK. I'm a light sleeper and my brother is the opposite. It'll be the only way I get some shut-eye."

The guy grinned. "No problem, Mr. Withers. We've already got your card details, so that's all been taken care of. Will you be requiring a wake-up call?"

"No, I think I'll sleep in. Long flight."

"Enjoy your stay," the kid said, and handed over the other swipe card. "Coffee machine and cable on demand in both rooms. We've got you down for staying one night."

Reznick smiled and nodded. He took Luntz by the arm and they rode the elevator to the seventh floor in silence. It was a long walk down the carpeted corridor. He swiped the card for room 788 and went inside. He sat Luntz down on the bed.

"Why the room change?" Luntz asked.

"Never you mind."

The truth was he didn't like the set-up. Not one bit.

The questions were stacking up as he paced the warm room while the man he should have killed sat with his head in his hands. Reznick needed to think this through without having to babysit this guy.

He reached inside his bag and took out what looked like a nasal spray, then calmly sprayed the highly concentrated sleeping drug into the man's left ear.

Reznick had to stop him from collapsing onto the floor. He picked Luntz up and placed him on the bed. The drugs would knock him out for at least four hours, leaving Reznick without that worry ahead of the handover.

The minutes dragged.

Reznick checked his watch repeatedly as he paced the room. He made himself a black coffee. Then another. The more he thought of the sequence of events, the more it didn't make any sense.

Shit.

He ran through the events in his head one more time. The encrypted message and accompanying documents had been received in the usual way prior to an assassination. The target was Tom Powell. He'd had the right room. He had followed instructions.

The best solution was, as Maddox said, for Luntz to be taken off his hands so Reznick could disappear back into the shadows. Maddox always made the right call at the right time. He'd lost count of the number of times that Maddox had gotten Reznick or one of the contractors out of a jam when an operation became problematic. But as of now, Reznick was in the middle of a fucked-up situation and needed to get out of Washington.

He switched off the lights and sat in the dark. He checked the luminous display of his watch. It showed 03:33.

What was keeping the handover team so long? It was more than an hour since he'd called Maddox, and still no sign of them. He wondered if Maddox had tried to contact him with an update to the plans.

He gulped down some of the cheap coffee and looked out of the window toward an apartment with the lights on, curtains drawn. Shadows moved inside. He tried to open the window to let in some air but it wasn't budging.

Damn.

Upstairs, the sound of a TV, the vibration carrying through the ceiling. Down below, a woman's strained voice. Outside, the drone of an air-con unit.

The waiting continued.

He made his third coffee.

The sound of the drugged man's deep breathing reminded Reznick of his own father lying in a drunken stupor in a crummy Washington hotel room, all those years ago. An image flashed up in his mind, of his father lying face down on the bed at the end of the day, exhausted and drunk, his best suit still on, the room stinking of booze. Reznick's father had hated his job at the sardine-packing factory in Rockland, hated his life, and he'd been haunted by memories of the war. It was plain for all to see. Each time his father, a man he'd revered, stood to attention in front of the Vietnam Veterans Memorial and saluted the names of his fallen or missing comrades, there was a terrible pain in his eyes. It was as though he was reliving the horrors again.

His father had never spoken of what he'd witnessed or what he'd done. He didn't have to. The war had left him hollow. The scars were etched onto his craggy face and burned into his shattered mind. Some part of his father had died in Vietnam, left behind like the young comrades who had given their lives in the jungles of a foreign country.

A soft moan from the sleeping man sprawled on the bed snapped Reznick out of his thoughts. The waiting dragged on and on.

Eventually, just after 5 a.m., the sound of footsteps in the corridor outside.

Finally, they're here.

He peered through the peephole. A well-dressed white couple who looked like Mormons were walking down the corridor. They stopped outside room 787, the room he'd originally been allocated.

Strange. Maddox said it was an in-house job. So who the fuck were they?

Reznick pressed his left eye tighter to the glass, eyelashes brushing the metal surround. He held his breath and stood statue-still. Into view came a second man. He was stocky and wore a dark suit and forensic gloves.

This is no pick-up.

The three of them said nothing, not even looking at each other. The woman stepped forward and knocked four times on the door of 787, as the two men stood hidden either side, guns now drawn.

Rat-a-tat-tat.

She waited a second before she knocked again. A few moments elapsed. Then the stocky man swiped a plastic keycard through the locking system and the three of them went inside, shutting the door quietly.

Reznick stepped back from the peephole and let out a long, slow breath. He felt trapped in the suffocating room. His mind raced. Who were they?

More than five minutes later, they all emerged stone-faced. The stocky guy remained outside room 787, but the couple walked toward the elevator.

Shit.

Reznick knew the couple had gone to speak to the kid at the desk. He figured he had four, maybe five minutes—tops—before they returned.

The stocky man stared straight at room 788's peephole for a few moments. The room Reznick was in with Luntz. He wondered if the man had seen him.

Impossible.

Then the man turned away and faced 787.

Fuck it.

Reznick stepped away from the door, slowly pulling his 9mm Beretta from his waistband, then padded like a tomcat across the room and got his Trident 9 suppressor from his "delivery" bag. He slowly screwed the silencer into the gun, and carefully clicked off the spring-loaded safety lever with his thumb. He was glad he'd already racked the slide of his gun, knowing the sound would alert the man.

Reznick walked silently back to the door and stared through the peephole again. The stocky man had walked five yards down the hall. But then, slow as you like, he turned and walked back until he was standing outside Reznick's door.

He held his breath as the man moved closer until his face became distorted, as if through a fish-eye lens. He seemed to be paying far too much attention to the door Reznick was standing behind.

Suddenly, Luntz let out a loud moan in his sleep.

Reznick winced at the sound. The man outside stopped chewing his gum.

Reznick didn't move.

The man began to chew his gum again, eyes unblinking. Then he leaned forward and pressed his left eye up against the glass.

Reznick raised the suppressor to the peephole, turned his face away, and squeezed the trigger. It made a muffled *phut*. A small jaggy hole—less than an inch in diameter—had been blown out of the chipboard door.

The adrenaline flowed.

He opened the door wide enough to drag the body into the room. The bullet had torn into the man's left eye. Blood oozed down his cheek from the gaping wound.

Reznick bent down and pulled the man in by the feet before he could bleed out onto the carpet in the corridor. He checked outside the door, and quickly picked up the wood and glass splinters lying on the floor before closing it. Then he pulled Luntz off the bed and replaced him with the huge stranger.

Reznick felt sweat beading his forehead. He rifled through the dead man's pockets and found an iPhone, but no ID or wallet. He went to the bathroom, picked up the hotel toothpaste, and twisted off the cap. Then he went back to the door and wedged it into the small hole, so at a quick glance from the outside it appeared intact.

Reznick grabbed his bag, picked up Luntz, and slung him over his shoulder. He weighed around ten stone. Light compared to the stocky guy. Then he opened the door and looked out. All clear.

He edged into the corridor, closed the door quietly, turned left down the corridor to a fire-exit sign, and went down the stairs to the basement. He reached into his pocket and switched on the jamming device that would nullify the hotel's door alarms, then left through an emergency exit.

Reznick emerged with Luntz at the rear of the building. He walked nearly half a block until he came to a narrow side street, where he saw a Mercedes parked up. He used the high-tech fob, which deactivated the car's locking system, the immobilizer, and the alarm system.

Reznick opened the back door and put the sleeping Luntz onto the seat, before strapping him in. He climbed into the driver's seat and checked inside the glove compartment. Nothing. He clicked the switch on the fob and the car purred into life.

Reznick pulled away slowly, not wanting to attract attention, and punched in Maddox's secure number on the dead man's cell phone.

"I'm on the move," he said. "The delivery has been compromised. Someone or something has left us wide open. I repeat, we have been compromised."

Maddox stayed quiet for a few moments. "Is the target safe?"

"Yes, he's safe. I got a visual on a crew of three. Two men and one woman. One of the guys is down. I'm calling from his cell."

"Jesus."

"Do you want to download the data from the phone?"

"We're already doing it."

Reznick pulled out the fob again, and flicked a side switch so no one could track the vehicle through the GPS on the phone. "So, what happened to the two guys you sent?"

A long sigh. "They've been taken out. The whole thing's fucked up. Head to the usual safe house."

Then the line went dead.

Four

The Gulfstream jet was cruising at forty thousand feet as it entered American airspace over the Eastern Seaboard. FBI Assistant Director Martha Meyerstein—in charge of the Criminal, Cyber, Response, and Services Branch—was the only member of her team awake. She looked around the cabin. The rest were getting some shut-eye on the long flight home from Dubai.

On her BlackBerry, Meyerstein speed-read the first email of the morning—from the Director, wanting a progress report on an ongoing investigation into public corruption involving a Californian senator, Lionel Timpson. She'd have to reply by the end of the day. Something else for her in tray.

She put down her phone, on top of a pile of intelligence briefing papers on the adjacent empty seat. Then she reclined and stared out of the window at the white strobe light on the wing tip.

Her mind hadn't shut off after the cyber-security conference.

Waves of tiredness swept over her. She tried to remember the last time she'd had a proper vacation, and realized it had been over two years. She was killing herself, but she didn't know any other way. This was the job she had craved for so long, after all. Her father, a top Chicago attorney, thought she was mad for embarking on a career with the FBI when she could have sailed into corporate law and a high six-figure salary. She was currently earning $157,000, with $20,000 extra in bonuses for reaching her targets. A great salary. She had a lovely house in Bethesda, Washington DC, around the corner from Fox pundit John Bolton; she sent her kids to private school and was pretty happy with her lot. But she knew, deep down, her father would much rather she'd entered the rarefied atmosphere of a top law firm.

Maybe he was right. Her privileged upbringing in the upscale North Shore suburb of Winnetka and an elite private education at the Latin School of Chicago—and then Harvard Law School—had led to numerous offers from law firms in cities from New York to Los Angeles. But instead of following in the footsteps of her three brothers, she had embarked on a fast-track career with the FBI after attending a lecture by an inspirational woman, a Dartmouth graduate, who'd headed up the Boston field office. She found she loved Quantico. And she loved the Bureau. It became her life.

Meyerstein was now the highest-ranking female within the FBI structure, which she was very proud of. But it had come at a steep price.

She stared at her left hand. The white band where her gold wedding ring used to be, her finger slightly indented from wearing it for more than a decade. The only sign of her old life. The only visible sign she had once been happily married—before her husband, James, a professor at Georgetown University's Center for Security Studies, left her for one of his students, a French girl he was mentoring.

Her phone rang and a couple of her team stirred.

"Martha, sorry to bother you, but we've got a problem like you wouldn't believe." It was Roy Stamper, who headed up the Criminal Investigative Division that she was responsible for.

Meyerstein sighed. "What kind of problem?"

"How long till you touch down?"

"Half an hour. What's going on?"

"Violent crime unit got a call from the Washington field office a few minutes ago. Luntz is missing."

"He's what?"

"We think he's been kidnapped."

"Wasn't someone watching over him?"

"Yeah, Special Agent Connelly. He's dead." Meyerstein felt her insides go cold. "He's been strangled."

Meyerstein remembered a fresh-faced young special agent at a briefing just over a fortnight ago. "The rookie from Seattle?"

"Right."

She closed her eyes for a moment. "Shit."

"Washington field office has a team over at the St. Regis as we speak."

"So what are the indications as to who or what is behind this?"

"Too early to say. But I've spoken to Stevie"—Stamper was referring to Stephen Combe, the special agent in charge of the Washington field office—"and he said it had the hallmarks of a professional job. But we've also got what appears to be a separate hit on a guy at the Clarence Suites, nearby. We think they might be linked."

Meyerstein listened in stunned silence as Stamper gave a summary of what had happened. When he finished talking, she gulped down the last of the cold coffee still left in her cup.

"The guy at the Clarence Suites was shot through the eye from behind a door."

"What are the police saying to this?"

"They aren't happy and are asking a lot of questions."

"We need to button this up. This is on a need-to-know basis. Who's the lead detective on the scene?"

"Maartens. I've spoken to him already and we're getting full cooperation."

"OK, we need to stand up SIOC for this." The Strategic Information and Operations Center—or SIOC, pronounced "sigh-ock"—was on the fifth floor of FBI Headquarters. It was the global watch and communications center, providing round-the-clock information on emerging criminal and terrorist threats to the US. "But first I want everyone in the briefing room in two hours."

"Leave it with me."

The massive office of FBI Director Bill O'Donoghue overlooked Pennsylvania Avenue from the seventh floor of the Hoover Building. It was located in a secure wing, three doors down from Meyerstein's own office, sealed off behind electronic doors with security cameras; a keypad code was required, which only the most senior agents had access to.

Meyerstein was ushered through the glass door etched with the silver FBI seal and into his huge office by Margaret, his PA, who had worked for the Bureau for almost twenty-five years.

"Take a load off, Martha," O'Donoghue said, not lifting his head. He was sitting behind his oversized mahogany desk, reading a raft of briefing documents ahead of his meeting with the Director of National Intelligence at 10 a.m. Probably why he was so preoccupied.

"Thank you, sir."

She sat down in a deep leather chair and looked around the office. His desk featured two phones neatly placed beside each other—one for internal calls and the other for the President—two gold lamps, and three framed family photos. One of the pictures showed a proud O'Donoghue, wearing a smart dark suit, with his wife and only son, Andrew, taken at Andrew's recent Princeton graduation.

Behind O'Donoghue was a floor-to-ceiling bookcase—flanked by an American flag and an FBI flag—with a huge TV in the middle. Most of the space was taken up by history tomes and political biographies of Roosevelt, Rockefeller, Churchill, and Truman, as well as law enforcement awards and photos. The prints adorning one of the walls looked like Rembrandts, while on the opposite wall were black-and-white photos of the San Francisco and Washington offices.

To Meyerstein's right was an oval conference table with six burgundy leather chairs. On the wall in front of the table, a plasma TV with a camera, used primarily for videoconferences with the President, the Attorney General, or any of the special agents in charge of the fifty-six FBI field divisions.

To her left, in the far corner of the room, a new blue-and-burgundy pinstriped sofa with three matching wingback chairs, beside a coffee table stacked with FBI books and magazines. Adjacent to where she was sitting, a mahogany credenza that had mementos received from visiting dignitaries.

O'Donoghue continued to read the documents as Meyerstein shifted in her chair. She cleared her throat, but still he didn't let on. He was always first in each morning just after 6 a.m., and he rarely left before 10 p.m. He had served in Vietnam as a navy pilot before joining a powerhouse Washington legal firm, eventually making partner. He even knew her father from his high-profile court cases. He was scrupulously polite, occasionally asking how her father was. She invariably said he was the same old lovable curmudgeon, which made the Director smile, knowing her father's fearsome reputation in court.

O'Donoghue, like Meyerstein, lived and breathed his job. He had been recruited to the FBI six years earlier as Deputy Director—and promoted to Director two years later—and had transformed the organization, ensuring a seamless flow of information between all the field divisions, HQ, and other government agencies, making it fit for the twenty-first century.

He was comfortable with broad-brush strategy documents and mission statements, but also meticulous with detail, hauling anyone over the coals for not following correct procedure. He was that sort of guy. But she had always found him to be very professional and unfailingly polite—though perhaps not on this occasion—albeit slightly aloof.

O'Donoghue let out a long sigh, leaned back in his seat, and fixed his gaze on Meyerstein. "OK, down to business. So far I've got the bare bones of what happened at the St. Regis. What's your take on this?"

Meyerstein cleared her throat. "This has all the hallmarks of a professional assassination. To take down a federal agent in such circumstances indicates planning and backup, either military or special ops. Perhaps, if I'm to speculate, we may be talking about a foreign government."

He went quiet for a few moments. "Any intel?"

"Not so far. But this is a bespoke job, not off the peg."

"Foreign governments, eh? Got any in mind?"

"Take your pick from any number of countries which hate America at this moment."

"What about Iran? They hate America."

"Well, they fit the bill. We foiled the Iranian plot to kill the Saudi ambassador in 2011. Is this payback? I don't know. So they can't be ruled out. But the National Counterterrorism Center is working on the problem as we speak."

"Look, I'm meeting with the Director of National Intelligence. He'll want some details. He'll also want to know how this was possible. How could this happen?"

"That's what I intend to find out."

"Then again," O'Donoghue said, shaking his head, "is it possible there's a problem in our ranks?"

Meyerstein saw where this was going. "I hear what you're saying."

O'Donoghue shrugged. "Just playing devil's advocate."

"I agree we can't discount such a possibility."

The Director leaned back in his seat and stared at her. "I'm intrigued you think a foreign government might be behind this. What's your rationale?"

"Luntz's area of expertise makes him valuable to any government. But the fact that he specifically asked to speak to the FBI so urgently makes me think something else is afoot—and that's why they want to silence him."

O'Donoghue nodded. "Taken from right under our noses. Very audacious. And dangerous."

Meyerstein nodded.

"Tell me more about Connelly. Was he new?"

"Just a few months with us, sir. Was based in Seattle for a couple of years before being posted here."

"Married?"

"Young wife, two kids."

O'Donoghue turned and stared out of his window over the Washington skyline. "I want the bastards who did this, Martha. You have whatever resources you want."

"Sir, my team will also be alive to the possibility another story is playing out. I'm of course talking about national security. We can't rule that out." Meyerstein got up out of her seat.

"Oh, Martha?" he said.

"Yes, sir?"

"Let's do this right. And let's nail those responsible."

"Count on it, sir."

Meyerstein walked out of the office and took the elevator down two floors to where Roy Stamper was standing waiting for her, unsmiling. He was wearing his customary navy suit, white shirt, navy silk tie, and highly polished black leather shoes. He had been with the FBI since he was headhunted after graduating from Duke, coming top of his class at law school. They had both started training at the FBI's academy at Quantico at the same time.

He wasn't a great mixer. Never had been. He was quiet, but unlike her errant husband, he was a great family man. Her own father, despite being a workaholic like her, was the same, trying to take time out of his punishing schedule to meet her mother for lunch or supper. Her father was devoted to her mother. He liked being with her. He liked being around her. They looked relaxed in each other's company. Martha could see that.

She'd never felt that with her own husband. He'd never wanted to share a glass of wine with her when she got home. He'd never wanted to go to the park with their children. He didn't want to do anything with the kids. It was as if they were an inconvenience to his academic life, getting in the way. She herself didn't have a great work–life balance, but when she was home, her family was the be-all and end-all.

That's what she admired so much about Stamper as a man. He loved his wife and his three kids with a passion. He was teetotal, and had once told her he was truly happiest when he had his family around him. He was that sort of guy. He didn't talk about women, he didn't chase women, he simply got on with doing his job. He rarely raised his voice. And apart from being one of the good guys, he was also a good listener.

They had worked their way up the ladder together. Although she was his boss, Meyerstein had always used him as a sounding board, knowing him to be discreet, offering wise counsel when the job threatened to swamp her.

"What a mess, Roy," she said.

"Tell me about it."

"So, have the schedules been created to ensure we'll be fully manned for the duration of this case?"

"Yeah, crisis management guy with SIOC—Guy Stevens—has sorted it out. We've been allocated OPSD." It was the main briefing room for major cases. "The rapid deployment team has created logs from the Washington field division, so we're all up to speed. They're setting up boards in our SIOC room as we speak."

They headed along the corridor, her heels clicking on the beige tile floor, then straight into the windowless and radio-secure Strategic Information Operations Center and into their allotted briefing room. Covering one wall was a huge screen, which could be manipulated to split into twelve different screens for showing the news channels or videoconferencing. It was currently showing a live feed from the St. Regis hotel.

A young male agent greeted her with a "Morning ma'am," and handed her a fresh cup of black coffee when she entered the room.

"Thanks," she said, as Stamper went to the far end of the room to speak to one of his team.

She felt jet-lagged and mentally exhausted, having only napped in the last forty-eight hours. Now she had virtually no chance of catching up on her sleep until Luntz was found.

A quick glance around the briefing room. Most of the faces were familiar, and she had worked with them on numerous investigations over the years. The task force had pulled together the finest investigative and analytical brains from numerous government agencies. They each brought their own areas of expertise.

There were two agents from Stamper's Criminal Investigative Division who specialized in kidnapping investigations; a profiler, Jan Marino, from the National Center for the Analysis of Violent Crimes; four agents from the Critical Incident Response Group, including behavioral and tactical; two critical incident and intelligence analysts; three members of the Computer Analysis Response Team, who would be responsible for searching any computers owned by Luntz or at his place of work; a member of the Cyber Division, to find out whether a threat had been made electronically and to see if computer systems had been hacked; and a handful of counterterrorism specialists. In addition, she recognized representatives from the Department of Homeland Security, the police, and the CIA dotted around the briefing room.

Meyerstein sipped the steaming-hot coffee, as she stood at the lectern taking a few moments to gather her thoughts.

"All right, folks," she said, leaning over to put down her cup on a nearby desk. "We've got three problems. Firstly, a government scientist has gone missing. We need to find him and we need to find him quick. Secondly, one of our colleagues babysitting him is dead. Strangled. We need to find the people responsible. Thirdly, the specter of a major security threat to this country."

The men and women all nodded solemnly. A few scribbled notes on pads of paper, while others worked on iPads.

She turned and faced the plasma screen. "I must warn you, this will not be pleasant viewing." She pointed at Stamper. "OK, Roy, let's roll it."

The huge screen showed graphic forensic pictures of the body of Special Agent Connelly, stuffed into the bottom of a closet. His face was gray-blue, distinctive marks around the neck.

"OK, freeze-frame the picture. Roy, what are we talking about?"

"Manual strangulation, but with a twist."

Meyerstein closed her eyes, feeling a headache coming on. "Meaning?"

"Initial toxicology reports were clean, but we retested the body fluids, which show traces of succinylcholine in the brain."

Meyerstein nodded. She knew all about the properties of the quick-acting substance that could render a person incapable of resisting any intruder. It was the drug of choice for intelligence services the world over. She looked around at the grim faces of her team before turning to face Stamper again. "This is a hit, right?"

"This has all the hallmarks of a neat job." Stamper was using "neat job" as a euphemism for a professional kill. "The drug's immobilized Connelly, and then he's been killed by someone's bare hands. He would've known what was happening to him but would've been helpless to do anything."

"Fingerprints? Cameras catch anything?"

Stamper pointed the remote control at the screen. "Grainy CCTV pictures of a white man in his thirties checking into the hotel."

"Freeze it there, thanks," Meyerstein said. "We got any idea who this guy is?"

Stamper cleared his throat. "Face recognition has confirmed this is highly likely to be a guy called Reznick. Used to be involved with the Agency."

Meyerstein looked over the assembled faces toward Ed Hareton, who had been seconded from Langley. "What's Langley saying, Ed?"

Hareton paused for a few moments as if thinking out his answer. "He's not on our books. Then they just gave me the usual spiel—'We don't do that shit.'"

Meyerstein sighed. "Does that strike you as a likely scenario, Ed?"

Hareton shook his head as the briefing room became deathly quiet, all eyes trained on him.

Meyerstein stared at Hareton for a few moments, letting her withering gaze linger. "So that's it?"

"No, I've made some calls. He did once work for us. But he hasn't worked for us in an official capacity for three and a half years."

Meyerstein felt her anger grow. Why did she need to wheedle the information out of him? What happened to post-9/11 inter-agency cooperation? "Does he now or has he ever worked for the CIA in an unofficial capacity? Sub-contracted, so to speak."

"There are indications—"

"I don't want indications or some Agency double-talk, Ed. We're looking for a missing government scientist and one of our colleagues has been murdered. Now, I'm going to ask you again—does he now, or has he ever, worked for the CIA in an unofficial capacity?"

Hareton shifted in his seat. "He once did wetwork for the government. What he's doing now, no one knows."

Meyerstein's senses had switched on despite her tiredness. "OK, now we're getting somewhere," she said sarcastically.

Hareton flushed a deep red, embarrassed.

It wasn't Meyerstein's style to humiliate individuals in front of their peers. But she needed answers, not prevarication. She turned to face the freeze-framed footage. "Well, he's certainly not retired. So, has he got any links to private security firms? Sub-contracting assassinations for foreign governments?"

Hareton shook his head. "He only ever worked for the American government."

Meyerstein looked across at Stamper. "What else, Roy?"

"Reznick checked in under a false name only hours before this happened. His fingerprints are all over this."

Stamper picked up the remote control again and played more footage. It showed Luntz and Reznick caught on camera outside the St. Regis in the middle of the night, after a fire alarm had gone off. He froze the image of a white guy—average height—wearing a blue shirt and pants. "We're scouring the hotel's internal CCTV as we speak."

Meyerstein studied the image, hands on hips. The man was ruggedly handsome—a day or two's beard growth, short dark hair, an impassive expression. "Tell me more about Reznick."

Stamper shrugged. "The guy's a ghost. Black ops. No one knows or is admitting whose responsibility he is, but like Ed says, we believe he's carried out countless assassinations on behalf of the American government for years. Former Delta Force. The unit is also known as CAG, short for Combat Applications Group, for those familiar with Fort Bragg. This guy, Reznick, is something else. Been there, done that, got the T-shirt. Also got a major beef with authority, according to his file."

Meyerstein sipped her coffee. "You want to elaborate?"

"It was noted by Colonel Gritz at Fort Bragg, who incidentally personally invited Reznick for the Delta assessment following glowing reports, that Reznick didn't like officers and was openly hostile during the Delta selection phase. Apparently he despised nearly all the officers he ever met."

Meyerstein put down the coffee and folded her arms. "Anything else?"

"Highly decorated. A bit of a legend among the Delta cadre, by all accounts."

"And then?"

"And then . . . Then he disappeared into the clutches of what we assume to be the Agency, working across the globe."

Meyerstein noticed Hareton shift in his seat.

"The files note that Reznick was directly responsible for killing Hamas commanders and al-Qaeda operatives hiding in Pakistan, and he has advised friendly governments on assassination for the last decade."

Meyerstein looked at Hareton. "Special Activities Division?"

Hareton shook his head. "The CIA has issued a denial, but I think we can take it as read."

"Full name?"

"Jon Reznick," Stamper said. "Lives alone in a house on the outskirts of Rockland, Maine. He pays his taxes. On his IRS return describes himself as a management consultant. He has two bank accounts."

"How much has he got in them?"

"Three hundred and forty thousand dollars in the main one. He has no stocks, but he owns his own home, estimated to be worth eight hundred thousand dollars, outright."

"What about the second account?"

"That is topped up each year to the tune of fifty thousand dollars. It goes on tuition fees at Brookfield boarding school for his daughter, Lauren Reznick, which comes in at forty-three thousand eight hundred dollars per year, and the rest on piano lessons, vacation money, that kind of thing."

"Is he married?"

Stamper sighed. "He was. Elisabeth Reznick was a partner for a law firm, Rosenfeld and Williams, Inc., who had their offices in the Twin Towers. She . . . she died on nine eleven. Pulverized to dust. No body found."

Meyerstein's mind flashed back to the day the world fell in on America. She remembered watching the nightmare images on the big screen in her office. The dust cloud over Manhattan.

"Tell me about his medical history."

"He was shot in the leg in Afghanistan, but he made a full recovery. Tough as hell."

"Has he been involved in anything high-profile?"

"Textbook stuff. We believe he headed up a team that went into Afghanistan to help the Northern Alliance topple the Taliban. He led Task Force 121—a Special Forces group answerable to no one, assembled from Delta, Navy Seals, CIA paramilitary operatives, and others—into Falluja to assassinate some hard-line Baathists. Then they had to fight their way out, street by street, for nearly six hours, after two Black Hawks were downed during the rescue mission."

Meyerstein pointed to a National Security Agency guy, Kevin Warwick. "So, Kev, what about Reznick's phone records? Has Fort Meade unearthed anything?"

"Untraceable number made a call to a cell phone which is registered in his name. GPS pinpointed his home in Maine. Someone called him a matter of hours before he appeared in Washington. We're still trying to pinpoint who it was."

Meyerstein stared long and hard at the "ghost" on the screen.

"So, where is he now?"

Stamper blew out his cheeks. "We know he took Luntz to the Clarence Suites, close to the St. Regis. Night-desk guy said a man matching Reznick's description checked in under the name Withers, with a man who matched Luntz's description. The body of what we believe to be an unidentified foreign national, without any ID, was found in one of two rooms booked under the name Withers. Forensics are on the scene. We're checking surveillance cameras in the street as we speak. Still drawing a blank."

Meyerstein let her gaze wander around the room. "Luntz is top priority. We must get him back. But to do that, we must find Reznick." She went quiet for a few moments as the assembled agents scribbled or punched in notes on their iPads. Then she turned to face Stamper. "What about Luntz's wife?"

"Two agents speaking to her right now."

"What's she saying?"

"She said he didn't talk about his work."

"That doesn't seem credible. Are you telling me he didn't mention anything about why he was heading to Washington?"

"Apparently not."

"Check out his computers, files, records, everything on Luntz. I want to know about him from his friends, neighbors, people at the lab. I also want Bangor field office to go over Reznick's home from top to bottom. We need to get into his life. Are there any cell phones? Laptops? Anything. I want to know everything there is to know about him."

Stamper nodded. "I believe he's got cousins that live in South Carolina. He's also got relations in Nova Scotia."

"Good. Let's get onto the Canadian Security Intelligence Service. We need to build up a complete picture of Reznick. Has he been in contact with anyone he knows?"

Meyerstein sighed as she looked at Stamper, knowing both of them would be away from their families until the investigation was resolved. She hated that part of her job.

She turned to face the assembled agents. "I want to make one thing clear. There must be no mention of our missing scientist or the murdered Fed." The agents and specialists nodded. "OK, people, I want calm heads on this. Let's get to it."

Five

It was still dark as Reznick headed off the freeway at Exit 24 toward Annapolis, Maryland, with Luntz still out of it in the back seat.

The car hit a pothole, and it jolted Luntz from his slumber.

"Where are we?" he asked.

Reznick said nothing as he glanced in the rearview mirror.

"Where are you taking me?" Luntz's head lolled like a rag doll as he spoke.

"Never you mind."

Luntz began to retch.

"What the hell's wrong with you?" Reznick said.

"I don't feel too good."

"Are you shitting me?"

"No, I'm not."

He retched again.

"Better keep it in."

"I'll try."

Reznick sighed. He couldn't wait to get shot of Luntz and let Maddox figure out what to do with him.

After a short while, he turned off Rowe Boulevard and pulled up at a deserted parking lot in the shadow of the Navy-Marine

Corps Memorial Stadium. He opened Luntz's door. "This is as good a place as any to be sick," he said.

Luntz stumbled out of the car. Then he fell to his knees and heaved the contents of his stomach onto the asphalt. He retched a few more times before wiping his mouth with the back of his sleeve. "I'm sorry."

"You finished?"

"I think so."

"You sure?"

"Yes, I'm sure."

He had a ghostly pallor that wasn't surprising in the circumstances.

"Please . . . can you tell me what you're going to do with me?"

"You're gonna be fine, trust me."

"Why don't you answer my questions? Why were you sent to kill me?"

"It's nothing personal."

"Who hired you?"

"Too many questions."

Reznick buckled him back up and slammed his door shut. He needed to get out of his maintenance uniform. He drove on for a few miles and located a 24/7 Walmart. He bought some fresh clothes, then changed in the car and drove off toward the safe house.

"Why didn't you kill me when you could?" Luntz asked from the back seat. "What stopped you?"

"You're starting to bug me now. Like I said before—too many questions."

A few minutes later, they were driving through a near-deserted downtown Annapolis, past the floodlit Maryland State House and over the King George Street Bridge.

The dead man's cell phone rang.

Reznick picked up. "Yeah."

A long pause. "We need to talk." The voice was electronically distorted.

Reznick realized it had to be an accomplice of the guy he'd taken out. The last thing he needed was to get into a discussion with *them*. "I think you've got the wrong number."

He ended the call and dropped the phone onto the passenger seat. But a few minutes later, only half a dozen blocks from the safe house, the phone rang again.

Reznick answered. "I thought I told you—"

"You have something we want."

"Not interested, thanks."

"Don't be so hasty. You need to hand him over."

"I think we're done."

The man let out a long sigh. "We have something of yours. Do you want to know exactly what?"

Reznick's chest tightened. "What are you talking about?"

"Do you recognize this woman?"

A few seconds elapsed before a familiar voice came on the line. "Jon? Jon, is that you?"

A feeling of dread washed over him. He was listening to the fragile and frightened voice of his late wife's mother.

He took a few moments to gather his thoughts. "Beth, what the hell's going on?"

"Jon, I'm so sorry . . ."

"Sorry? What do you mean *sorry*?"

Silence.

"Beth, what's wrong?"

An unsteady breath before she spoke. "Some men . . . some men took me from the house and—"

The man's voice came back on the line. "I have a gun pointed at your mother-in-law's head as we speak. You give me what I want and you'll see the lovely Beth again. But you must listen very carefully to what I have to say."

"Who the fuck is this?"

"Wrong answer. Maybe this will focus your mind."

A shot rang out as Reznick drove on in stunned silence.

The man came back on. "Do we have your attention now? I hope so. OK, Jon, hopefully you realize that we're serious people. So, I'm going to get straight to the point. It's not just Beth we took. We also have your daughter."

Everything seemed to slow down as he tried to comprehend what was happening. The word "daughter" sent Reznick spiraling into a private hell.

His beautiful daughter. How could this be happening? Wasn't she still at school? He realized he'd gone into shock.

"She's very pretty. But if you want to see her again, you need to do exactly as I say. I'll call you back in two minutes."

The line went dead as an unbearable emptiness opened up inside Reznick.

He pulled over on a tree-lined residential street four blocks from the safe house. A black anger began to build deep within him, ready to devour him at any moment. Part of him wanted it to. But then, slowly, it subsided as his training kicked in.

He began to think and reason, moving beyond a visceral reaction as he tried to figure out exactly how to respond.

Reznick smashed his fist on the dashboard. "Fuck!"

How on God's earth had they kidnapped both Beth and Lauren? His daughter boarded at an exclusive school in western Massachusetts. But then he remembered that she was staying over in New York with Beth as a pre-Christmas treat before she returned home to Maine on Christmas Eve.

So, was she being held in New York? But how had these guys known about his family in the first place?

He wracked his brains. He'd only had a handful of friends over the years, and they'd drifted away from him since Elisabeth's death.

Only his oldest friends in Rockland—guys he'd grown up with in the 1980s, when his hometown had been a tough fishing port struggling with boarded-up stores on Main Street, and motorcycle gangs and their dogs running amok in the bars—knew about his daughter. The bottom line was he wanted to protect her from his world and show her only the good things.

His mind flashed back to an evening at a local bar, the Myrtle. The only time the subject had been openly broached by someone outside his tight-knit circle. Danny Grainger, a lobsterman and obnoxious ex-classmate from high school, who hated his life and liked to drink himself into oblivion six nights out of seven, had approached Reznick and asked about his daughter. He'd heard that Reznick was in the military. Reznick knew he was spoiling for a fight and would have gladly obliged. But he just smiled and said his daughter was fine and thanks for asking, and left it at that.

The answer had seemed to placate Danny and he'd smiled his best drunk's smile, put his arm around Reznick, and proceeded to talk at length about how he didn't recognize the working-class town of Rockland these days. The once-tough waterfront of fish-packing and commercial docks now transformed—especially downtown, around Main Street and the harbor—by countless art galleries, museums, fancy restaurants, and the North Atlantic Blues Festival. But Reznick hadn't given him—nor anyone, that or any other night—a clue about where his daughter was. Reznick knew that in his line of work, the best way to get to people was to get to their family. Easy targets.

Luntz cleared his throat loudly in the back seat, snapping Reznick back to reality. "What the hell is going on?" he said.

Reznick turned around and pointed a finger in Luntz's face. "Not a fucking word."

Luntz looked close to tears as he shook his head.

A few moments later, a chime on the dead man's iPhone signaled a message. Reznick opened it—a short video clip. His mother-in-law was lying tied to a steel pillar, in a dingy basement or warehouse, hands behind her back, a blindfold over her eyes. He noticed the emerald stone around her neck, the one her late husband had given her as a fiftieth birthday present. He watched her bony shoulders begin to shake, then her lip, before a gun was pressed to her head and her brains splattered onto the pillar.

He closed his eyes as revulsion swept over him. He closed the message as his breathing quickened.

Reznick needed to get control back. Needed to focus. He thought of Lauren, only eleven years old. He couldn't be sure they had her. But deep down, he sensed they weren't bullshitting.

He had to contact Maddox.

Reznick picked up the iPhone and punched in the number. Then, just as he was about to press the green phone icon to dial, he stopped. He needed to take things slow. He needed time to think. And the more he thought about it, the more it began to dawn on him that he couldn't trust anyone else on this. The fewer people who knew, the better.

He had to do this his way. This was his daughter: she was priceless. He couldn't allow one false move that could jeopardize her. All it would take was a phone call to Maddox—a call they'd be monitoring.

The cell phone rang again.

"If you don't want the same thing to happen to your daughter, listen and listen good. You will take what I want to Miami. You will drive him there so as to avoid any problems with airports or trains. In just over twenty-four hours' time, we will contact you on this number, and talk about an exchange. If you speak to the police, the

Feds, or anyone, you will receive another video—of your daughter getting a bullet in the head. Don't disappoint me, Jon."

———

Reznick began the long drive south on I-95. His mind flashed back to Beth's dreadful final moments. A woman who had suffered so much with the loss of her daughter on 9/11. A woman who had tried to rebuild her shattered life, despite not having a body to bury. A woman who had looked after Lauren in the years after Elisabeth's death. What a terrible end to a fine woman.

His mind flashed back to the first time he'd met Elisabeth's parents—dinner at the Café Carlyle on the Upper East Side, half a block from their townhouse. A pianist had played jazz standards as the wine flowed, and Elisabeth had draped her arm around him as Beth smiled.

Waves of guilt swept over him. He alone was responsible for Beth's death and his daughter's kidnapping. His shadowy world had encroached on his family.

His mood darkened further. The anger coursed through his veins, growing like a cancer, threatening to eat him alive. On and on he drove. The man in the back seat, Luntz, tried to make conversation. But Reznick was too busy trying to figure out what the hell to do.

The hours dragged.

He drove on, tormented, down through the Carolinas. Eventually, he pulled off I-95 and headed into Florence, South Carolina. He still had relatives who lived nearby, although he had never met them. His mother's bloodline could be traced back to Scots who had been forced off their land during the Highland Clearances in the nineteenth century. They had immigrated to Nova Scotia before they crossed the border. His mother could trace her roots back to one Jimmy MacKinley, who had moved his family to Maine, where he became a fisherman. The rest of the MacKinleys headed down to the Carolinas. Poachers, trappers, and outlaws, unable and unwilling to be tamed. Backwoodsmen. Renegades. Wild people. They lived off the land. It was their home.

He pondered on that as he found a parking garage and stole a black Lexus with tinted windows. Afterward, they went to a diner and ate in silence, then Reznick got back onto the freeway, headed south. As the day drew to a close, as he crossed the Florida state line, a plan had begun to formulate in his mind.

Simply turning up and handing over Luntz wasn't an option. *They* held all the cards. What he needed was someone he could trust to keep Luntz safe—someone who could help him out.

He knew such a man. A man he'd trust with his life.

Just before midnight, Reznick drove into Fort Lauderdale, South Florida. Luntz was out cold in the trunk, trussed up like a chicken, and had been for the last hour.

Reznick pulled up half a block from the neon-lit, spray-painted entrance of the Monterey Club. The bar was located south of downtown, next to a tattoo parlor, part of the same complex that sold classic bikes.

The owner of the bar was an old Delta operator, Harry Leggett, who'd been his best man at his wedding. Tough, funny, and a complete nightmare after ten bottles of Heineken. Leggett was the only one from Delta his late wife, Elisabeth, had liked.

It was Leggett's sister Angie, who'd worked alongside Elisabeth, who had introduced her to Reznick.

His mind switched back to their first date. It was imprinted on his mind. He'd been home for two weeks' leave, and Angie had suggested they meet up as a foursome for a drink at McSorley's Old Ale House, a spit-and-sawdust dive in the East Village. Elisabeth talked fast about everything under the sun, from running the New York Marathon, to fighting off a mugger in Central Park with pepper spray, to her expensive education at the Chapin School. He'd surprised himself by liking her immediately. They just clicked. He had never entertained the thought of settling down until he met her. She was beautiful, neurotic, open, relaxed in his company and, he noticed, quick at self-deprecation. She was from a different world. She talked of Cubism and modern art. He hadn't had a clue what that was all about. But there was an immediate connection.

He'd listened to her go into minute detail about the distinction between tax avoidance and tax evasion. They'd drunk warm beer in half-filled mugs and eaten a cheese platter with raw onion and hot mustard. When she asked him about his work, he didn't tell her about Delta, but said he worked overseas a lot for the government. She didn't press him further. He'd liked that, but guessed that Angie might have filled her in on the details. Then he'd talked of Rockland and how it was a great town these days. He'd told her about new art galleries popping up almost overnight and how it was changing the image of his hometown. He'd spoken about the calming nature of the sea, the smell of the fresh fish that had just been landed, and of crowded Main Street, thronged with visitors in the summer months. He'd told her that when he smelled the ocean, he knew he was home. And that he was safe. She'd listened intently. She said she'd always wanted to live by the sea; work was in Manhattan, but she could see herself giving it all up for a less stressed life.

The possibilities seemed endless.

He'd felt like a different person. The following day, they met up again and walked in the park. Within a few months—and quite out of character—he'd found himself proposing to her at the Crystal Room in the Tavern on the Green, overlooking Central Park. They were married the next year. The wedding reception was at the Plaza on August 14, 1999, a blazing hot day. Twenty Delta operators wearing impeccable gray morning suits turned up and sat in the corner of the main ballroom, guzzling beer and laughing uproariously as the band played Carpenters covers. Elisabeth's family, blue bloods who gave large donations to the Met and the Museum of Modern Art, had looked aghast—although Beth seemed to enjoy herself more than her husband. The highlight of the evening had been an inebriated Leggett attempting to mimic Michael Jackson's moonwalk as the band played "Billie Jean" and then collapsing in a heap, leaving the Delta crew in stitches.

The sound of thrash metal from Leggett's bar brought him back to reality for a few moments. Tiredness was starting to swamp him. He popped a couple of Dexedrine and closed his eyes. His mind flashed back to 9/11. The news footage of the collapsing towers. The smoke. The dust cloud. The twisted metal. The mayhem.

The worlds of Reznick and Leggett had been inextricably linked that fateful day.

Elisabeth and Angie were both tax attorneys and worked in the same law firm in One World Trade Center. Both had perished on 9/11. Leggett's sister was one of the jumpers—trapped by the flames, she'd leapt from the eighty-ninth floor to her death. The downward spiral of his old friend had begun on that day.

Reznick and Leggett had both used the same coping strategy: they cut themselves off from the outside world. They found solace in their own ways. The first thing Reznick had done was ask Beth to look after Lauren. He couldn't cope with looking after a baby. There was no body to bury and he wasn't sleeping. And he'd wanted Lauren to be safe in Beth's Manhattan townhouse. He was consumed by anger and grief. He couldn't provide the stable family home she needed.

He'd retreated back to the solitude of his home outside Rockland. He sat on the beach where he'd sat with Elisabeth and Lauren for hours at a time. The memories haunted him. Plagued him. He would sometimes climb down to the rocky shoreline when it got dark, and listen to the waves crashing onto the beach. But then he'd be engulfed by a black mood, and he'd scream in a burning rage until his lungs nearly burst. It was like it would never end. He drank too much and he didn't see a soul for months. He didn't want to.

Then one day, out of the blue, he'd called Leggett. They met up in New York, and hugged and cried and talked about their losses. It was clear that Leggett was drinking insane amounts. He knocked back two bottles of scotch a day, interspersed with numerous beers. But it didn't end there. By the start of 2002, Leggett had begun to self-harm, cutting his wrists and arms, and he was hospitalized. Eventually, he seemed to have sorted himself out and got back with Delta, but by 2004 he'd had enough, and retired to Florida.

Raucous laughter snapped Reznick back to the present. He stared across at Leggett's bar. Standing outside it were kids wearing black, smoking cigarettes, drinking from bottles of beer, arms draped around some statuesque bar girls.

The night air was warm and sticky. He checked his rearview mirror and side mirrors, but he didn't detect any tails or cops. He was running a risk with a stolen car with South Carolina plates. He decided he would take that chance. His major concern just now was that he couldn't take Luntz into the bar. That would be asking for trouble.

He weighed up his options and realized he didn't have any. He decided to leave the car where it was, as he was only going to be gone for a couple of minutes. He shut the window and stepped out into the sultry night. Pressing the car's central-locking fob, he walked up to the bar's entrance.

A tattooed skinny guy with tousled blond hair stepped forward and smiled, partially blocking his way. He was holding a cigarette in one hand, a bottle of Bud in the other. "Sorry my friend," he said. "We're closed."

"I'll bear that in mind, son," Reznick said as he brushed right past him and headed inside to the cool of the bar.

A crazy old hippie was belting out some punked-up blues classics on an old guitar, as stoned college kids lounged around on sofas, drinking beer and laughing loudly.

Reznick walked up to the bar and ordered a Heineken. He handed the tattooed, muscle-bound barman a twenty-dollar bill and told him to keep the change. The kid took the money and Reznick took a long drink. The cold beer quenched his thirst.

"I'm looking for Harry Leggett," he said.

"Who's asking?"

"Name's Reznick."

"You got a first name?"

He gulped down the rest of the Heineken. "Just tell him Reznick's in town."

A smile spread slowly across the barman's chiseled features and he handed Reznick back his twenty-dollar bill. "Your money's no good here, man. It's on the house." He extended his hand. "Pleasure to meet you, sir. Ron Leggett. Remember me? We met a few years back, up in New York."

Reznick shook his hand. "Christ, Ron, I didn't recognize you. How's your father these days?"

"A pain in the ass, if you must know." He asked a barmaid to hold the fort for a few minutes. The girl nodded sullenly as Ron opened a couple more Heinekens and joined Reznick on the other side of the bar.

Ron pulled up a stool and sat down. "Man, Dad's gonna freak when he sees you," he said, taking a large gulp of beer. "I take it you're not here for the music."

"Is your dad around?"

The kid pulled out a pack of Winstons from his shirt pocket, tapped out a cigarette, and lit up. He inhaled half an inch of cigarette before he flicked ash on the floor. "Yeah, he's around. Just not here. An old buddy turned up this morning and they went fishing this afternoon. He likes to kick back a couple times a week. He's probably sleeping it off on his boat."

Reznick's gaze was drawn behind the whiskey optics, to a faded color picture of Leggett that showed some guys drinking in the bar. He didn't recognize any of the faces. "Your dad's got a boat?"

"Yeah, a brand-new fifty-foot Cabo," Ron said. He took a deep pull on his cigarette and crushed it in the ashtray. "It's awesome. Pure teak inside. Man, my dad loves that boat."

Reznick smiled but said nothing.

"Real pleasure to meet you again." He leaned closer, voice low. "My dad once told me that you were the only man he truly trusted. Said you never made a wrong move, you always made the right call. And you never, ever let him down."

Reznick averted his gaze. "I don't know about that." He looked at the boy's rippling physique. "So, how's life working out for your dad?"

"I work all the hours here, and he spends most of his time on his boat."

"I hear you."

Ron fired up another cigarette, dragging hard on it. He blew the smoke out of the corner of his mouth, away from Reznick. "It's a job." He slugged back some more beer. "But my heart's set on becoming a Marine. An officer."

"You any idea what it entails?"

"A bit."

"You know the motto at the Officer Candidates School at Quantico?"

"No, I don't."

"*Ductus Exemplo.*"

The kid shrugged.

"Look it up. It's Latin."

Ron smiled blankly.

"I really need to speak to your dad now. Is his boat nearby?"

"Yeah, he's got a nice new berth down the marina. Walking distance. Man, he'll freak when he sees you."

Reznick drove the Lexus—with the man he should have killed still in the trunk—to a parking garage three blocks away. He popped open the trunk. Luntz was still out of it, and probably would be for a few more hours. Locking the car, he headed down to the waterfront.

A short while later, he walked past the Elbo Room on Fort Lauderdale Beach. The sounds of whoops and cheers and thumping music spilled out from the bar.

He walked on for a couple of hundred yards, the lights of the yachts and restaurants in the marina in the distance. A few minutes later, he found himself on a wooden gangway to Dock E beside the Intracoastal Waterway, right next to the dock master's office.

An old guy hosing down the deck of one of the boats nearby, cigarette at the corner of his mouth, nodded to Reznick. "You down to do some fishin'?" he asked. "If you are, you're too late. But I'm taking my boat out at first light if you wanna come back and do some serious fishin'. Snared fifteen marlins yesterday alone."

The smell of fish bait, kerosene, and barbecued meat hung in the muggy air. It reminded him of night fishing when he was a boy, his father reminiscing about 'Nam, the Mekong, and his buddies who hadn't made it home, trying not to think about his next shift at Port Clyde Foods cannery. He'd always hated his factory job. He'd wanted Reznick never to work in any of the Rockland fish-packing plants. He'd once taken him in to watch him work. The smell had made Reznick sick. He remembered watching his father's dead-eyed expression—so different from the pictures of him back in Vietnam. He'd watched his dad work at the packing tables, using a pair of sharpened knives to cut the heads and tails off the fish coming in before packing them in cans, being bellowed at by a weasel foreman. His father could never answer back, as he'd never work in any of the plants in Rockland again if he did. It was piecework, so the faster he went, the more money he made. He worked from 7 a.m. until 10 p.m. every day, with hardly any breaks.

It was there and then that Reznick had vowed he'd never do that job.

Reznick saw the lights from a nearby yacht partially illuminating the dock. "Maybe next time."

"You got a boat here?"

"Looking for a friend of mine. Harry Leggett."

The old guy pointed to the pristine fifty-foot yacht berthed nearly twenty yards away. "That's Harry's boat."

"Thanks for the tip."

"Any time," he said, now mopping the deck of the boat.

Reznick walked farther down the gangway and climbed on board the yacht, using the aluminum rails to help him. Bait tanks and tackle storage boxes lined the cockpit. In the center was a fighting chair mounted on an aluminum-reinforced plate, for marlin fishing.

Reznick knocked on a small window on the cabin's doors. He got no answer. He tried a couple more times but still nothing. He peered through the window and saw a modern galley with granite surfaces.

"Hey, anyone home?" Reznick said. "Harry—you in here, you old boozehound?"

No reply.

Reznick opened the door and switched on the lights. Ron was right: the yacht was teak everywhere. There were two single berths made up, and a small settee.

"Hey, Harry, you wanna shake a leg?"

The sound of the water lapping against the side of the yacht. But he also heard the sound of a TV.

Reznick knocked hard on the door to the stateroom and went inside. It was dark, except for the huge flat-screen TV blaring. The place stank of liquor and cigarette smoke. "Fucking hell," he said. A Fox News anchorwoman was talking shrilly about the costs of healthcare. He reached over and flicked on the light switch.

A half-empty bottle of tequila lay on its side, the contents soaked into the thick beige carpet. There was an empty bottle of scotch on the bedside table.

Reznick slumped on a sofa. He couldn't believe he had missed Harry. He must have headed out for a late-night bar crawl with his buddy.

He felt anger gnawing at him. He was running out of options, and fast. He needed Harry to take Luntz off his hands, no question. But as he looked around the detritus of his Delta comrade's broken life, he wondered if Harry was really the man to help him.

The more he thought of it, the more angry he got with himself for even considering his old friend, a burned-up alcoholic, as suitable to watch over Luntz—or anyone, for that matter. He couldn't even look after his own life.

The news anchor droned on. *"America will have to make some hard choices . . ."*

His heart sank as he began to face up to the consequences of his own hard choices.

Reznick closed his eyes, head in his hands. He listened to his heavy breathing. He could barely hear himself think over the braying voice on the TV talking about the repercussions of the size of the US debt. "*There will be a price to pay some day . . .*"

He sat up and stared again at the empty booze bottles.

The newscaster's booming voice was talking about a Taliban resurgence in Helmand province. Reznick leaned over and picked up the remote control, turning off the TV. He sat in contemplation for a few moments. He thought he could hear something. It was like a tap running. He cocked his head and wondered if it sounded like a shower.

He looked over toward a recessed door, which was partly concealed by old cardboard boxes. He got up, stepped over the empty bottle of tequila, kicked aside the boxes, and opened the door to reveal a huge en-suite bathroom. The room was steamed up. "Harry, are you drunk? You in here all this time?"

Reznick walked over to the shower and yanked open the door.

His heart nearly stopped. Lying in the fetal position inside the shower was a man with a familiar crew cut. Reznick bent down and saw the tattoo on the left forearm. The Delta insignia—a black dagger and the word "Airborne" above it. He remembered the night they'd both decided to get tattooed, after completing the Operator Training Course.

He turned the body over. The dead blue eyes of Harry Leggett stared back at him. He edged closer and smelled the booze.

Harry's skin was bluish-gray. Reznick's gaze was drawn to his firing hand—his right—and a large callus in the web of the thumb. The telltale sign of a former Delta assault team member, even after all these years. He had the same.

Then his attention was drawn to something so small and insignificant, it could—and most certainly would—be missed by the cops when they eventually found the body.

Behind Harry's left ear was the tiniest of pinpricks.

Reznick felt his throat constrict. It was a mark he was all too familiar with. Someone wanted whoever discovered the body to think Harry had been on booze and pills. But Reznick could see with his own eyes. His blood brother, Harry, had been suicided.

Reznick began to shake. He thought his heart was about to burst. He fought back the tears as he slid his hand under Leggett's head, cradling it like a baby, as the shower water poured down. He felt a volcanic anger take hold as he stared at the lifeless eyes. The same eyes that had shed tears of joy and laughter. The lines more pronounced, almost like claws around the skin. He pulled Harry's head to his chest and he began to weep. Unashamed.

"Who did this, Harry?" He clutched him tight to his beating heart. "Who did this to you? Tell me!"

He felt numb as dark thoughts began to cloud his head. Someone had got to Leggett. Not so long ago—perhaps within the last few hours. Just ahead of Reznick. He wondered if he had been followed south. The whole thing was so fucked up it wasn't true.

Reznick carefully lowered Leggett's head down to the plastic floor of the shower. Water cascaded into the dead man's open eyes. "I've got to go, Harry. I need to leave you here." He stared down, a lump in his throat. "I'll be seeing you." He touched his friend's cheek. Cold.

The raw anger inside began to subside. He zoned out, as he had been trained to do.

Reznick looked around the teak-paneled cabin, trying to figure out his next move as he gathered his thoughts. His prints were all over the place. On the rails, on the handles, in the cabin. The body would be discovered come first light. And they would have him pegged for killing his old buddy.

This was a cute operation. But Reznick hadn't called ahead. So how had they known about Harry?

Six

Reznick took Harry Leggett's son into a back room at the bar, locking the door. The boy had the same sunken eyes as his father. He sat the kid down and told him the news straight. He watched as the kid went a ghostly white before breaking down in tears.

"I don't fucking believe you, man. Are you kidding me?"

Reznick draped an arm around the boy's broad shoulders. "Ron, look at me. If there was anything I could've done, I would. Your father meant the world to me."

The kid was sobbing hard.

"Let it out, son."

Reznick remembered the wretched emptiness of the day his own father died. He remembered watching them lower his coffin into the grave, former Marines looking on. He'd been a young man himself and had put on a strong face. A mask.

The boy's body was shaking and quivering as he sobbed his heart out.

"I don't have the right words, Ron. But I want you to know that your father loved you."

The kid wiped away the tears with the back of his hand. "What happened?"

Reznick leaned in close and sighed. "Listen to me, Ron," he said, keeping his voice low. "What I'm about to say is difficult to get your head around."

"What do you mean?"

"There were no visible signs of injuries. But it was made to look like it was a drunken accident."

"I don't understand."

"I can't go into it . . . but I know the signs. He might have been jabbed by an anesthetic-type drug. One that paralyzes, makes it look like a person has collapsed and had a heart attack. It's a method of assassination."

The kid looked at him aghast.

"Is this related to your work or people you know?"

"Maybe."

"Maybe? What does that mean?"

"It means I don't really know."

The boy shook his head, tears streaking his face. He stared at Reznick. "You caused this, didn't you?"

"Ron, you've every right to be angry. I'd be angry too."

"Someone is after you, is that what it is, and got Dad instead?"

"There are forces at work in this country about which you have no knowledge. Do you understand?"

"My mom always thought something like this would happen. The people you work with get tangled up in your personal life—she always worried about shit like that."

"Ron, you said a guy turned up here this morning, asking to speak to your dad. I need you to tell me about this guy."

Ron wiped his eyes with the back of his hand. "You think he did this?"

"I don't know. Maybe."

The kid stared at Reznick. "What do you want to know?"

"Have you seen the guy before?"

"No."

"Did he have a name?"

"Chad . . . I think he said his name was Chad."

The name sent alarm bells ringing. "Chad?"

"Yeah, Chad. You know him?"

"Ron, look, I know this is tough, but can you describe this guy to me?"

The kid dabbed his eyes. "Long blond hair, dark tan, mean-looking dude."

"Mean-looking, right. Did he have a pronounced accent at all?"

"What do you mean by that?"

"I mean, did it stand out in any way?"

"Yeah. He sounded like a big Texan boy."

Reznick nodded. "I know this isn't easy, but is there anything else you can remember about this guy? I'm talking physically."

"He had a huge fuck-off scar on his face, if that's what you mean. Nasty-looking motherfucker."

Reznick's blood ran cold. The description was a perfect match for a guy he knew. A guy Leggett had known. A guy called Chad Magruder, a former Delta crazy who had been on countless missions with Leggett and Reznick before he was found guilty of raping a woman after breaking into her home in Raleigh.

"Did he arrive by car? Think very carefully."

"Yeah, the dude's car was right outside, half blocking the entrance. Look, sir, I want to help you find whoever did this."

"I understand that absolutely. But just try and think for a minute—what kind of car was he driving?"

"I think it was a black SUV."

"Are you sure?"

"We've got surveillance cameras out front. I can check."

"Show me the footage."

The kid stared blankly, before averting his gaze and getting to his feet. "Follow me."

Reznick followed Ron through to a small windowless room near the rear of the bar. There was a table with a keyboard and two small monitors. One was blank and one showed the exterior of the bar, some kids still goofing around, smoking and laughing. Ron punched in the approximate time the guy called Chad had arrived. Scrolling through the footage, minute after minute, he got to 9:04 a.m. and a black SUV pulled up, partially visible. The car reversed into view.

"Let this section play," Reznick said.

A few moments later, a tall and wiry man walked into shot— long blond hair, shades on, Cowboys baseball cap, black shirt, jeans, and scuffed boots.

"Freeze that!" said Reznick.

He looked long and hard at the grainy image. It was Magruder all right.

"OK, I think that's the guy you told me about," Reznick said. "Can you back up to when the car arrives? I'm sure there's something on the rear windshield, a big sticker, when he reverses."

The kid scrolled back and froze the image.

Reznick peered at the screen. "Ryan's of Weston?"

The kid scrunched up his face. "Yup."

"What the hell's that?"

"Rental company based in Weston."

"Where's Weston?"

The kid blinked away the tears. "On the edge of the Everglades. Not far. Maybe twenty miles or so."

Reznick looked at the boy before hugging him tight.

The kid began to sob into Reznick's chest. "Why'd he kill my dad?"

Reznick sighed. "God only knows."

As he headed back to the parking garage, he realized having Magruder on the scene was bad. He crossed a busy intersection, took a right, and saw the blue neon sign for the garage up ahead.

What the hell are you doing, Reznick? Stuck in the middle of Fort fucking Lauderdale, when your little girl needs you. Goddamn, why hadn't he gone straight to Miami and focused on playing along with those guys, and getting his daughter back?

Lauren was out there somewhere, alone. Probably terrified at the hands of God knows who.

"Hey, buddy, you lost?" a man's voice said.

He turned around as a cop car pulled up beside him, the arm of the officer in the passenger seat hanging out the window.

"Just looking for a bar, officer."

The cop chewed gum as the driver talked into a radio. "Yeah—what bar you looking for?"

"Any bar'll do."

The officer smiled, chewing hard on his gum. "You not from around here?"

"No, sir. From out of town."

"Out of town, huh? Where you staying?"

"Supposed to be staying on a friend's boat. But he's gone out night fishing instead. So, you know how it is, a man's gotta pass the time some way."

The officer stepped out of the car. "Sir, do you have any identification on you?"

Reznick reached into his back pocket and handed him the second fake driver's license. The cop scanned it before nodding.

"Long way from Burlington, Vermont."

Reznick smiled.

The officer shrugged. "Seems OK. But I'll need to check these details over on our computer, sir. Won't take a minute, OK?"

Reznick nodded. "Take your time, officer."

The cop got back in the cruiser and called in the name. A couple of minutes later, the radio crackled to life. "Yeah, it's clean."

The officer stared at Reznick. "What d'you do up in Burlington, if you don't mind me asking?"

"A bit of this, a bit of that. Maintenance mostly."

He handed the ID back. "Sorry for keeping you, sir. A routine check, I'm sure you'll understand."

"Not a problem, officer."

The officer nodded to the driver and they headed off, taking a right at a set of lights.

Reznick let out a long sigh at the close call. If the car had been stopped, he'd have had to take the cops down. Not ideal in any circumstances.

He walked on for a few minutes, before heading down a side street and finding his way back to the parking garage. Up on the second floor, he popped open the trunk of the Lexus. Luntz was breathing hard. Reznick untied him and undid the gag. "Let me out of here," Luntz said, sweat beading his forehead. "Please don't lock me in here again."

Reznick stared down at the blinking, terrified scientist. "It all depends on if you behave yourself. Do you understand?"

Luntz blinked away tears and nodded.

Reznick yanked Luntz out of the trunk by his T-shirt and stood him up. He looked unsteady on his feet. "You OK?"

Luntz shook his head. "No, I'm not OK." His eyes were glazed.

"Do what I say and we're gonna get through this, d'you understand?"

Luntz stared blankly at him and said nothing.

"OK, let's go," said Reznick as he marched him across the concrete floor toward a Volvo.

"Please, where are you taking me? Please, I'm scared. I'm scared you're taking me somewhere to kill me."

"That's not gonna happen. Just trust me." Using his high-tech fob, Reznick disabled the alarm and the immobilizer. Then he opened the passenger door and strapped a disorientated and blinking Luntz in. "Don't move a fucking muscle."

Reznick went around and opened the driver's door. Pulling out his Swiss Army knife, he bent down and popped open the plastic cover around the steering wheel. On the left-hand side was the ignition. He unscrewed the two bolts that held the metal cover in place, and jammed the knife's smallest blade into the slot. The engine purred into life.

He slid into the driver's seat, put on his seat belt, and revved the engine a couple of times.

Where to now? Should he follow up the Magruder lead to the town of Weston, on the off chance of getting lucky?

His thoughts turned to Magruder's name. Unusual. Rare, even. How many Magruders could there be in a provincial town in South Florida?

Reznick pulled the iPhone out of his back pocket and punched in "411" for directory assistance.

"What number are you looking for?" a woman's voice said.

"Hi, looking for a number in Weston, Florida. Is there anything for Magruder?"

"How are you spelling that, sir?"

"Magruder. M-A-G-R-U-D-E-R."

"Hold the line, sir." Vivaldi's *Four Seasons* started playing for what seemed like an eternity. It was probably only a couple of seconds. Eventually, the woman came back on the line. "Yes, sir, I've got one in the town of Weston, Florida."

"One number, that's great."

"Yeah, we've got a Shelley Anne Magruder, two three eight seven Lake Boulevard, Weston. Number is nine five four, three eight four, seven two seven two."

He made a mental note of the address and number and ended the call. Then he buckled up, switched on the sat nav, and punched in the town of Weston.

The woman's voice on the sat nav directed him out of Fort Lauderdale and onto the I-95 ramp toward Miami and the Port Everglades. He cranked up the air con, and the blast of cold air began to refresh him. Then he switched on the radio. Some country station was playing.

He turned it up as he remembered the first time he'd met Magruder.

It had been a cold spring day, snow still on the ground—during the selection and assessment for 1st Special Forces Operational Detachment–Delta at Camp Dawson, West Virginia. It started with the same bullshit eight-hour standardized psychological tests: *Do you like brunettes? Do you have black, tarry stools? Do you think people are talking about you? Do you hear voices? On the whole, do people understand you? Do you think of yourself as a serious person? Are you introspective?* That kind of lame, pseudo psychobabble.

They wanted to screen out the crazies. But they must have been asking the wrong questions that morning.

Magruder, a tall wiry man, was clean gone. He had insane amounts of nervous energy. He stood out as an obsessive, even among the obsessives of Delta. He had a stellar reputation for marksmanship, even among the Delta crack shots. He attended shooting competitions across America and beat everyone in sight. He practiced magazine change and dry firing, time after time. He'd read his Operator Training Course manual multiple times, and kept abreast of tradecraft and explosives. Everything was an opportunity to improve. To get better. He carried more weight in his rucksack; he studied martial arts to the highest level, beating the shit out of some of the best fighters in America.

But what no one knew at the time was that Magruder was damaged. Unlike Reznick, who had enjoyed a typical outdoorsy childhood in Maine—hiking, hunting, and fishing with his dad—Magruder had endured a torrid, violent childhood. His father, a trucker, had physically abused him for years. Beatings bordering on torture.

While other Delta guys drank like maniacs when off duty, Magruder—who wasn't married, and lived alone in a trailer—was content to nurse a bottle of beer for hours and then retire quietly for the night.

He didn't talk about sex at all and seemed embarrassed as the rest of Delta watched porn, drank beer, and talked about women.

Then a succession of violent rapes occurred in Raleigh, including incidents at North Carolina State University, by what police thought was a lone stranger. The hooded man had climbed through the victims' windows, dressed in black, and raped the women at knifepoint.

Police arrested Chad Magruder, who was reported to have been deferential to the detectives when he was charged with three counts of rape. He was convicted, and most people who'd read about the case in the newspapers—including Reznick—thought the key would have been thrown away.

The truly terrifying thing was that no one had ever thought Magruder was mad. A bit quiet—obsessive, sure—but one of them.

"Why are we heading in this direction?"

"Never you mind. Look, I don't want to hear any more from you."

"Please, can't you just drop me off and let me go?"

"Knock it off and we'll get on a whole lot better." Reznick let out a long yawn.

The sat nav guided him down a dark, near-deserted street toward a huge house overlooking the lake, partially hidden behind a trimmed hedge. The number 2387 on the gate, a silver Mercedes convertible in the drive. But no sign of the black SUV caught on the cameras outside the Monterey Club.

He came to a stop outside for a few minutes. A police patrol car came into sight at the far end of the lake.

Reznick drove on as the cruiser passed in the opposite direction. Neither of the two officers glanced out of the window. He continued for another half-mile before he turned around and headed back toward the house.

He pulled up about a hundred yards away behind a BMW, but with a line of sight to the front door and the asphalt driveway. Then he switched off the engine and lights before letting out a long sigh.

"Why are we stopping here?" Luntz said.

Reznick turned and stared at him. "Do you want to spend Christmas with your family?"

"Yes, of course."

"Then you're going to have to do exactly what I say. And you're going to have to trust me. With your life."

Seven

Fifteen miles southwest of Baltimore, Thomas Wesley was driving past block after block of soulless glass and steel towers in a sprawling business park. His nighttime drives were becoming a routine, killing time until he started his shift as an overnight stocker at Walmart. He yawned and checked the luminous orange clock on his dashboard. It showed 3:47 a.m.—thirteen minutes until he was due at work. It had only been three months since he'd taken the minimum-wage job. But already the mind-numbing hellishness, coupled with his coworkers' small talk about reality TV shows he didn't watch and fad diets of movie stars he didn't know, made him hanker for his old life.

Up ahead, the office sign of Xarasoft—his old employer, a company he had given twenty-one years of his life to—glowed bright yellow. Only a few lights were on, in the foyer of the mirrored glass tower.

Wesley gazed across the parking lot at the other monolithic towers that populated the business park. There were cameras scanning everywhere. Most of the companies were technology firms and were contracted—like Xarasoft—to the National Security Agency.

He'd had a good life—a voice analyst who worked for the NSA as a contractor. Six-figure basic salary. Huge bonuses. Foreign vacations. The works. Now he was so fucking broke he couldn't even pay his utility bills.

His coworkers at Walmart had no idea what he used to do. They never asked. Even if they had, he couldn't tell them the truth about his top secret work. They probably wouldn't believe him anyway.

Wesley saw a light go on, four floors up at his old company. He wondered if they were communicating in real time with the NSA, perhaps ingesting one or two intercepted bulletin board postings, instant messages, IP addresses, or vital *FLASH* traffic that had been flagged up.

He felt depressed as he contemplated his old life.

His wife thought it was only the Prozac that was keeping him able to face the world. But there was something else keeping him going—the reason he wouldn't give up trying to get people to listen to what he knew. *A conversation he had begun to piece together from fragments of nigh-impossible-to-intercept scraps of information.*

He listened to the voices. He used voice-comparison technology and listened over and over again in the small booth in his home office, headphones on, stripping the recordings down to the core voices. He wasn't sleeping during the day. His wife worried about him. But she didn't know what he knew.

Two days ago, he had uncovered a smooth and terrifying narrative among the disembodied voices. The problem was no one was listening.

Wesley took out his BlackBerry and set about composing the latest encrypted email to Lance Drake, a Republican congressman on the House Intelligence Committee—and an old Yale drinking buddy. He stared at the screen for a few moments before sending the message. Then he put away his phone and closed his eyes, thinking of his fiftieth birthday party only a year earlier, when the congressman and other close friends had attended a barbecue in his backyard. Now those same people he'd thought were his friends, people he'd had a beer with on a Saturday night, guys he'd gone bowling with once a month, didn't return his calls or go out for drinks.

His cell phone rang and Wesley almost jumped out of his skin.

"Thomas, what the hell are you playing at?" It was Drake.

Wesley cleared his throat. "Lance, appreciate the call back."

"Do you know what time it is?" The congressman's voice was an angry whisper.

"Yes, I know what time it is. Did I wake you?"

"The buzzing of my fucking BlackBerry on my bedside table woke me up."

"Lance, why haven't you answered my emails?"

"Why haven't I answered your emails?" The tone was heavily sarcastic. "Do you want me to level with you?"

Wesley said nothing.

"You've sent me precisely twenty-seven emails—all virtually identical—in the last forty-eight hours alone. Not to put too fine a point on it, I'm starting to question your state of mind."

"My state of mind, huh?" Wesley felt a knot of tension in his stomach. "There's nothing wrong with my state of mind."

"Thomas, they say you had two psychological evaluations before you were fired, and that you show certain *personality traits*."

"That's bullshit."

Lance let out a long sigh. "Thomas, look, I know how smart you are. But the fact of the matter is, you screwed up before. You made the wrong call."

"Is that what they told you? That's bullshit."

"They say you were flat-out wrong."

"They're lying."

"Listen, I've not got time for this, Thomas."

"OK, let's focus on the here and now. Forget about that. What I'm about to tell you is something that sounds a bit far-out, I understand that."

"Thomas, please, it's late."

"Just bear with me. I've been busy working on developing a new bit of software. It helps achieve tight bandwidth compression of the speech signals like you wouldn't believe."

"Thomas, I don't understand this technical stuff you're throwing at me."

"Before my security clearance was taken away, I began to piece something together. Lance, all I ask is that you take heed of what I'm saying. I believe there is a very real threat to America."

"Why haven't I heard of this?"

"Good question. But that's just half of it. There's more I've discovered recently. I've been listening to the voice again. I think I've identified the person. You wanna know who it is?"

"In the name of God, Thomas. You don't work for the NSA or Xarasoft anymore. Are you telling me you've taken secret recordings off-site?"

"I'm not going to say. What I will say, Lance, is that if you just meet up with me and put me in front of that committee, then they can decide. I swear, you have to listen to what I've got."

"I can't believe what I'm hearing. Look, why don't you take what you've got to the NSA?"

"I have. I sent them the details anonymously, but I haven't heard back. Nothing."

Drake sighed again.

"Lance, I did over two hundred hours of speech-data tests, and I know I'm correct. The cover audio I picked up was an innocuous pop song, but underneath was an encrypted conversation. I stripped away all that shit. But, Lance, it's not just the conversation

I've decrypted. I believe a covert message has been embedded within the digital audio signal."

"What?"

"I'm still working to decode that side of things. America needs to wake the fuck up."

"I can't believe what I'm hearing. You were sacked for wrong analysis."

"I told you that was lies. Do you really think I don't know what I'm talking about—is that what it is?"

"They're using words like 'paranoid' and 'deluded.' Look, maybe it's best if you don't email me anymore."

Wesley shook his head. "They've got to you, haven't they? Someone has told you that this guy is nuts, and for your career, leave him alone. Is that what's happening?"

Lance was silent.

"I want to meet up with you."

"That ain't gonna happen."

"Lance, what's more important? To do things the right way, or do the right thing?"

"Look, this is getting us nowhere."

"So what do you suggest I do with what I've got? No one is listening."

"Thomas, we're done. I'm sorry. Don't bug me again with this."

Eight

The ranch-style house in Weston appeared algae green as Reznick peered through the night-vision binoculars. He was slouched down low in the car, watching and waiting, with Luntz sat in the back seat.

His mind flashed back to the landscape of Falluja at night.

Blinding lights. Screaming and pleading. The smell of open sewers. The dust. The filth. The Black Hawks flying low, strafing the neighborhood. The green-smeared vision of night sights, as Task Force 121 scoured the warren of streets and alleys in the darkness, looking for insurgents.

He lost count of the number of kills. He became desensitized until he almost didn't care. They'd trained him that way. It had become second nature. But, somehow, he still managed to keep a small part of his soul intact. Even when his team killed an insurgent, and cut off the man's bloodstained clothes to check for tattoos to help identify the body, Reznick always remembered what his dying father—haunted by memories of Vietnam—had said when he'd told him he was going to join the Marines: "*Never be blasé about death. Don't forget, every man you kill is somebody's son.*"

The words had stayed with him. Echoed down the years. He always clung to that, even as he felt his soul was turning black. Even when they were scanning the dead man's irises and fingerprints with a portable biometric scanner. It was always *somebody's son*.

The front door opened and Reznick snapped back to reality. A woman who looked in her thirties emerged wearing a smart jacket, dark slacks, and kitten heels, speaking into her cell phone.

Reznick watched as she locked the door, turning the handle a couple of times. She climbed into the silver Mercedes, slamming the door shut. Then she reversed out and drove off, past the lake.

He had a split-second decision to make. Follow or fold? Was Chad Magruder inside? He felt conflicted.

"Fuck," he said.

"What is it?" Luntz asked.

"Be quiet."

He stayed put for a few moments, until she was nearly out of sight. Then he started up the engine but kept his lights off. Time to see where she led him.

He pulled away slowly, and waited for a couple of minutes before he switched on his lights. He soon caught sight of her car farther along the north side of the lake. He hung back as much as he could as he negotiated the quiet, palm-lined residential streets. They skirted downtown Weston, which was like a Mediterranean village, all pastel colors and low-rise buildings.

Then she took a right at some lights and drove down Racquet Club Road, past the Hyatt. A few moments later, she pulled up outside a motel overlooking another lake.

Reznick drove on, and took a left into a parking lot on West Mall Road. It had a clear line of sight over to the motel a couple of hundred yards away. He picked up his night-vision binoculars and peered into the darkness toward the deserted motel parking lot. The woman was sitting in her car, lights on, engine running, cell phone pressed to her ear, occasionally nodding her head.

The woman then ended the call, got out of her car, and walked into the reception of the motel.

Reznick edged the car around the corner and back onto Racquet Club Road, then got himself into position at the far end of the motel parking lot, shielded by an island of shrubs and palms. He switched off his engine and lights, slouching in his seat. Then he picked up the binoculars.

Did she work there? Maybe she was an innocent. But what if . . . what if his daughter was being held there? Was that too far-fetched? The thought triggered an adrenaline rush to his heart. His breathing quickened.

The seconds ticked by, then the minutes.

Just as he was about to get out of the car and head into the motel, the woman emerged alone. She got in her car, switched on her lights, and pulled away, oblivious to Reznick.

What now? Follow her or sit tight? He couldn't barge into the motel and go room to room. The cops would be called and he would be taken in. And then what?

"Goddamn."

Reznick decided to sit tight. He wondered if the woman had taken a message to someone inside. Was that it? Was Magruder holed up inside? He thought back to news footage of Magruder being led away in handcuffs from the courtroom, impassive, eyes dead.

The time dragged like a chain at the bottom of a sandy seabed. He waited. And waited. And still he waited. More minutes being eaten up. But no one left or entered the motel.

"Fuck," he said.

He turned the car around and drove back downtown. He stopped to pick up some sandwiches and provisions from an all-night deli to keep them going for the next few hours, intending to head back to the ranch house to find out who the woman was and see if Magruder turned up.

The plan changed.

As he headed past the downtown shops, he took a right at the lights onto Main Street. His gaze was drawn to a Mercedes, parked diagonally opposite a Starbucks under a huge palm. He checked the plates. It was hers.

Reznick drove on for a couple of hundred yards, pulled a U-turn, and parked fifty yards behind the Mercedes. He had a perfect view of the coffee shop on the corner. The clock on his dashboard said it was 5:37 a.m. He switched off his lights and picked up his binoculars, switching off the night vision as the lights were on in Starbucks.

Scanning the inside of the store, he saw the Magruder woman sitting at a table with a couple of coffee mugs. She was expecting company. But a few minutes later, the woman walked out of the Starbucks alone. Her clothes looked expensive, well cut.

Who was she?

He slouched down in his seat as she walked toward her car, opened it with a fob, and drove away up Main Street.

Reznick felt torn again. Should he follow her or sit tight? But there were two coffee mugs on the table. He decided to stay where he was, and he peered through the binoculars at the interior of the Starbucks. A young woman was wiping down the tables.

A couple of minutes later, the Starbucks door opened and a lean guy who looked in his early forties walked out. He wore faded jeans, cowboy boots, and a black T-shirt; he had long blond hair, a thick scar on his face.

It was Chad Magruder. Reznick felt his flesh crawl.

He watched as Magruder lit a cigarette, walked farther up Main Street, and then disappeared up a street to the right. Reznick switched on the ignition and headed the same way. A few moments later, he passed Magruder climbing into the black SUV—the same one Reznick had seen on the surveillance tape at the Monterey Club.

OK, you bastard. Where are you going?

Five hundred yards up ahead, Reznick pulled into a space outside a deli and switched off his engine and lights. He checked his wing mirror, and a minute later Magruder drove past, oblivious, cigarette dangling from the corner of his mouth.

Reznick waited a few moments before he pulled out and followed the SUV. Magruder was about one hundred yards ahead and it looked like he was heading for the freeway. Five minutes later, he was driving up a ramp and onto I-75. The traffic was heavy even at that ungodly hour.

Reznick was now four cars back, and he crossed lanes for a couple of miles to try to stay out of Magruder's rearview mirror. They were headed south in the pre-dawn darkness. Time dragged. He saw a sign for Miami. Then Magruder changed lanes and slowed down, only two cars ahead, glancing in his rearview mirror.

Counter-surveillance move.

Reznick stayed in his lane, knowing not to dart off in another direction. He remained calm as Magruder continued to check his mirror for tails. Then Magruder turned around and stared at the car behind him.

This bastard is cute.

Traffic was down to a crawl. Ten minutes later there was another sign for downtown Miami and Magruder changed lanes again, taking the Miami Avenue exit. Reznick dropped back and followed Magruder toward the huge skyscrapers of Miami's business district. All the time, Reznick kept his distance. Glass and steel office towers loomed over Brickell Avenue.

Then Magruder hung a sharp left and headed into an underground parking facility. Reznick went around the block twice before he too headed into the basement parking lot.

Reznick caught sight of Magruder's car in a disabled space right beside the elevators. His left arm was out the window, cigarette dangling from his fingers, his cell phone pressed to his right ear.

Reznick passed within fifty yards and took a ramp to the upper-level parking. He drove around the deserted lot for a couple of minutes and then headed back down to Magruder's level.

Cruising past, he stole a quick glance in his rearview mirror. At that moment, Magruder stepped out of his car, dropped his cigarette, and crushed it with the heel of his boot. Then he placed his cell in his back pocket and headed toward the steel elevators.

Reznick drove into a space straight ahead, beside a massive concrete pillar. Engine still running, he looked in the rearview mirror and saw Magruder press the elevator button. He picked up the binoculars and turned to see Magruder get into the elevator. Then he trained the binoculars on the light indicating the floor. It eventually stopped at the forty-second.

Reznick switched off the engine and turned to Luntz. "I need you in the trunk."

"Please . . . I'm scared as it is. I won't cause any trouble."

"You need to get in the trunk. For your own safety. Like I said before, you need to trust me."

Luntz reluctantly agreed and got back in the trunk. "How long will you be?"

"Not too long, I promise. Not a sound though."

Luntz lay down and Reznick shut the trunk. He centrally locked the car and then took the elevator to the forty-third floor. From there, he headed down a flight of stairs. There was a metal sign on an outer door for Norton & Weiss, Inc.

He looked around the outer lobby. A camera panned the entrance, which had locked glass doors and a metallic keypad beside the handle. He headed back down in the elevator and got back in the car, taking another Dexedrine.

It wasn't long before Reznick felt wired. He waited, grinding his teeth as the pills kicked in big time and the adrenaline flowed. He no longer felt hungry.

Half an hour later, Magruder appeared, running his hands through his hair. *Nothing like a vain psycho*, Reznick thought. But instead of heading to the car in the disabled bay, Magruder walked toward a Suburban with blacked-out windows. *Why the change of car?* Had Magruder just been given a new job? And how did Norton & Weiss fit into it?

Reznick sunk down low, and waited until Magruder had left the garage before turning on his engine. He caught sight of Magruder driving fast through the dark downtown streets before he headed across the MacArthur Causeway to South Beach.

Reznick needed to hang back and not get too close, but he nearly lost him not wanting to run a red light on Washington Avenue. Eventually, he took a left and then caught sight of the Suburban one hundred yards up ahead, cruising up Jefferson Avenue and onto 18th Street, past the Holocaust Memorial and down Convention Center Drive. Then along a side street and past the rundown, neon-lit Sunset Motel.

Magruder parked one block away, with a clear diagonal line of sight to the motel.

Reznick drove on to Dade Boulevard, and double-backed onto Alton Road before pulling up on West Avenue. He was out of sight, but now less than two hundred yards from Magruder, whose car was facing the opposite direction.

A panhandler came into view. He was walking the near-empty streets wearing a filthy jacket, a Yankees cap, and some fancy sunglasses, taking the occasional slug from a bottle of Night Train.

It was then that Reznick had an idea.

Nine

Reznick switched off his engine, got out of the car, and walked up to the panhandler. The old guy's eyes were wild and bloodshot—he smelled of piss, rancid booze, and cigarettes.

"You wanna make an easy fifty bucks, old man?" he asked.

The panhandler gave a nonchalant shrug, as if he were used to getting such offers every day.

"Gimme your jacket, hat, shades, and your bottle, and this fifty is yours," Reznick said, flashing the bill.

The man grinned, exposing nicotine-stained stumps for teeth. "Why would I do that?"

Reznick took another fifty-dollar bill from his pocket and shook his head. "A hundred bucks."

The panhandler nodded as he took off his jacket, hat, and shades. Then he handed over his bottle of booze and snatched the money from Reznick's hand in one movement. "Nice doing business with you, my friend."

Reznick put on the stinking coat, the cap, and the sunglasses. "Get some soup in you, for God's sake," he said, but the panhandler was already sauntering toward 19th Street, straight for the nearest liquor store. Farther down the street, Reznick caught sight of the black Suburban parked up.

Magruder's window was down, phone pressed to his left ear.

Reznick shuffled across the road and headed slowly in his direction. When he was within ten yards, Magruder turned around, phone still pressed to his ear, but he ignored the sight of the panhandler approaching.

Reznick ambled up to the Suburban's open window, hand outstretched as if for money.

"Get the fuck away from me," Magruder said.

Reznick punched him hard in the side of the head and Magruder's eyes rolled back. His cell phone fell out of his hand, but Reznick caught it before it hit the ground. Magruder was out cold.

He leaned over and rifled in Magruder's waistband, retrieving a Beretta. Then he opened the door and patted down his jeans, discovering a serrated hunting knife taped to the back of the man's left calf.

Reznick pulled out the plastic cuffs he had in his back pocket and tied up Magruder's hands and feet before pushing him over onto the floor of the passenger seat. Then he dumped the panhandler's stuff at the side of the road and slid into the driver's seat. He drove around the quiet South Beach streets for a few minutes, away from the main drags of Ocean Drive and Washington Avenue, looking for the right spot. Past empty parking lots, art deco hotels with neon-lit signs, and dimly lit side streets. Then down palm-fringed residential streets, until he saw a realtor's sign outside a boarded-up house on Michigan Avenue, between 12th and 13th Streets, adjacent to Flamingo Park. It was painted a sickly yellow and seemed abandoned. He examined it to see if it was suitable.

It didn't look bad at all. A rusty chain-link fence covered in flaking black paint surrounded the property, including a padlocked driveway.

Reznick waited until a couple of people walking by were out of sight. Then he reversed back onto the sidewalk until the car was pressed up against the padlocked gates. Leaving the engine running, he got out and picked the lock, opened the creaking metal gates, and got back in the car, reversing up the driveway. Then he hauled the deadweight of Magruder up the overgrown driveway, and kicked in a wooden panel on the first floor.

Dragging Magruder inside, he took a few moments for his eyes to adjust to the darkness. He was in what looked like a ransacked kitchen. It smelled as if an animal had died there.

A pile of rotten blankets lay on top of a mattress. Strewn on the tile floor were cigarette ends, old crack pipes, and empty cans of beer and bottles of wine, as if some panhandlers had been squatting there. Reznick placed Magruder on the mattress and then ripped up some filthy rags. He wrapped them tight around Magruder's head, covering his mouth and nose, only the eyes exposed.

Picking up a half-empty bottle of wine, he poured out the contents, and went over to the sink and filled it up with water. Fixing the suppressor to his Beretta, he kicked Magruder in the back.

The bastard came to. Eyes crazy. He tried to stand, but the blow to the head and the fact that he was trussed up meant he was immobilized.

Reznick leaned close and pointed the gun at his head. "Time to answer some questions, Magruder."

"Reznick?" The rag muffled his voice. "What the fuck, man?"

"Shut up."

"What've you got me tied up like a hog for, man?"

Reznick slapped him hard across the face. "I said shut up. Now, listen to me very closely. I want some answers."

"What's this all about?"

"Leggett. What did you do to him?"

"I don't know what you're talking about, man."

Reznick slapped him hard on the other side of his face.

"I think you do. Now, you're gonna tell me, or you're gonna taste some water, do you know what I mean?"

The fear in Magruder's eyes was real. He knew what Reznick meant.

"Hey, look, I don't know what you're talking about, man, I swear. Reznick, what's this all about?"

Reznick pressed his right foot hard onto Magruder's chest as the man writhed on the floor. He tipped the water from the bottle into Magruder's mouth and nose through the rags. The water glugged into Magruder's throat, down into his stomach. The veins in his neck were nearly bursting through his skin, his eyes wild with terror. They had both been trained to withstand waterboarding. They knew that it was just a simulated drowning. But the reality was: every man has a breaking point.

He stopped pouring after ten seconds.

"I want to know what you were up to. Were you ordered to do a job? Were you asked to neutralize Leggett?"

Magruder shook his head furiously.

"What did you do to him?"

He was sobbing and half-choking.

"Where is my daughter? Tell me what you know."

Magruder closed his eyes. Reznick poured more water through the cloth. Magruder flailed, and Reznick pressed a foot into his chest again. Then he stopped and gave Magruder a few moments to try to recover. This time, the terror had become blind panic.

"I'll ask again, where is my daughter?"

Magruder shook his head.

Reznick removed the soaking rag as Magruder spluttered and heaved. "Answer, you fuck."

Magruder coughed up water and retched for nearly a minute before he spoke. "Please, Reznick. Believe me, man, I didn't have a choice. I was told to do Leggett and turn up in Miami today."

"Turn up for what today?"

Magruder began weeping. "Man, I'm sorry."

"Tell me what you know or you'll die, right here and now. Who gave you the orders?"

"The guys . . ."

"What fucking guys? The guys in that tower in downtown Miami?"

Magruder nodded, sniveling and sobbing hard. "It's a front. Jon, believe me, I would never—"

"A front for what?"

"I don't know. I've done various jobs for them. A Russian oligarch. An Arab woman. They pay me a lot of money. A *lot* of money—in cash. I need the money, man. I owe a lot of people."

"I asked what kind of front."

"That it's a legal firm."

"How did you get to hear about them?"

"They approached me in jail about a year ago, and said they could get me out if I went to work for them."

"How are you out of jail?"

"They got me out."

"Who's *they*?"

Magruder began coughing, hacking up water and phlegm. "I don't know."

"You must know. Who's in fucking charge there?"

"All I know is that I get a call, and I head there, and I speak to a guy called Vince. White guy. Real intense. And when I mean intense, I mean *real* intense, you know what I'm saying?"

"All I need to know is where my daughter is."

"I know nothing about that."

Reznick's mind was racing. "What were you parked on 19th Street for?"

"They wanted me to acquaint myself with the area, that's all."

"Were you told to kill me?"

Magruder closed his eyes, retching and coughing at the same time. "I was just told something was going down, to get to know the area, that's all, and then await instructions."

Reznick put the rag back over his face and poured out the rest of the water. He stared down at the other man. "Where is my daughter?"

Magruder was bug-eyed with terror. Reznick could see he was close to the edge. He removed the rag again as Magruder spluttered and brought up water.

"I swear, I don't know about your daughter."

"You fucking liar. You piece of shit. You know about her, don't you? Where is she? Tell me!"

Magruder's eyes were turning in his head. He was nearly unconscious.

Reznick pressed the gun to his head. "Last time—what do you know about my daughter?"

"Absolutely nothing. I swear, man. I did Leggett. And I was gonna be given one hundred thousand dollars cash to do it, in return for my return. You understand?"

Reznick stared at the former Delta operator. For a split second, he felt pity for a man who was tougher than anyone he'd ever met. By now, Magruder was shaking but saying nothing.

Reznick went over to the sink and filled the bottle full of water again. "You want some more?"

Magruder shook his head.

"One last chance—where is my daughter?"

"I don't know your daughter, or where she is."

Reznick replaced the rag and poured. Magruder's face scrunched up as if in pain, and he clenched his teeth. Then he groaned and moaned, shaking uncontrollably.

"Don't pull that shit with me, do you hear me?"

Gargled gasps for air, his chest heaving up and down. Time seemed to slow.

Reznick leaned over and slapped him hard across the face. "What the fuck is wrong with you?"

No breathing. No sound. No movement. Reznick rolled him over and felt his wrist. He didn't feel a pulse.

He turned away and kicked over a chair. "Goddamn you." He felt sick to the pit of his stomach. He paced the deserted house, head in hands. He hadn't meant to kill Magruder, despite him taking down Leggett. He'd just wanted to make him talk.

Ten

It was still dark when Lieutenant Colonel Scott Caan's alarm clock rang at his rented home near downtown Hagerstown, Maryland. He groaned and leaned over to switch it off after a fitful sleep. He wasn't a morning person. Never had been. He took a few moments for his brain to adjust to the new day before he got up and headed to the bathroom. He splashed some cold water on his face and looked at himself in the mirror. Toned, lean, eyes clear. He felt in the best shape of his life. But he was still waiting to hear from his handler.

He didn't dwell on that. It wasn't his role to worry about them. He had to focus on his part. He pulled on a T-shirt and gym shorts, and laced up his Adidas running shoes. Then, like he always did, he headed downstairs to his gym in the basement and did five miles on the treadmill, twenty minutes pumping iron, and ten minutes on the rowing machine, topped off with fifteen minutes hitting a punching bag, jabbing and hooking until he thought his heart was going to pack in.

He checked his pulse. It was within acceptable limits for aerobic workouts. He was in great shape. He was ready. Had been for weeks.

Sweating profusely, endorphins running around his body, he took a hot shower. He closed his eyes and wondered if he needed more sleep. He reckoned he'd managed, at best, four hours last night.

Caan enjoyed the warm water pummeling his skin. He knew it wouldn't be long. *Any day now.* He wondered if his coworkers were asking why he hadn't been in for the last three weeks. He thought of the eight long years he had given to the company. The sacrifices. The hours. The time he could never get back. But he knew it would all be worth it.

The more he thought about it, the more he realized how well he'd done, concealing his secret life from his coworkers. He was playing a long game. They thought he was just the quiet guy who was diligent and liked to go for runs at lunchtime. The guy who worked long hours and never complained, or bitched, or made any trouble. The guy who did his job and never, under any circumstances, attracted attention. But they didn't know him. They didn't know him at all.

He turned off the shower, dried himself, and put on a clean set of clothes that had been carefully chosen for him: checked button-down shirt, dark jeans, thick blue sweater, Timberland boots.

After cleaning his teeth and combing his short dark hair, he put on his black down jacket and clipped on his pager. Then he headed to a diner three blocks away.

Outside, the cold air nearly took his breath away, a sharp frost on the ground. The forecasters had warned of a serious cold front heading down from Canada, perhaps bringing a major snowstorm for Christmas. He had been keeping an eye on the forecast for days, checking the weather in New York and Washington, DC.

He was glad to get into the warmth of the diner, where he ordered a hearty breakfast of waffles, bacon, and poached eggs with his black coffee. The chubby waitress wearing gold tinsel in her hair brought him his food and said, "Enjoy your breakfast, sir."

Caan smiled but said nothing.

As he sat there eating alone, he felt alive for the first time in years—perhaps since his childhood. He had a purpose. He had been given a plan.

He only received coded instructions. But, in the last couple of years, they had begun to talk specifics: timescale, methodology, resources. It had all been carefully formulated. He knew what was at stake.

His pager bleeped and he felt his stomach lurch. The last time it had bleeped was a week ago, instructing him to go to Baltimore. Was this the day? Unclipping the pager from his belt, he saw the coded message he had been waiting for. It read simply: *Blue skies in Madrid.*

This was indeed *it.*

"Want a refill, sir?" the waitress asked, seeing his mug was empty.

Caan clipped his pager back on and smiled. "I'm good, thanks. Gotta dash."

"You have a good day now."

Caan smiled back and left enough cash on the table for the server. He made the short walk home. He went into the spare bedroom and picked up the suitcase that was already packed, and lugged it downstairs and placed it carefully in the trunk of his beat-up Datsun. Then he got in the car and headed east on I-70, toward the state-of-the-art storage facility on the outskirts of Baltimore.

He felt himself zoning out as he drove, and the sound of a car horn startled him. He checked in his rearview mirror for signs of any tails. But there was nothing. The rest of his journey was just as uneventful.

After about an hour, he drove off the freeway and onto the quiet streets of a business park. He saw the sign for the I-Store facility he had visited a week earlier. The guy behind the reinforced screen was chewing gum. Caan showed his fake ID and took the elevator to the third floor, then punched in the four-digit code before pressing his thumb up against the biometric scanner. There was the sound of mortise locks clicking, and he opened the locker. Inside was the gym bag he had deposited seven days ago.

He carefully picked up the bag and headed for the exit.

"You get what you were looking for?" the guy at the desk asked politely.

"Yes, thank you."

"Have a good day, sir."

Caan opened the trunk of his car and placed the bag inside, then slammed it shut. And so began the two-hundred-mile journey to New York City.

About an hour in, as he headed east on I-95 into Delaware, he checked again for any tails in his rearview mirror. He changed lanes a few times, but nothing.

He afforded himself a smile. *Not long now*, he thought.

Eleven

The sun peeked over the rooftops as Reznick returned to the Volvo. He felt wired. He couldn't believe Magruder had gone so quickly. That wasn't how it was supposed to work. Magruder was the only one who might have had information about Lauren's whereabouts. It seemed inconceivable that he had known nothing.

Fuck.

The whole thing had descended into a living nightmare.

He popped open the trunk. Luntz was lying in the fetal position, eyes screwed up against the sun.

"You OK?" Reznick said.

"Just."

"Get in the back, stay quiet, and be good."

Luntz clambered out. He looked unsteady on his feet and Reznick helped him into the back seat before strapping him in. "This is insane."

Reznick fired up the car. "You hungry?"

"I don't think I can eat. I feel sick."

"Trust me, you need to eat."

Reznick drove to a nearby 7-Eleven and took a subdued Luntz in with him. He ordered two hot breakfast sandwiches and black coffees, and picked up some donuts for later. They wolfed down the sandwiches in the car.

"Feel better?" Reznick said.

Luntz nodded as he chewed his food.

The sun was edging higher in the sky and Reznick squinted, using his left hand to shield his eyes from the glare. Suddenly the iPhone rang. He didn't recognize the number.

"Dad . . . Dad, it's Lauren."

Reznick's heart missed a beat at the sound of his daughter's voice. "Lauren, are you OK? Talk to me, honey."

Silence.

"Lauren! Speak to me!"

More silence.

"Lauren! Lauren!" Reznick closed his eyes tight. "Lauren! Are you there?"

"Yes, she is," a man said. The same voice he'd heard before. "And she's alive. For now, anyway."

"Listen to me. If you harm her in any way, and I mean in any way, I will hunt you down and rip out your fucking heart."

"Shut up! We're running the show. So, here's how it's gonna work. You hand over the scientist and you get Lauren back. Any attempt to call in the police or Feds will result in Lauren being killed. Are we clear?"

"Crystal."

"I don't want to harm her. But I will if Luntz isn't handed over. I'll call you in an hour with the delivery point."

The man hung up.

Luntz broke the silence. "Was that them?"

"Who's *them*?"

"The people who want me."

Reznick said nothing.

"They have your daughter, don't they?"

"You talk too much."

"You're going to hand me over, aren't you?"

"Just be quiet."

Luntz stared straight ahead. "I'm a family man, too. My wife and kids need their dad back."

"So does my daughter."

Luntz looked away.

"Someone wants you dead, real bad. Why is that?" Reznick asked.

"I know things."

"Stop playing fucking games. Why do people want you dead?"

Luntz was quiet for a few moments before he spoke. "I need to speak to the FBI."

"About what?"

"I believe lives may be at stake. American lives. And that's why you need to hand me over to the FBI."

"Not while they've got my daughter."

Reznick was running out of time and options. He knew he couldn't just sit and wait for them to call and bounce him all over Miami. But he couldn't give up Luntz, as the scientist was the only bargaining chip he had.

There was only one real option. He had to take the fight to them. The problem was that the only lead he had was the downtown firm he'd followed Magruder to—Norton & Weiss.

"Please, don't hand me over to those people," Luntz said. "You've got to believe me, I'm begging you." He clutched the photo pendant tight and pressed his hand to his chest. "I swear on my son's grave that I'm telling the truth."

Reznick looked into Luntz's sad blue eyes and could see he wasn't lying. He could see the older man's complexion was clammy and pale, clearly not well. Probably exhausted, as well as traumatized.

Tiredness was also beginning to cloud Reznick's head. His thoughts seemed to be slowing down.

"I feel sick," Luntz said.

"Just hang in there."

He could see that driving around with Luntz was asking for trouble. Sooner or later, a cop would pull them over. It was getting too risky, having him around. The bottom line was that he needed to dump Luntz. Get him somewhere safe.

Reznick's mind raced as he realized he was clean out of ideas. He needed someone who knew the area—but who?

Suddenly, out of nowhere, a name sprang into his head. *Tiny.* Ex-Delta operator Tiny.

Reznick thought back to a telephone conversation he'd had with Leggett, a year or so earlier. Harry had said he'd bumped into Tiny in a bar. Tiny was working the door. But what was the name of the bar? And where exactly? Had to be relatively close to Fort Lauderdale.

He took the cell phone from his jacket and punched in the number of Leggett's bar. A young woman answered.

"I need to speak to Ron Leggett right away," Reznick said.

"Who's this?"

"Just put him on. I'm a friend."

A few moments later, Ron came on the line. "I'm sorry, things are—"

"Ron, don't hang up. I think your phone will be bugged, so I want you to go to the tattoo parlor next door and ask to borrow the owner's cell phone for five minutes. And get the number."

"I don't understand."

"There's no time to explain. Just do it."

A short while later, Ron came back on the line and gave Reznick a number.

"I'll call you back on that number."

He hung up, and Reznick punched in the digits.

Ron answered immediately. "What do you want?"

"The man who killed your father has been taken care of."

A long silence opened up, as if the kid didn't know how to react. Was he in shock? "Are you sure?"

"Positive. Now listen—I need a little help. Your father mentioned to me that he visited an old friend. Big guy. We called him Tiny."

"I know the guy. Met him once. I was with my dad. The guy was working the door."

"Which bar? Where?"

"South Beach. Fourteenth Street."

"You sure?"

"Yes. I got the name—Mac's Club Deuce. It's open twenty-one hours a day. Just off the main drag."

Reznick headed straight there.

It had been more than ten years since they'd worked together in Special Forces. But when he turned onto 14th Street and saw a hulking figure drinking a coffee outside, he recognized him immediately. Charles "Tiny" Burns.

Reznick turned right and parked down an alley near the bar. He turned and stared at Luntz. "Do not attempt to escape."

"Where are you going?"

"Never you mind."

Luntz blinked away tears as Reznick locked the car and headed around the corner.

"Charles," Reznick said. "How the hell you doing?"

Tiny turned around and took a few moments to twig who it was. His face broke into a broad smile. "You gotta be kiddin' me! Jon—what the hell are you doing here?"

"You don't wanna know, believe me."

Tiny roared with laughter and gave Reznick a hug that nearly crushed the breath out of him.

"Goddamn, man, you've no idea how good it is to see you," Reznick said.

Tiny gripped his hand tight. "Man, how the fucking hell are you?"

"Better for seeing you. Look, I've got a problem. And I need help. If you can do this, you need to leave right now."

"Jon, what do you want?"

"Where do you live?"

"What?"

"Do you live here on the beach?"

"No, man. A former Delta operator, Bobby Sloan . . . you know him?"

Reznick shook his head.

"Well, he loaned me his trailer. It's shit, but it's a home."

"Perfect. I need you to look after someone for me. I've got business here in Miami. But it has to be right now."

Tiny nodded silently.

"I need someone that I can trust, just like you trusted me. You remember Falluja?"

"Every night I fall asleep I remember Falluja."

"Who got you out of that hole?"

"You did."

"I'm not gonna sugarcoat it—I'm calling in my favor. I'll also give you a thousand dollars to look after this guy for twenty-four hours."

Tiny stared down at the ground for a few moments.

"Will you do it?" Reznick asked.

He looked up and smiled. "Goddamn right I will. I'd do anything for you, man."

"Gimme your trailer plot and the address."

"Pitch eighty-seven, Del-Raton trailer park, up the coast at Delray Beach."

Reznick pulled out a wad of cash from his back pocket and handed it over. Tiny didn't count it, merely put it in the front pocket of his jeans. Then Reznick handed over the keys to the stolen Volvo. "Got the guy in the back."

When they got to the alley, Luntz glanced around, blinking.

"I want you to drive back home and look after him with your life," Reznick said.

Tiny slid into the driver's seat and fired up the engine. "Nice ride. Do you want my car?"

"I'll find my own."

"What's going on?" Luntz said.

Reznick crouched down. "This guy is a friend of mine. He'll look after you. He'll keep you safe."

Luntz nodded. "I don't know if I can—"

Reznick's phone rang, interrupting Luntz mid-sentence. He didn't recognize the caller ID.

"Yeah?"

"Mr. Reznick," a woman's voice said. "This is the FBI. We need to talk."

It hadn't taken the Feds long to close in. It was the absolute last thing he needed.

"I am Assistant Director Martha Meyerstein. I'm based at FBI Headquarters in Washington, but I'm here in Miami. I need to know if you still have the government scientist."

"I don't know you."

"You do now. I want to talk. But first I need to know if the scientist is alive and with you. Look, you must trust me."

"I don't trust people I don't know."

"I'm asking you to trust me. We have reason to believe that there is a serious plot underway. You must return him into the custody of the FBI. This is a matter of national security. Do you understand?"

Reznick looked at Tiny, who shrugged. "I'm listening."

"Firstly, we would like confirmation that he is alive."

"Yeah, he's alive."

Meyerstein let out an audible sigh. "Can I call you Jon?"

Reznick said nothing.

"Jon, can I speak to the scientist?"

"Not possible."

"Jon, as an act of good faith, we would really appreciate it if you could let the scientist confirm that he is alive. That's all."

Reznick stifled a yawn.

"We just want to have him tell us his name, date of birth, and his wife's name."

Reznick's gut instinct was to be loyal to the flag. And the two words—"national security"—bothered him. He had served his country over the years.

He pressed the phone to Luntz's face. "FBI wants you to confirm your name, date of birth, and wife's name. Go right ahead."

Luntz blurted out, "Fourteenth and Collins!"

Reznick yanked the phone from him and ended the call. "Not smart." He grabbed Luntz by the throat. "One more false move and you'll die."

He slammed the door shut. "Tiny, get this guy the fuck outta here. Take him to your place, keep him safe and sound. I'll be in touch."

The car sped off with Luntz in the back.

Reznick's first move was to steal a Mazda parked farther down the alley. He headed away from the beach and back across the causeway into Miami. He saw a sign for Brickell Avenue and headed into slow-moving traffic, towering skyscrapers either side.

He recognized the green sign for the parking garage he had followed Magruder into. He drove down the ramp and pulled up beside the elevator doors. He looked around. In the far corner he saw a brown UPS truck, its engine idling.

Reznick got out of the car and walked up to the truck. The driver wound down his window.

"Think you got a flat, buddy," Reznick said.

"You gotta be kidding me." The man got out of his vehicle, frowning and cursing under his breath. Reznick pressed a gun to his head.

"Hey, what the fuck?!"

"In the back of your truck. Now!" He hustled the UPS driver into the back, among the parcels and boxes. The man was shaking and terrified, cowering in the corner of the van. "I'm not going to hurt you. But I need your clothes."

The guy didn't protest. He just stripped off and threw his clothes at Reznick.

He was then tied up with duct tape. "Not a sound for half an hour. If I hear a peep out of you, you get a bullet in your head." The man nodded furiously, sweat beading his forehead.

Reznick took off his jacket and pulled on the brown UPS shirt with matching baseball cap. He picked up a parcel and the delivery clipboard. "Not a fucking word." Then he stepped out of the truck and carefully locked the door. Once he had made sure there was no one around, he walked over to the elevator and punched the "Up" button.

He stepped into the empty elevator and pressed the button for the forty-second floor. The door closed, and less than twenty seconds later he was at his destination. He walked up to the glass doors in the outer lobby. On closer inspection, a black metal buzzer on the silver keypad had *Norton & Weiss, Inc.* engraved in small writing.

Behind the huge glass doors, a small, bespectacled young man wearing a suit looked up from his computer. Reznick pressed the buzzer as he smiled at the guy.

The kid got up from his chair and ambled across to the intercom. "I'm sorry, sir," he said. "Our firm doesn't accept visitors."

"It's a delivery from Washington. Urgent."

The young man shook his head. "I'm not expecting any deliveries today."

"Look, I need a signature, man," Reznick said. "I've not got all day. Real urgent."

The kid bit his lower lip as if he were thinking it over.

"Look, I ain't got all day, pal. You wanna sign?"

He cracked open the door. Reznick barged inside and pressed a gun to the startled young man's temple. "Be very quiet."

The kid stumbled backward as the door clicked shut.

Twelve

The main office was mostly open plan: a cool, gray-blue interior, laptops and iPads on half a dozen desks. Reznick could see there were two other offices.

"Where's everyone else?"

"Please . . . I'm the only person in just now."

Reznick pushed him into one of the wood-paneled inner offices. Legal tomes and journals lined the walls.

"What do you want?"

Reznick pressed the gun to his head. "Tell me about your company."

"We're a law firm. What the hell is this?"

Reznick pulled back the slide of his Beretta. "Don't take me for a fool, son."

The kid flushed crimson. "I work the back-office stuff. That's all I can say."

"What was Magruder doing here earlier?"

"I have no idea what you're talking about."

"Stop bullshitting me, son. If you want to do this the hard way, that's fine."

"Please, we're a law firm. There must be some terrible mistake."

Reznick slapped him, hard. "Now, if you don't tell me what you know, you'll be checking out of this world earlier than you thought."

"Please! Please!"

"I want some fucking answers. Do you understand?"

"Please, don't . . ." He composed himself. "Please believe me, I have nothing to do with it."

Reznick shook his head. "Wrong answer." He moved the gun back to the kid's forehead.

"Christ almighty!"

"He's not going to help you. No one is. Now tell me what Magruder was doing here."

The kid began to whimper as he cowered. "I'm . . . I'm not who you're looking for."

"Why can't you answer a simple fucking question? Tell me about Magruder."

A long silence opened up before the kid spoke again. "All I know is he did a job for us. I don't get involved in that. Look at me—do I look like I get involved in that side of things? I'm an analyst, OK?"

"So, what's this setup?"

"We're a private company. We receive commissions to do security consultancy for the government."

"Stop the bullshit. What do you really do?"

The kid closed his eyes. "We subcontract wet jobs. I'm logistics. Satisfied?"

"Who funds this operation?"

"I don't know anything about that. My boss does. He runs the show."

Reznick grabbed him by the throat, gun still pressed to his head. "Where's your boss?"

The kid's eyes were screwed up tight with the pain. "He's out of town."

"I don't believe you."

The young man's eyes filled with tears as he shook his head.

Reznick pressed his face right up to the kid's. He could smell the fear. It was as if it were seeping through his pores.

"I just killed Magruder." The look on the kid's face was that of sheer terror. "Now, I'm not in the mood to discuss matters at length. I want answers. And I won't stop until I find my daughter. So, where is she?"

"I swear, I don't know anything about your daughter."

Reznick stared him down. "Magruder said he was going to kill me. So, how was he going to carry this out?"

"All I know is that you were going to be directed to the Sunset Motel."

"And then what?"

"Magruder was told to await instructions. You would then . . ."

"I would then what?"

"You would then be told to call a cab. And Magruder would be dispatched to pick you up before the official cab company and kill you. He was meant to take the guy you have to the rendezvous point, where they'd be waiting."

"Where's the rendezvous point?"

"Not a clue."

"Who's running this show?"

"Brewling. Mr. Brewling."

"Does he work for the *Company*?"

The young man shook his head. "Used to. A lot of contacts there."

"So you subcontract the dirty work?"

He nodded.

"Will Brewling be at the rendezvous point?"

"I don't know. I just sit in this office all day. That's what I did at Langley. I never worked out in the field."

"Figures. Who does Brewling use, apart from Magruder? Any Miami crew involved?"

"Some Haitians. I think they're all FRAPH."

Reznick knew all about the feared paramilitary group, the Front for the Advancement and Progress in Haiti, formed in 1993 by a CIA informant. In 2004, Reznick had been part of a secret Delta mission to track down and kill prominent FRAPH members living in the Dominican Republic. The irony was that he had been assigned to kill the same people the US had trained in the early nineties. FRAPH spread terror. They broke into homes, and tortured and killed their political enemies. Thousands were slaughtered. Faceless bodies were left strewn in the backstreets of slums. It was known as "facial scalping," the victim's face peeled from ear to ear with a machete. Many of FRAPH were former members of the Tonton Macoute.

Was that who had his daughter?

"How do you know for sure they're Haitians?"

"Look, that's what I know."

"You got a name for these Haitians?"

The kid shook his head.

"Tell me where they are."

"I think—"

"I don't want 'think' or 'maybe,' I want a precise location."

The kid bit his lower lip. "Somewhere in Miami Beach."

Reznick stared out toward the outer office. At the desk where the young man had been sitting, there was a BlackBerry with a flashing red light. A recent message had been received. He went over to the desk, pulling the weeping kid with him.

———

He picked up the BlackBerry and scrolled down the messages. Nothing of any interest. But he was curious, so he scrolled through the applications and saw Smart WiFi, eOffice 4.6, and e-Mobile Contact. Then he saw an app he didn't recognize or know anything about: Dexrex SMS.

"What the hell is this?"

He opened it up and saw it required a username and password. Reznick raised his gun to the young man's head. "Username and password now, fucker!"

The kid began to shake. "Username is *Lemonheart*, password is *Genesis*. As in the Bible."

"As in the shitty rock band," Reznick spat.

He typed in the letters on the tiny Qwerty keyboard. Then an extra security question was asked. "Childhood nickname?"

"Please . . . I'm not authorized to—"

"Childhood nickname!"

"Droop."

"Droop?!"

The young man blushed. "I walked around with droopy pants as a toddler."

"Jesus Christ. And you used to work for the CIA?" Reznick shook his head as he keyed in *Droop*. Almost immediately, a huge archive of decrypted instant messages—all sent to and from the BlackBerry—was downloaded.

The last sent message caught his eye: *Proceed to 5131 North Bay Road for safe delivery of cargo after pickup.*

Reznick showed the message to the young man. "What's this address? I thought you said you didn't know anything."

The kid stared at the screen for a couple of seconds. He scrunched up his face as if trying to remember what the address meant.

"What the fuck are you touching?" Reznick said, pulling him back.

Reznick crouched down and saw a silver switch underneath the table. The little bastard had set off an alarm.

Suddenly, the kid was scrambling across the floor to a jacket slung over a chair and reaching inside. He pulled out a pistol and turned to point it at Reznick.

But Reznick was already one step ahead. He fired two shots and watched, as if in slow motion, as the young man crashed to the floor. Blood oozed out of the kid's chest through his shirt, seeping into the carpet. Reznick stared long and hard at the dead body. He'd been given no choice.

He committed the North Bay Road address to memory. Then he went down the stairwell three floors, rode the elevator to the first floor, and then raced down the stairs to the basement garage to get back to the car.

Heart pounding, he pushed through the basement door—and froze. A guard was pointing a gun straight at him.

"Don't move, motherfucker!"

Thirteen

In the control room of the FBI's Miami field office, Martha Meyerstein was staring grim-faced at a bank of screens showing real-time CCTV footage from the Brickell Avenue tower as the drama unfolded. Standing at her side was the special agent in charge of the Miami Field Division, Sam Clayton. His arms were folded and his sleeves rolled up.

Her team were on their phones, either chasing down leads or reaching out to other intelligence agencies. But it was clear that the ongoing police incident, which had thrown up red flags as it matched Reznick's description, was the breakthrough they needed.

She recognized Reznick's features as he stood, hands on head, dressed in an ill-fitting, brown UPS shirt. The middle-aged security guard was speaking into the radio attached to his shirt, gun fixed on Reznick.

"We've got the fucker," Clayton said.

Meyerstein ignored the comment, as Reznick was now staring straight into the security camera. The dark circles under his eyes made it look like he hadn't slept in days. A heavy growth of stubble on his face, mouth turned down.

"What's the ETA?" she said, turning to look at Clayton.

"Approximately two minutes."

"You mind me asking why it's taking them so long?"

Clayton sighed. "Some hip-hop convention. Miami-Dade police have to help out Miami Beach police, who are swamped with calls. Tens of thousands of them are flooding the city—hogging the beach, Ocean Drive, Washington Avenue. But there are two cars already downtown, and they should be there real quick."

Meyerstein stared at the screens as the guard wiped his brow. "I don't like it. And what's happened to Luntz?"

"Our guys are scouring the footage in the parking garage as we speak."

"Good. What about our two Fed teams?"

Clayton blew out his cheeks. "North Miami Beach to downtown. Ten minutes if they're lucky."

"They need to get a move on."

Meyerstein couldn't take her eyes off Reznick. He was staring into the camera, and it felt as if he were staring straight at her. As if he knew she was there. She pushed the thought from her mind.

"What about the guy Reznick killed inside this building? And what about his company, Norton and Weiss?"

"Don't know the identity of the kid who ran into Reznick. All we know is that Norton and Weiss, Inc. is a law firm run by a former CIA guy, Brewling. He wasn't on our radar. We had him down as retired. Name ring a bell?"

"Brewling? Didn't he work under Buckley way back in the eighties?"

"Was his sidekick in Beirut, no less. Led the covert operation to free Buckley when he was kidnapped by Hezbollah. It was a fuck-up and, as you know, Buckley was killed. Brewling retreated to Langley."

Meyerstein didn't take her eyes off the screens. "That figures. Does he live in Miami?"

"Just north. Very upscale area. Indian Creek Island. But he's not there."

"Well, let's find him. We need to speak to him."

"We're working on it."

Meyerstein felt frustrated just watching visuals. "Why is there no sound? Can't we hook up to this guy's radio through his security company?"

"We're still trying. Shit, he's making his move."

Meyerstein watched as Reznick took a step forward. She knew what was coming. In an instant, Reznick had grabbed the man's gun and used his left hand to redirect it away from his body, before slamming his right fist hard into the guard's jaw. It was a Krav Maga move Meyerstein herself had been taught by the Israeli military.

The guard was out cold.

"Oh Christ, what the hell?" She watched as Reznick headed out of view. "Is it possible to get some other camera angles, people?"

A computer guy shouted across, "That's all we've got!"

Her cell phone rang and she saw O'Donoghue's name on the screen. "Damn, that's all I need."

Sat in the FBI's Miami conference room, Meyerstein connected with O'Donoghue, who was taking charge of the emergency videoconference from inside his huge office at FBI Headquarters in Washington. She quickly brought him up to speed with developments down in Miami.

The Director spoke first. "Martha, we have begun discussions about this ongoing investigation with the President's National Security staff, the Director of National Intelligence, and the Department of Homeland Security. We are all very concerned that this is resolved ASAP. How did you let him get away?"

Meyerstein felt herself flush and took a few moments to compose herself. "With respect, sir, this is no average Joe. Jon Reznick is trained to cope with almost anything. Look, I don't think this is a time for pointing fingers. This is a very complex investigation."

"Miami is not a big city. Why can't we trace Reznick, and in turn our scientist?"

"Reznick is jamming the signals, pure and simple. We just can't pinpoint where he is."

The bright red light on the phone on the conference table began flashing. "Bear with me a second, sir. I'll put this on speaker so we can all hear."

She pressed the speaker button so both O'Donoghue and everyone in the Miami conference room could hear. "Martha, we got something."

It was Kate Reynolds, a bright, up-and-coming special agent in her late twenties—a political science graduate who'd been signed up while at John Hopkins. Reynolds had been seconded to the Hoover Building from the Kansas City field office, and was now at the lab Luntz worked at. She reminded Meyerstein of herself at that age. Fresh, eager, and not yet worn down by the pressures of the job, but Meyerstein also detected a toughness and no-nonsense approach that she could relate to.

"Kate, we're in the middle of a videoconference with Director O'Donoghue, just so you know," Meyerstein said.

Reynolds gave a nervous cough. "I'm working alongside the lab's senior management team. We're going through the records of everyone who's worked in the lab, and we have three members of staff who've left in the last three years. Two have been accounted for, tracked down to new jobs. But there's one guy who worked with Luntz and who seems to have dropped off the radar."

Meyerstein said, "Kate, you got a name?"

"Lieutenant Colonel Scott Caan, a US army scientist. Hasn't been seen in the last couple weeks."

Meyerstein spoke first. "That's great work, Kate. Now let's find out everything about him. Phone records, medical history, friends, coworkers—let's get into his life and see what we can find."

Special Agent Reynolds said, "Sure thing."

O'Donoghue was nodding, taking notes. "You lead on this, Martha. And no more excuses."

The feed from O'Donoghue's office went blank.

Meyerstein cleared her throat and turned to her team in the Miami conference room. "A guy disappears from a government lab. No word from him. Luntz contacts us and is under FBI protection before he is due to meet us about his concerns. There are red flags here. Agreed?"

Everyone nodded.

"Kate, are you still there?"

"Yes, ma'am."

"I'd like a full report in an hour. The bare bones will do. Get me a picture of Caan and send it now." Meyerstein turned to her team again. "As soon as the photo arrives, I want it run through face recognition software. I want it analyzed in-depth, and then let's get Caan's picture to every field office in the country. He's out there somewhere."

The phone on the conference table rang. The caller ID told her it was Roy Stamper. Meyerstein picked up.

"Martha, I've been following up a couple leads with Miami Beach police," he said, the sound of loud traffic in the background. "We've got something real interesting."

"Where exactly are you, Roy?"

"A back street in South Beach. The body of a white male. Looks like he's just been waterboarded."

"You gotta be kidding me."

"Nope. Not exactly an everyday occurrence."

"You got a name for this guy?"

"We got a name and a direct connection to Reznick."

"I'm listening."

"The dead guy is Chad Magruder. Ed has got back to me with confirmation that he was Special Activities Division. Has a sister who lives out in Weston, nice town on the edge of the Everglades."

Meyerstein felt her stomach knot. "Tell me all you've got on this connection."

"You're gonna love this. Magruder and Reznick were in Iraq together. Black ops. But it doesn't end there."

Meyerstein glanced up at the conference room screen as medics attended to the unconscious security guard at the Brickell parking garage. "Yeah, I'm listening."

"Four hours ago, a suspicious death was called in from Fort Lauderdale."

"Go on."

"Local police found a dead guy on a boat. Guy named Leggett. Old Delta operator, just like Reznick. Best man at his wedding."

"Good work, Roy."

She ended the call and relayed the news to her team. "It's obvious Reznick is the common thread. Two dead former Delta buddies of his. A dead young man who worked at Norton and Weiss. A missing scientist. And, let's not forget, one of our colleagues, Special Agent Connelly from Seattle, is also dead." She detected a renewed sense of determination among her team. "We might've let Reznick slip through our fingers. But that's the first and last time it's gonna happen. I want to find both Reznick and Luntz. I want everyone on it. I want all agencies brought up to speed. And I want results, not excuses."

Fourteen

The first thing Reznick did after speeding away from the office tower on Brickell was to head across the causeway to South Beach. He dumped the car at a parking garage and hailed a cab, eager to get to his destination as soon as possible. The cab driver was a young Brazilian woman who looked like a model.

"North Bay Road," he said, climbing into the back seat.

She nodded and sped off, headed west, away from the crowds thronging the main drags, past fading pastel-colored apartment buildings. She didn't talk, but glanced occasionally in the mirror.

They passed Flamingo Park and turned onto Alton Road. His cell rang.

"Don't hang up, Jon." It was the Fed woman again—Meyerstein. "The longer this goes on, the harder it'll be for me to try to help you. I want to help you find your daughter. We know about her. And we know what happened to her grandmother. I know that's what's driving you on this."

"Keep talking."

"Jon, I have scores of people working to track down Lauren."

"Don't bullshit me. You want Luntz."

"We want them both back safe and sound. Jon, you've got to trust me on this. It's the only way."

"Yeah, right."

"Jon, as I said before, national security is at stake. This is a very grave situation."

"What about my daughter?"

"We'll find her, I promise. But we're dealing with a highly—"

Reznick ended the call. He knew they had either managed to track the cell phone or were close to pinpointing his location, despite the jamming. And he also knew that they would have swamped the area with cops looking for suspicious vehicles, cars, and people.

The huge palms, hedges, and foliage nearly shrouded the huge mansions behind their high walls. He was half a dozen blocks from the address.

"Just drop me off here," Reznick said.

The driver pulled up and turned around. "Fifteen dollars, please," she said, smiling broadly.

Reznick pulled out two one-hundred dollar bills. "Gimme your phone and I'll give you two hundred dollars and this shiny new phone for your trouble."

The driver shrugged. "Yeah, whatever," she said, taking the money and the phone and handing her Sony cell phone over.

"If someone calls within the next hour, give them the number of your phone, can you do that?"

"You kidding me? For two hundred dollars? Absolutely."

She smiled as Reznick slammed the door shut. Then he watched her drive away, knowing he had bought himself some time as the Feds tracked the phone in the cab.

Fifteen

With his gun tucked into the back of his waistband, concealed by his T-shirt, Reznick went up North Bay Road on the shaded side of the street. He knew it wasn't ideal, walking around in the affluent neighborhood. Every cop in Miami Beach would be looking for him with a full ID and photo. He had to get out of sight. And quick.

A man with an overweight golden Labrador passed by, then an elderly, Lycra-clad male jogger, his sunglasses glistening, iPod earbuds leaking bass-heavy dance music. Reznick didn't make eye contact. Up ahead, he saw a large white mansion behind high, wrought-iron gates. Cameras with small red lights filmed the gate and part of the perimeter wall and street. He crossed to the opposite sidewalk to stay away from the prying cameras.

He knew there would be infrared motion sensors on the grounds of such a house, and alarmed doors and windows. He stood under a huge palm tree diagonally opposite the house as a gold Lexus passed by.

Reznick felt the sweat run down his back as he pulled out the electronic jammer from his pocket. He switched it on to "Lock." Within seconds, the red lights on the surveillance cameras had turned off.

He had created a forty-yard dead zone disrupting three main bandwidths and all Bluetooth and Wi-Fi signals.

Reznick slid the device back into his pocket and waited for a few moments to make sure the coast was clear. Then he crossed the street and went down a small deserted lane at the side of the house, before taking out the suppressor and screwing it into the Beretta. When it was all clear, he climbed over the wall and dropped down onto a stone path.

Out of nowhere, two Dobermans bounded toward him. They flew at him, teeth bared, salivating, their black eyes locked on his body. Calmly, Reznick took out his silenced gun, aimed, and fired. A couple of muffled shots and both dogs were dead.

He edged across the lawn toward the side of the house and found an unlocked door. Inside, the house was bathed in an ethereal orange light coming through huge bay windows.

He stood still, listening for any movement.

Silence. But that didn't mean anything.

He moved through the main floor, scanning each segment of the space. He had been trained to visually "pie off" a room—a military term for slicing a room into triangular sectors. It was usually carried out by a team, with each man having his own point of domination. One-man room clearing was a different animal altogether. The risks were far greater—there was no backup.

Room to room, gun in hand.

The terrible thought crossed his mind that he had the wrong house.

Reznick headed down a highly polished hallway, which led to a spiral staircase. His senses all switched on, he slowly headed up the flight of stairs, one step at a time. Again he went from room to room, until he came to a closed door. He made sure to stay clear of the "fatal funnel" directly in front of it, to prevent being shot from behind the door. He also made sure he stood on the non-hinge side.

He reached out and softly turned the handle, pushing open the door.

Reznick went back into the hall and stood stock-still, not breathing. He listened. But again he heard nothing.

He continued along the hallway, which led to another spiral staircase. The wooden stairs creaked as he climbed to the third floor. He continued to pie off the space. The landing curved around and led to the bay side of the house. There were several rooms, all the doors shut.

One at a time.

The first room was a huge bedroom, bed perfectly made up, modern art on the walls, beige and cream throughout. The second room was a smaller bedroom and was painted a cool blue. He stood outside the third room. Then he turned the handle and pushed open the door. It was a study overlooking the bay. Dark wood, leather chair, dark brown walls, and the smell of cheap cologne.

Reznick approached the fourth door side-on, gun in the air. He sensed something, and stopped. He crouched down low, peering under the crack at the bottom.

A creak inside, and a shadow moving.

Reznick froze. He could hear the beating of his heart.

Suddenly, shots fired through the door, narrowly missing him. He hit the floor and fired five muffled shots through the top half of the door.

The sound of a body falling on the other side.

Reznick kicked in the door, gun drawn. A guy lay on the ground. Blood seeped from his mouth and two bullet wounds— one in his chest and one in the throat. The man's eyes were open, but he was dead and gone.

Goddamn.

Reznick turned, exited the room, and headed slowly down the hallway toward one final door. He waited a few seconds before he kicked it open and looked around. It was a huge bathroom, floor-to-ceiling frosted windows. He stood still.

He could hear the sound of whimpering close by. It was coming from behind a door within the bathroom.

He gently pushed open the door. Cowering on the floor of the wet room was an old woman.

"Please don't hurt me!" she implored.

Reznick walked over to her and pressed the gun to her head. "Who the fuck are you?"

The woman was crying. "Please, don't hurt me."

"Where's my daughter?"

"I don't know anything. I'm just the maid."

"Stand up!"

Slowly she stood up, hands on her head. From the cheap nylon slacks and plain cotton shirt, Reznick could tell she was indeed the domestic help.

"Who was the guy I just shot?"

"Bertrand. He looks after the security of the house when Claude is away."

"Who's Claude?"

"Claude Merceron."

"Where is he?"

"I have no idea. They don't tell me anything. I just cook and—"

"Shut the fuck up." Reznick grabbed her by the shirt. "Who else is in the house?"

"No one. It's just me now."

Reznick frog-marched her downstairs to the main room. He pointed to a large, black-and-white framed photograph of two middle-aged men shaking hands. "Who are those guys in the picture?"

"Mr. Merceron is on the right," she said.

Reznick studied the photo. He noticed the dark, cold eyes. "Who's the other guy?"

"That's the Haitian consulate general."

"So what is Merceron?"

"Sir, he's a diplomat within the consulate in downtown Miami."

"Is this a recent picture?"

"Yes, quite recent."

"Where was it taken?"

"I don't know."

Reznick stared at the photo, the chubby face with the black eyes imprinted on his brain. "I think you know more than you're letting on. Where's my daughter?"

The woman averted her gaze. "I told you I don't know."

"You're lying! Where is my daughter?"

"Please, I have two young children. I'm on my own. They need me."

"So does my daughter. Tell me where the fuck she is or your children won't have a mom to look after them."

"Please . . ."

Reznick pressed the gun to her head.

The woman wept. "I'm telling the truth. I haven't seen your daughter. But I do know something was happening here the night before last. I was told to keep to my room. I came down to the kitchen to make myself a sandwich and fetch a glass of milk. And Bertrand was angry to see me. So was Mr. Merceron."

"Why?"

"I think they'd been down in the basement."

"OK, now we're getting somewhere. Tell me about this basement."

"I never go down there. Only Bertrand and Mr. Merceron."

"You never go down there at all?"

"Never."

"Show me this basement."

The woman led Reznick through to a huge modern kitchen. She pointed to a pine dresser in the corner adorned with cookbooks and small china ornaments. "Underneath there," she said.

Reznick pushed the dresser aside and a few ornaments smashed to the ground. A sealed iron hatch like a manhole was revealed. There were two rectangular holes either side to open the cover. "Where the fuck are the keys?"

"Bertrand has them. I swear I don't know where they are."

Reznick pressed the gun to her head again. "Tell me."

She pointed to the huge freezer.

Reznick rummaged inside. In the third compartment down, beside packets of frozen fish and frozen fries, he found two large keys. "You weren't being entirely truthful, were you?"

The woman bowed her head and began to say a prayer, tears rolling down her face. She made the sign of the cross. "I'm sorry."

"Yeah, so am I."

He crouched down beside the hatch and carefully slid both keys into the rectangular slots. Then he turned them anti-clockwise.

Reznick lifted the hatch with the keys still inside the slots, revealing a ladder leading down. He pulled out his penlight, and the narrow beam of light penetrated the darkness, revealing a cavernous concrete space. He ordered the maid down first. She protested, but he pushed her down the ladder. He followed her, and directed the beam of light around the empty space. He saw a switch and flicked it on, bathing the room in cold, silver light.

Reznick looked around. The basement was supported by four large concrete pillars, and his gaze was drawn to an open hatch just behind one of them. He walked over to it, and shone the penlight into some kind of sub-basement.

Reznick forced the maid to lead the way down the hatch into the darkness. She mumbled a prayer under her breath. Placing the penlight between his teeth, he climbed down and found himself in a dank and dimly lit dungeon that had to be below sea level. A sickly smell pervaded the air and a rat was gnawing on something in the corner. The damned thing didn't move when he shone the light directly on it. He saw that the rat was tearing at a bone.

Reznick moved the beam around. Dead chickens and voodoo dolls were hanging from meat hooks attached to the ceiling. He turned and shone the penlight toward the far end of the room. He saw what looked like a small shrine. A voodoo shrine. Unlit candles, wooden carvings of men, and the blood and bones of dead animals were scattered around the basement floor. At least, he thought they were animal bones.

Bolted to the floor beside the shrine was a heavy wooden chair with iron wrist and ankle cuffs attached.

Reznick felt sick. He checked the rest of the room but it was completely enclosed. He headed back up the ladder with the maid, and then up the second ladder to the kitchen. He shut the hatch and breathed in the fresh air.

He felt a mixture of anger and emptiness threatening to engulf him. He thought of Lauren in such a sickening place and wanted to scream. Had she been kept here? Was that it?

Reznick stared out of the kitchen window at a sleek, sixty-foot sport yacht tied up on the jetty at the bottom of the garden. The stainless-steel trims glistened in the sun. "Tell me about visitors to this house. Have you had any visitors? Any white people in the past week?"

The woman nodded.

"Tell me what you know."

"There was one white man. I don't know his name. He came here to speak to Mr. Merceron. I made them dinner and that was that."

"What did he look like?"

"Gray hair. Dark suit. Very expensive. He wore sunglasses and didn't take them off, which I thought was unusual. I didn't really see much of his face. Very thin."

"What about a girl? Was there a young white girl here in the last week?"

The woman made the sign of the cross and mumbled a prayer. "I don't know about any girl."

"Where is Merceron? Is this where he lives?"

"Two or maybe three times a week."

"Has he got another place in Miami?"

"I know he used to stay at the Setai."

"I want to know where he is now!"

"I don't know. He doesn't use this place as often as he did. Maybe to chat things over with Bertrand."

Reznick pointed to the cruiser tied up outside. "Is that his boat?"

"Yes."

He grabbed the woman by the arm, and marched her out of the huge, glass French doors and down the wooden jetty. He stepped onto the teak deck, holding the maid by her arm, and went down into the galley.

Reznick looked around. A walnut-paneled stateroom with cream sofas, mahogany furniture, African art on the walls. A wrap-around minibar at the far end, with bottles of Chivas Regal, Johnnie Walker, and Cristal on show.

He checked the guestrooms. But they were empty, no sign of Lauren.

Reznick and the maid got off the boat and headed back to the house. As they approached the kitchen door, the cab driver's cell phone burst into life, blasting out an RnB ringtone.

"Hello, Jon. You've been busy, haven't you?"

Reznick's blood ran cold. It was the guy who had Lauren. "Cut the bullshit, I want Lauren. I want to meet up."

"Just want to say how cute that cab driver was who dropped you off. She was a real honey. You wanna know what happened to her, Jon?"

Reznick's heart sank. He stared out over the dark blue waters of Biscayne Bay, the towering skyline of downtown Miami in the distance, and wondered where the hell they'd taken Lauren.

"Let's put it like this—the same thing will happen to your daughter if you don't bring us the scientist tonight."

"Where and when?"

The man sighed. "I really don't know if I can trust you anymore."

"I said, *where and when?*"

"I'll call you an hour before the exchange with the place."

"I want to speak to my daughter. How do I even know she's alive?"

The man began to laugh. "You don't, that's the thing."

Sixteen

The interstate traffic heading into Washington, DC was down to a crawl. Thomas Wesley thought of the lunch date he was about to crash; he felt nervous and wondered how his old friend, Congressman Lance Drake, would receive him.

Hadn't Drake made it clear during the phone conversation in the middle of the night what he thought of them meeting up? And, perhaps more importantly, why would he want to be seen with a disgraced loser who'd been sacked from his high-ranking job working with the NSA? Drake was on the up, after all. He was a "star of the future" in Republican circles.

Wesley's mind flashed back to their college years. Back then he'd known Drake as a wild college boy who knocked back tequila shots, washed down with bottles of cold beer. Now if he turned on Fox, Congressman Drake was riffing on guns, God, and "old-fashioned values."

It was strange. While at Georgetown, Drake had never expressed right-wing or even liberal sympathies. He'd been apolitical. More interested in getting loaded on booze and fooling around with "hot chicks."

Wesley, on the other hand, was known as the college nerd. He reveled in all things technological, wrote software code through the night, and never skipped class. Occasionally, he would be dragged along to an on-campus party with Drake and his drunken friends. But more often than not it was to The Tombs—a *Ratskeller* at the main gates of the university—for Buffalo wings and pitchers of beer and Hoya basketball. He didn't mind, as Drake and his friends were usually pretty hilarious and fun to be around. But smoking weed and hanging out with crazy girls seven days a week didn't hold as much appeal for Wesley as it did for Drake. For Wesley, the only girl who interested him was the one who became his wife. Drake thought that was weird. But, despite their differences, they'd rubbed along well together and been good friends.

He looked at the photo of his wife that hung from the rearview mirror. It had been taken at a friend's wedding in DC. Her black hair cut in a soft bob; her head back, laughing. She was truly beautiful when she smiled.

His wife didn't want kids and wasn't in the least bit maternal. She wanted her career as a teacher. He'd accepted that. But, over the years, as he saw his friends change and start families, he'd realized he desperately *did* want a family. Children to hold and love and cherish. To bring into the world, show them all the great things.

His hands-free car phone rang. The display showed it was his wife calling from work.

"Hey, honey," he said, "I was just thinking about you."

"Hope they were good thoughts."

"Gimme a break, will you?" He smiled.

"Sorry I missed you this morning, but I had to get out the door before six."

"Don't worry. I managed to pour the milk into my Cheerios without spilling anything on that beloved hardwood floor."

She laughed. He loved her laugh. "Are you driving?" she asked.

"Yeah, I'm heading to Washington."

"I thought you were working a day shift today."

"I'm taking a day off from the delights of Walmart. I need to speak to Lance in person."

A long silence opened up.

His wife spoke first. "I thought he wasn't interested."

The tone of her voice told Wesley she was annoyed. "I'm just going to turn up and speak to him. Hopefully change his mind."

"Thomas, what's gotten into you? You can't do that."

"Why not?"

"Why *not*? Because he's a powerful congressman now, and not a buddy from the old days. Thomas, you're not in his world anymore."

"Honey, he needs to know exactly what I know. I don't know what else to do. I—"

"Why can't you just let it go?"

Then she hung up, leaving Wesley to wonder if this was really such a good plan after all.

⌣ ⌣

The Beaux-Arts facade of the Old Ebbitt Grill—next to the White House—let Thomas Wesley know that he'd found the right place.

A cherished memory flooded back. He had visited the bar once when he was at Georgetown. It had been his first date with the girl who would become his wife, and he'd deliberately picked the place to impress her. They drank champagne, and ate grilled filet mignon with mashed potatoes, sautéed spinach, and red wine sauce. They sat and laughed and talked about nothing in particular for hours, all through the afternoon.

He walked through the revolving doors clutching his briefcase and looked around. He saw dark mahogany and velvet booths, brass and beveled glass—just as he remembered it.

"Good afternoon, sir," the maître d' said. "Are you joining us for lunch?"

"I'm joining Congressman Lance Drake for lunch in the main dining room," Wesley lied. "Has he arrived?"

"Absolutely," the man said, picking up a menu. "Follow me, sir."

The main dining room was all wooden crossbeams, starched white tablecloths, antique gas lamps, and an air of refined decadence. At the far end, Drake was sitting alone at a booth, wearing a navy single-breasted suit, maroon silk tie, his hair slicked back. He was talking too loudly into his cell. A half-empty glass of white wine was on the table, a chilled bottle of Chablis in a silver ice bucket by the booth.

Wesley sat down opposite Drake as the maître d' gave a respectful nod and handed him the menu.

"The waiter will be over to take your order in a few minutes, sir."

"Very good," Wesley said as the maître d' disappeared into the melee of the restaurant.

Drake stopped speaking mid-sentence and shot him a dirty look. "I'm sorry to cut short this conversation, Frank, but an old friend of mine has just turned up, right this moment. Do you mind if we catch up later today, is that OK?" He waited for a few moments and then said, "Frank, great idea, I'll see you then." He ended the call and put the phone beside his wine glass. Then he leaned forward, and Wesley could smell the drink and smoke on his breath.

"What in God's name do you think you're doing here? I thought I'd made my position clear."

Wesley smiled. "Good to see you too, Lance."

"Who told you I'd be here? It sure as hell wouldn't be my staff."

"Your itinerary on your phone laid out what you're doing for the next three months."

"Have you hacked into my phone?"

Wesley sighed. "You weren't listening to me, so I knew I needed to speak to you face to face. So, here I am."

They stopped talking when a waiter approached their table and asked to take their orders. Wesley asked for a bottle of mineral water with two glasses, while Drake told the waiter that they weren't quite ready and to come back in ten minutes.

When the waiter was out of earshot, Lance leaned forward again. "I've a good mind to report you for this. You'd never work again. You'd be banged up for fucking years."

"Lance, does Christine know about this lunch with one of your Harvard interns?"

Drake took a long sip of his wine and smiled. "Is that what this is about? You're blackmailing me?"

"Absolutely not. But I feel like I'm banging my head up against a brick wall time after time on this. This is too important."

The waiter returned with two glasses and a large bottle of water. He poured the water and gave a respectful nod before leaving them to it.

"Look, I'm not interested in what you've got to say. Have you got that?"

Wesley shifted in his seat and his foot knocked into something. He looked under the table and saw it was Drake's briefcase. He took a sip of cool water. "Lance, how long have you known me?"

Drake rolled his eyes. "Look, what does it matter how long I've known you?"

"It matters because you know that I do things right, and I always do the right thing. You wanna cut me some slack?"

"Look, I'm sorry what happened to you. Really I am. But I'm not the person who can help you with this. It sounds like what you've got is classified. We'd be breaking the law."

Wesley reached under the table and, out of sight, pulled the tiny blue iPod Shuffle out of his jacket pocket. Then he opened up Drake's briefcase and dropped it in.

"What did you do there?" Drake asked, glancing under the table.

"Check your briefcase. There's an iPod. Listen to Track One."

"You better take it out right now." Drake's voice was barely a whisper. "Do you hear me? If I listen to what you've obtained, that would mean—"

"Listen to it, and I'll be out of your face. I promise."

Drake let out a long sigh and finished the rest of his glass of wine. "OK, let's for argument's sake say that I agree. What does it contain?"

"It lasts about three minutes. It's been cleaned up. Digitally remastered, if you like."

"Why me?"

Wesley leaned forward, hands on the table. "You have the clout, pure and simple. I've tried and I got nowhere. I don't know where else I can turn." He leaned closer, his voice a whisper. "I think once you know the identities of the people in the conversation, you'll call in the specialists at the NSA or FBI to try and decode the covert message it contains. On the surface, the message is undetectable. Which points to a highly sophisticated operation. And I'm convinced we're talking about an attack on America."

"OK, let's be clear on this. I'll listen to it. But I'm only doing this because what you're saying concerns me. I love my country with a passion."

"And I respect that, Lance."

"But I want to be clear that I can't guarantee anything. I will listen to this when I get back to my office, and then I'll call you."

Wesley finished the rest of his water. "That's all I wanted, Lance. I appreciate that."

The waiter returned and poured out more wine. Drake waited until he had finished and was out of earshot. "Who else knows about this?"

"Me, you, and the Inspector General at the NSA."

Drake went quiet for a few moments, then he looked toward the entrance and gave a small wave to a stunningly attractive, twenty-something blonde.

He fixed his gaze on Wesley. "Leave this with me and I'll get back to you. But if anyone asks, I don't know anything about it, OK?"

Wesley knew when it was time to leave. He stood up, and patted Drake on the shoulder like old friends do. "Appreciate that."

Then he walked past the young woman, who flashed a pearly smile, before heading out into the harsh glare of the early-afternoon sun, knowing his old friend wouldn't let him down.

Seventeen

Dark thoughts were starting to crowd Reznick's mind. He was driving south on Alton Road in a BMW 650i convertible he'd taken from Merceron's garage. He was no nearer to finding out where his daughter was. He felt bereft, and his anxiety was mounting as the minutes ticked down.

He knew he had to make the call. He punched in Maddox's number from memory.

Maddox answered on the second ring. "Who is this?" He hadn't recognized the number.

"Who do you think?"

"Where the hell are you?"

"Miami."

"I don't believe this. I gave you a simple job. We now have a rising body count. The Feds are after you and the target is missing. Reznick, I know what this is about. I heard about Lauren and her grandmother. I'm sorry, Reznick, for that. But you have a job to do. You need to bring in the target in the next hour. Do you understand?"

"That might be tricky, Maddox. And there's another dead. I just shot a guy half an hour ago."

"Reznick, we need to draw a line under the whole thing. Look, I'm glad you finally called. We can help you get Lauren, make no mistake about that. But you need to bring in the target. We'll work this out."

Reznick said nothing.

"There's something you need to know about Luntz."

"What about him?"

"Did some checking of my own. The IDF dog tag is bullshit. His name isn't Luntz."

"What?"

"We've been played. All of us. Our communication was compromised, you were right on that. But there's no such person as Luntz. He doesn't exist."

Reznick's tired mind tried to keep up.

"The guy you have runs a private bank that deals exclusively with the rulers of Saudi Arabia. He's tried to conceal the financial trail for 9/11. He tried to cover the tracks of the hijackers. And that's why his number is up."

Reznick felt as if an oncoming truck had hit him. Images of the falling towers and the dust cloud flashed into his mind. "He came up with a credible story. How did you get this information?"

"I've said enough."

He felt sick. How was this possible?

"We need to bring him in, Jon. There are other elements at work. We need closure on this today."

"I need to think about my daughter. How does she fit into this?"

"Reznick, as far as we can ascertain, they have your daughter somewhere in South Florida—I'm hearing near Key West—but they just want to get this guy back and get him out the country. Those on high in a foreign government are protecting him. We can't allow them to succeed, Reznick. We need to get rid of this guy."

Reznick pulled up at a red light, car idling. His mind was struggling to take it all in. He felt conflicted. He didn't know what to believe. "Key West?"

"Here's what I propose. Hand him over, and I'll negotiate with these guys to get your daughter back."

"I don't know what the hell has gone down here, Maddox, but I feel like I'm closing in on them."

"Reznick, you need to focus. You can't go out on a limb. You can't do this by yourself. Look, I've flown down to Miami. Do you know The Tides on Ocean Drive?"

"I've heard of it."

"Let's meet up there and we can run through our options. You tell me how you think we go about getting your daughter back. You call the shots. But you need backup, Reznick, don't you see that? You need logistics. One man can't do this alone."

Reznick knew he was close. Merceron was the key. But the contradictory information Reznick had been dealt made him fear the worst for Lauren. He was bombing around Miami trying to get a lead. Now Maddox and his team seemed to have Key West in their sights. Was it really possible that Luntz had pulled the wool over his eyes? Was Luntz really a shadowy banker who had concealed the 9/11 money trail? None of it made any sense.

"Reznick, are you still there?"

"Yeah."

"Is the target somewhere safe?"

"Sure."

"Good—we're in business. Bring him to The Tides within the hour. He'll be taken care of. Then our priority will be Lauren."

Reznick was running through the scenarios in his head.

"Reznick, are you still there, goddamnit?"

He saw a sign for an Internet café, its dark green awnings partially shading the sidewalk. His mouth felt dry and his stomach growled. "Maddox, I need more time on this. I've got to think this through."

"Reznick, you're out of time."

"Perhaps. Look, I'll call you."

"Wait. You need—"

"Speak to you later, Maddox."

Reznick parked the car in a nearby alley and went into the café. He ordered a bottle of still water, a Christmas cookie latte, and a large grilled cheese sandwich. He handed the barista wearing a Motörhead T-shirt a twenty-dollar bill and told her to keep the change, which brought a smile to her face.

He headed over to a table with no other users and sat down, back to the wall. He drank the bottle of water and wolfed down the sandwich, then logged onto the Internet and googled the name "Claude Merceron." It pulled up 10,529 search results. He clicked on the top link and it took him to a short biography with a picture.

He went back and clicked on the image search tab—823 separate photos appeared. Reznick scrolled through them. Some showed Merceron sitting at his desk in the Haitian consulate in downtown Miami, in front of the distinctive Haitian flag.

Shit.

The guy really was a diplomat. That meant diplomatic immunity. Untouchable.

Four pictures showed him handing over a million-dollar check raised by the Haitian community in Miami for the disaster-relief appeal.

Reznick studied the man's profile. He looked around mid-fifties, short hair with a peppering of gray. Those black eyes again. He was physically imposing. He exuded quiet authority, perhaps even menace.

Reznick thought back to the basement on North Bay Road. The voodoo symbols. The blood and bones. The smell of rotting flesh.

He clicked back and opened up a few of the articles written about Merceron. He read about his charity work and business interests. Then blogs from Haitian exiles came up, speaking about his fundraising efforts for underprivileged children in Little Haiti. But Reznick knew that charity work didn't mean shit.

Thirty minutes later, as Reznick felt increasingly jaded, he came across an interesting article. It was a *Miami Herald* piece about Merceron's vision for Haiti following the 2010 earthquake. He was pictured sitting on a roof terrace.

Reznick scanned the caption on the photo. It read: *Diplomat Claude Merceron's birthday party, March 7, 2010, Florida.* No indication of the venue.

He stared long and hard at the image, and wondered if the party had been held at the consulate in Miami. Was that where he could be found? Then he remembered a high-tech device that could help him.

He accessed the website for specialist software and tried to download the program Opanda IExif, which would perhaps help him find the location. But he wasn't in luck. Almost immediately, an error message came up on the screen saying *Incompatible Extension*.

His heart sank. "Goddamn," he said, not keeping his emotions in check.

"You got a problem, sir?" He turned and saw it was the girl who had served him.

"It's OK, I'll figure it out."

Reznick could feel her looking over his shoulder.

"The firewalls and security measures on all our computers will stop any new installations. And that includes exchangeable image file format readers."

"I appreciate your help, thanks."

Reznick turned and stared back at the error message on the screen.

"Why don't you just download it to your cell phone?"

He leaned back in his seat and turned again to face her. "Unfortunately, my phone is used for work purposes and has been configured in a certain way. I know for a fact it won't accept that."

She smiled and shrugged her bony shoulders. "That's too bad."

Reznick shrugged. "I'll figure it out. Do you mind if I have an espresso and some of that carrot cake?" He handed her a twenty-dollar bill. "Appreciate your help. Keep the change."

"Thanks. You mind me asking what you need that program for? Not gonna case some joint through geotagging are you?"

Reznick showed his palms in mock surrender. "You got me. Am I that transparent?"

She laughed.

"Actually, I'm wondering where a picture was taken," he said. "I'm a location scout. Just curious where it is."

"You kidding? You in films?"

Reznick nodded.

She flushed crimson. "Oh, wow, how cool is that?" She handed him her iPhone. "Hey listen, you're in luck. Download the program to my phone if you want."

Reznick smiled graciously. "Very kind, thanks. Are you sure?"

"Go right ahead."

For a split second, Reznick felt bad for spinning such a line. But what she didn't know wouldn't hurt her.

He downloaded the program. Then he googled Claude Merceron again, and scrolled through the image results until he got to the one with Merceron being interviewed on the roof terrace.

Reznick opened the image. His heart hiked up a notch. *Please, gimme a break, he thought.* Almost immediately, the GPS longitude and latitude references and the time stamp came up. He clicked on the link that said *Locate Spot on Map by GPS*, and a Google map appeared with a red dot at South Ocean Boulevard, Palm Beach. The tag read: *The Palm Beach Club.*

Reznick kept his feelings in check. He didn't want to get ahead of himself. It didn't mean a goddamn thing if Merceron wasn't there.

The club's website showed a liveried doorman smiling outside a sprawling, five-story whitewashed mansion, its marble entrance shrouded by palms. It was founded in 1959 and drew its clients from wealthy businessmen and political leaders who had "made Palm Beach their home," including Senator Jimmy Labrecq, Governor Collins, and a smattering of retired hedge-fund head honchos from Manhattan. The photos showed the health club, the cigar bar, the roof terrace, the three restaurants, and the butterfly-shaped pool.

He added the club's main number to his cell phone.

The girl arrived with his espresso and carrot cake, which Reznick finished in seconds.

He handed her back her phone. "Appreciate your help," he said again.

"You got everything you were looking for?" she asked.

"Absolutely."

Reznick fired up the car and pulled up the club's number on his cell.

"The Palm Beach Club," a man said. "How can I help?"

"Good afternoon. My name is Bill Crenshaw. The governor asked me to give you a call—he's sponsoring my membership next month. I've just bought a place down in Palm Beach, and he thought it would be a good idea for me to have a look around the club first."

"That's not a problem, Mr. Crenshaw. I can arrange for you to meet with Mr. Symington, our general manager, tomorrow."

"That doesn't work. I've got a flight first thing tomorrow morning and I'm pressed for time, so it would have to be later this afternoon or this evening."

"Very good, sir. Please hold the line, Mr. Crenshaw, and I'll check to see if Mr. Symington is free later."

A few moments of classical music before the man spoke again.

"Sorry to keep you waiting, Mr. Crenshaw. That's not a problem. The general manager has set aside his diary for this evening, if that's all right with you, sir."

"Excellent. I look forward to seeing what you have to offer."

Reznick ended the call.

———

The shadows were lengthening as he drove along Collins Avenue. Up ahead, he saw Barneys. He parked the car and went inside. There he bought a pair of shades, a dark blue linen jacket, expensive faded jeans, a brown leather belt, and a pair of burgundy loafers.

He checked into a small hotel nearby and quickly showered. Then he put on his new outfit and stared at himself in the full-length mirror. He looked like a different person. Hair neat and groomed. Smart clothes.

He headed downstairs and dropped off the keycard for his room at reception. Then he got back into the car, popped a couple of Dexedrine, punched the details of the club into the sat nav, and drove back over the causeway into Miami.

The sun was low in the sky as Reznick headed north out of the city. He got onto the freeway and sped on, past sun-scarred housing projects on one side, country clubs on the other. The lights of oncoming cars dazzled his eyes as the sky darkened.

Eighteen

It was dark and the air was warm and muggy when Reznick drove across the Southern Boulevard Causeway onto Palm Beach Island. He hung a left onto South Ocean Boulevard.

He cruised past the upscale Four Seasons, and after a couple of hundred yards he saw a sign for the Palm Beach Club. He drove on for nearly a mile before he doubled back, slowing down as he approached the main entrance.

Reznick scanned the locale as he pulled up outside. The club was sandwiched between two sprawling mansions and edged by huge, manicured hedges. Surveillance cameras on poles scanned the grounds.

He pulled out a pocket telescope from his bag and stared down the well-lit gravel driveway at the huge red-sandstone building. Three young valets—wearing white shirts, gold vests, black pants, and shiny black shoes—were standing ready to park members' cars.

Suddenly, he heard a couple of honks from a car horn and saw a flash of lights from a passing car, no doubt angry at where he'd pulled up.

He slouched down low as he watched the valets goof around in the driveway. Two cameras were focused on the entrance.

He checked his watch and saw it was 6:38 p.m. Over the next fifteen minutes, a handful of expensive cars—a couple of Jaguars, a Porsche, and a Rolls—turned into the driveway. Reznick watched as the drivers got out, helped by the valets. Some were dressed in conservative business suits, and others in chinos, blazers, and pink shirts, *à la* Ralph Lauren. Old and new money. Traditional and nouveau riche. All white. No women in sight.

He waited another five minutes. No new arrivals.

He drove back down the oceanfront road, did a U-turn, then headed back to the club. He turned into the driveway. Gravel crunched beneath the wheels as he drove toward the valets.

Reznick pulled up outside the ornate entrance, which featured a huge Christmas tree.

A young valet with floppy bangs walked around the car. Reznick wound down his window.

"Welcome to the Palm Beach Club, sir. Can I take your car, sir?"

"Look after it, son," he said, tossing him the keys.

The kid grinned and jumped into the car as Reznick was escorted inside. A huge lobby opened up before him—wood paneling, black-and-white tile floor, recessed lighting. Hanging on the walls were oil paintings of presidents who had been members of the club down the years.

Reznick was greeted by the club concierge and asked to wait in the lobby while he fetched the general manager. He sat in a dark-brown leather chair and looked around: grandfather clock in the corner, hunting scenes, tartan carpets. He picked up the *New Yorker* magazine sitting atop a pile on a glass table next to him, and flicked through it.

He checked his watch as the minutes passed, ignoring the relentless ticking of the grandfather clock. A full seven minutes after he had arrived, a man approached him, hand outstretched. He wore a single-breasted, well-cut dark suit, a white shirt, pale yellow tie, and shiny black Oxford shoes. "Mr. Crenshaw," he said, shaking Reznick's hand. He had a surprisingly strong grip. "Patrick Symington, general manager. Lovely to have you here tonight. How was your journey?"

"Not a problem. Always good to be back in Palm Beach."

"Indeed. Are we staying for dinner?"

"Sadly no. It'll have to be a super-quick tour. I've got a late-night meeting in Miami before my flight first thing tomorrow."

"Very good, sir, if you'll follow me."

Symington led the way through the paneled hallways into a drawing room overlooking the ocean, wine-red seats all around. A couple of club members turned and smiled, nodding in his direction.

"What sort of line of work are you in, Mr. Crenshaw, if you don't mind me asking?"

"Hedge fund management."

A smile crossed Symington's lips. "We have an eclectic cross section of Florida's business community. A couple of ex-presidents are members too, as well as numerous senators and congressmen. I'm sure you'll feel right at home."

Reznick nodded.

He was taken to the second floor, where there was a swimming pool and a gym. Then the third floor, where there was an enormous library and a twenty-five-seat cinema. The fourth floor had private rooms and apartments for members staying over, and a couple of bars. Then finally the fifth floor, where he was taken to a bar.

"Are you sure we can't at least fix you a drink, sir?" Symington asked.

"Actually, I think I will. A Scotch. Macallan, please."

Symington signaled a waiter over. "A Macallan for Mr. Crenshaw."

Reznick and Symington made small talk about the balmy December weather for a couple of minutes until his drink arrived on a silver tray. He picked up the glass and took a sip of the whisky. The warm amber fired up his belly.

"Very nice. Is that everything in the club?"

"We have a cigar bar up top, if you are interested, sir."

"That would be great. Can someone take my malt there and I'll have a Montecristo to go with it. Can't think of a better way to relax before my meeting later tonight."

"Absolutely, sir."

Symington called over the waiter and told him to take the whisky upstairs and to fetch a Montecristo cigar. He led Reznick up to the next level as the waiter followed.

"It attracts a terrific clientele. Of course, your membership application should go through immediately once we receive the governor's nomination."

Symington turned and smiled before escorting Reznick through a dimly lit corridor. As he opened the door to the cigar bar, the sound of easy-listening piano music filled the air. "A very popular spot later on in the evening," he said.

A wraparound walnut bar. A barman holding a tumbler up to the light to check that it was clean. Dark brown sofas and a burgundy carpet; more oil paintings of people he didn't recognize on the walls. The smell of cigar smoke.

"Very nice place you have here."

Symington walked out another door and onto the terrace. Reznick recognized Merceron immediately, and his heart began to beat a bit faster.

The diplomat was sitting at a table on the open terrace, next to an imposing figure in a white suit. They were both smoking massive cigars and drinking brandy. A gentle breeze blew in from the ocean, rippling a few napkins and carrying the sound of the waves crashing onto the beach.

Symington led Reznick past Merceron and the other man, to a seat on the opposite side of the terrace. The waiter placed his drink on the table.

Reznick sat down and stared out over the dark ocean. "This is a perfect spot for me to take twenty minutes out. Been a helluva day."

Symington made a small bow. "I'll bring you your cigar."

Reznick shook his head and smiled, picking up his glass. "Actually, I think I'll pass on the cigar and stick with the single malt, if that's OK."

Symington gave a small nod. "Very well, sir. I'll be back to see you in twenty minutes." Then he turned on his heel and headed inside.

Reznick waited for a few moments before he knocked back the scotch in one go. The warmth coursed through his veins. He looked over at Merceron and the other man, but they were deep in conversation. Then he turned around and looked into the bar. The barman was still busy polishing the glasses. Reznick didn't think Merceron's table was in the barman's line of sight, which was good news.

Apart from Reznick, and Merceron and his friend, the terrace was empty.

He took off his jacket and put it on his lap. Then he assembled the Beretta and the suppressor under the table, away from the prying eyes of Merceron and the other man. Satisfied the silencer was screwed in securely, he flicked off the safety lever with his thumb and pulled back the slide.

Reznick looked over toward the bar. The barman was wiping down the surfaces and had switched on the Bloomberg channel. He watched as the barman headed out of the bar and through the doors that led to the stairs.

This was his chance. He had a few minutes, if that.

He concealed the gun under his jacket as he got up from his chair and ambled over to Merceron's table. Smiling, he looked at the man sitting with Merceron. The guy's neck was thick, veins bulging. He was clearly a bodyguard.

"Mr. Merceron and I have some urgent business to attend to," he said.

The man looked at Merceron, who in turn shook his head. The bodyguard stared at Reznick long and hard. Then he broke into a broad smile, exposing excellent white teeth. "And what's it regarding?"

Merceron raised his eyebrows at the question, and then grinned at Reznick as if he were stupid.

"None of your goddamn business."

That wiped the smile off their faces.

The bodyguard stared sullenly up at him, a sneer on his face. "Who the hell are you?" He began to reach for his inside pocket.

Reznick smashed his fist hard into the side of the man's neck, just below and slightly in front of his ear. The bodyguard's head lolled forward. He had been rendered unconscious by the blow. The man would be out of it for a good ten minutes, maybe more.

Reznick stared down at Merceron, who wasn't grinning anymore. He dragged heavily on his cigar as if he didn't care, but a slight tremor in his hand betrayed his fear. Reznick pulled up a seat, and sat down at a ninety-degree angle to the diplomat, his back to the bar. He pointed the gun under the table.

"Hands on the table."

Merceron said nothing. He crushed the cigar in an ashtray and expelled the rest of the smoke through his nostrils. Then he sat with his hands on his lap.

Reznick pressed the gun to Merceron's crotch. "I said, hands on the fucking table."

"I don't think we've met. And you are?"

Reznick leaned over and struck Merceron's windpipe with his fist. He winced and clutched his throat, struggling to breathe.

"You'll do as I tell you. Hands on the table."

Merceron's eyes filled with tears after the shock of the blow, and he placed his hands on the table as instructed.

"Where is my daughter?"

Merceron swallowed hard and took a few breaths before he spoke. "Do you honestly think you can get away with this? In my club?"

Reznick stood up and picked up a white cotton napkin, stuffing it into Merceron's mouth. Then he pressed the gun to his shoulder and shot him once. The scream was muffled.

"Now, tell me where my daughter is."

Merceron yanked the napkin out of his salivating mouth and snarled, "You're going to die, my friend."

Reznick raised the gun to Merceron's throat. The diplomat began to laugh uncontrollably, tears streaming down his face. Then he spat at Reznick.

Reznick wiped the spittle off with the back of his hand and wiped it on his shirt.

"Go fuck yourself," Merceron said.

That was the final straw.

Reznick kept the gun trained on Merceron as he pulled the belt from his jeans.

"What the fuck are you doing?"

Reznick wrapped the belt tight around Merceron's neck. Tighter and tighter until Merceron looked as if his eyes were going to pop out of their sockets. The leather was biting deep into the thick folds of skin, and Merceron's mouth opened wide as his breathing became constricted.

"I'll tell you what I'm gonna do," Reznick said, teeth clenched. "I'm gonna squeeze the life out of you, you fat fuck, unless you tell me what I want to know. You wanna know what that feels like?"

Merceron was gasping for breath, shaking his head frantically. Reznick had found the man's tipping point.

"OK, enough! Please!" the diplomat rasped.

"Where is she?"

"My wife's boat, your daughter is on the boat!"

"Name of the boat? And where is it?"

"The yacht is called *Pòtoprens.*"

"I need the coordinates."

"It's anchored one mile south of Key West."

Maddox was right.

Reznick loosened the belt as Merceron struggled for breath, coughing and retching. He stared at him for several moments, wondering if he was telling the truth. The problem was that if Merceron was telling the truth, he could easily call up the yacht and get them to move.

"I don't believe you."

Merceron closed his eyes and held his throat as blood continued to spill from his bleeding shoulder wound. "I'm telling the truth."

"Who asked you to do this?"

"It was a favor."

"A favor for whom?"

"A guy. He works for the government."

"Name?"

"I can't give you his name, I've never met him. I do work for him. I do contracts." The sweat was running down Merceron's brow. He eyed the gun with bloodshot eyes. "Your daughter is on the yacht."

Reznick raised the gun. "How do I know that?"

"Check my phone. Open up the marine traffic application. It gives the coordinates of the yacht."

Reznick picked up the iPhone from the table and tapped the marine traffic app. It displayed a map of the Keys, with a red arrow showing the real-time GPS coordinates of the yacht *Pòtoprens*, as well as the speed and course it was taking.

"That's where she is. On my mother's life, I swear."

Reznick looked into Merceron's terrified dark eyes. He wanted him to feel what it was like. He wanted him to suffer. He felt a rage build deep within him. Then he pressed the end of the suppressor to Merceron's head and squeezed the trigger. A muffled *phut*, and brains and blood splattered all over the starched white tablecloth and napkins.

He hauled Merceron's body feet first through the empty terrace to behind the bar, leaving a trail of blood on the hardwood floor. He saw an open trapdoor and shoved Merceron's hulking body down there head first, crashing into bottles and metal kegs. The same procedure for the bodyguard, spraying some anesthetic spray in the guy's ear first, ensuring he'd be out of it for hours. Finally, he wiped down the floor and all the surfaces with the bloody white tablecloth and the barman's wet rag, which he dropped down into the cellar with the two bodies before locking the hatch and putting the key in his pocket.

The barman still hadn't returned. If he were lucky, it would be hours before they were discovered.

Reznick needed to disappear.

He washed his hands behind the bar, took Merceron's phone, and headed through the cigar bar and down the stairs, all the way to the huge lobby and out the doors. He waited for the valet to bring the BMW around, tipped fifty dollars, and sped off into the night.

He headed south on the freeway, leaving the lights of Palm Beach behind in his rearview mirror. He drove hard. His mind was on fire—he had to get to Lauren. But as he got south of Miami, he realized the traffic was getting slower and slower.

Eventually, it stopped moving. Gridlocked.

He wound down his window and looked across at a guy in the next lane, arm dangling out of his pickup truck.

"What's the problem?"

The guy just shrugged. "Four-car accident apparently, buddy. Some kids racing each other."

Reznick closed his eyes as the engines around him revved in the sultry evening air, hoping and praying his daughter was still alive.

Nineteen

It was 2 a.m., and the wailing from a passing ambulance, coupled with the incessant drone of traffic noise in Lower Manhattan, was starting to bug Lieutenant Colonel Scott Caan. As he stood in the fourth-floor apartment in Tribeca, he stared down through the slats of the wooden blinds at the icy, cobbled street below. A boisterous group of young women wearing Santa hats, high heels, and tinsel around their necks were hailing a yellow cab. One pulled up and they all piled in, laughing and screaming obscenities.

His cell phone rang.

"The time has come, my friend," a man said. "We have every confidence in you. *The job is yours if you want it.*"

The code words had been spoken.

Caan felt numb, as if in a trance. He ended the call and stood and stared at the phone for a few moments, stunned. Then he quickly got himself together. He slipped the cell phone into his shirt pocket and went over to the kitchen drawer, where he pulled out an electronic screwdriver.

This was it. This was what he had waited so long for.

At the far end of the room, beside the bookcase, he bent down beside what looked like an air vent, six inches off the floor. He unscrewed the metal grille covering it, reached inside, and pulled out the toolbox he had hidden there when he'd been here a month ago for his recon mission. He carefully placed the toolbox on the coffee table. Then he went to the bedroom closet and took out the suit holder, which contained the blue maintenance uniform. He laid out the clothes on the bed and went back into the closet for the boots and overcoat.

Everything was ready for this moment.

He took off his shirt and pants and laid them neatly on a chair. Then he put on the uniform, laced up the black safety boots, and put on the thick, dark overcoat, dropping his cell phone into one of the pockets.

Caan looked at his reflection in the mirror and smiled. He was ready. He was going to make his mark on the world. But not like anyone had imagined.

He took a deep breath and headed into the living room, picked up the toolbox, and walked out of his apartment, carefully locking the door. Then he walked down the three flights of stairs and through the lobby doors, out into the sub-zero streets. He sucked in the cold air, his warm breath visible in the chill of the early hour. It was good to breathe fresh air again.

He shivered as he headed across a striped crosswalk and past Puffy's Tavern, which was still open. Onto Hudson Street and then left, in the direction of the Civic Center. Past a smart brick building, and down the frozen street until he reached the Jacob K. Javits Federal Building, east of Tribeca. It housed twenty federal government agencies, and thousands of employees worked in the heavily guarded building.

It also housed the New York City district field office of US Citizenship and Immigration Services. He knew that in a few hours' time, there would be a long line of immigrants already lining up along Worth Street, ready to go through the security checkpoint and enter the building.

Caan walked across Foley Square toward the lights from the large first-floor windows, knowing security would be watching his every move on CCTV monitors and through the blast curtains. The Federal Protective Service relied on low-wage contract personnel to provide security for federal buildings across America.

This one was no different. And it was a major weakness.

He had read the 2009 Government Accountability Office report. It had cited frequent security lapses in incidents across the country, including investigators carrying weapons into key federal installations.

It was a no-brainer to pick such an installation.

His throat felt dry as he went through the glass doors to the airport-style security screening area. The lobby was high ceilinged, glass, and very modern: bright glare from the intense lighting; roped-off areas to process the thousands of visitors every day.

The night security detail was as he'd been told. Four guards, three of them morbidly obese. One was sitting monitoring an X-ray machine, another had an electronic wand, and the other two were watching proceedings.

Caan stepped forward and swiped his fake ID through a reader. A gate opened, and a guard chewing gum checked his photo.

"Step right this way, sir," he said.

Caan walked through the metal detector to the other side as his toolbox was put through the X-ray machine. No beeps. Then the guard with the electronic wand stepped forward and ran it across his body. Still no beeps.

"You're good," the man said.

The toolbox was being opened up on a large table, and the guard rummaging inside motioned him across.

Caan felt a knot of tension in his stomach.

"Can you explain to us what's inside, sir? It's showing several metal containers."

"Not a problem. I'm air-conditioning emergency maintenance." He picked up the aerosol container. "This is a bubble-up leak detector. We spray this stuff onto refrigeration pipes to test for any leaks. Apparently you got a problem. Pain in the ass, but this gets the job done."

The guard lifted up an electronic device. "And what's this?"

"Diagnostic equipment for temperature and air leakage."

The guard turned and checked a computer screen. "It says here on the call-out log, you're doing five bits of essential maintenance."

Caan handed over the faked paperwork he had been given. "That's right. Old buildings always have these goddamn problems. Never a dull moment."

The guard looked at his superior, who waved Caan through.

Caan nodded and smiled. "See you guys later."

They nodded back, expressionless.

Caan walked across to the elevators and headed to the basement. He knew from the blueprints where he was going. He stepped off the elevator and walked down a long corridor, harsh artificial light illuminating the way, his footsteps echoing on the tile floor. When he reached Maintenance Room 3, he swiped his card and went inside. Lockers and storage cabinets, and the smell of diesel and disinfectant. He took off his coat, hanging it in an open locker, and picked up a metal ladder and his toolbox. Then he headed up on the service elevator to the twenty-third floor.

He counted off the floor numbers until the elevator door opened. He headed along a deserted corridor, and opened out the ladder at the first designated location. He pulled a power screwdriver from the toolbox, climbed up two steps, and took off the grille covering the air vent. Then he got his toolbox and climbed up four more steps—his head now inside the vent—and took out one of the ten aerosol cans, which looked like leak-detection sprays but were in fact primed to detonate their contents by radio signal.

He felt the cold metal on his warm hands and smiled. Then he reached up and carefully attached the aerosol can to the roof of the air vent.

Satisfied it was firmly in place, he replaced the grille and climbed down the ladder, then repeated the process at the other side of the air duct. Over the next three hours, he did exactly the same thing on the seventh, tenth, twelfth, and fifteenth floors.

When he finished, he took the service elevator back down to the basement and put the ladder back in place. He put on his overcoat and picked up the near-empty toolbox, then headed for the exit.

"You all done, chief?" a guard asked.

"It's all sorted. Have a good night."

Then he walked around the corner and hailed a cab.

"Where to, buddy?" the driver asked as he climbed in the back.

"Penn Station. And make it quick."

As he rode a packed escalator up toward the Amtrak concourse, his nerve ends were twitching. Scanning the huge arrival and departure boards, he saw that he had twenty minutes to board the 6:30 a.m. Acela Express to Washington, DC, which was departing from the gate on the left.

Caan had been through the station numerous times before. It was a shithole and an embarrassment to the nation. The Long Island and New Jersey commuters flooded down the escalators after their early-morning trains pulled in. It was a relief to get to the lounge for first-class passengers.

Inside, Caan saw for the first time the man who was shadowing him. He was clean-shaven, wore a blue fleece, dark jeans, and Timberlands, and was carrying a black gym bag. He fitted the description perfectly.

The man didn't make eye contact. He bent down to tie his shoes. *The sign.* Then he followed Caan into the empty restroom.

The man placed the bag at his feet as he stood at the urinal. Caan went over, picked up the bag, and locked himself in a stall. He unzipped the bag and put on the fresh set of clothes that was inside. Then he left the toolbox in the stall for the man to dispose of, along with the discarded maintenance uniform.

Back in the lounge, Caan settled into a comfortable seat to read the *New York Times* with his complimentary latte and blueberry muffin. A short while later came the announcement that his train was boarding, and he followed a baggage handler and the other passengers to the train. He stepped on board and entered the first-class compartment. The decor was all silver and grays. He found his allocated leather seat and sat down, letting out an audible sigh.

His shadow took a seat four rows in front of him.

As the train picked up speed and headed out of the city, Caan gazed out into the darkness. He'd been dreaming of this journey for the last twenty-four months, since the planning had started. He couldn't believe how well the New York side of the operation had gone. What was to come would be the icing on the cake.

All the years he had lived a lie. The job he'd loathed. The country he despised. He had concealed his true feelings about America. But now his wildest dreams were on the brink of coming true.

Twenty

Reznick pulled over at a gas station outside Miami and grabbed a couple of hours' sleep, before heading south on Highway 1. He looked at his sat nav, which told him it was a 165-mile drive to Key West. It would take the best part of four hours. And he would have to stick to fifty most of the way, as he didn't want to be pulled over.

He pressed on south as dawn finally broke on the sun-bleached road.

As he left the mainland, the blue-green Atlantic was on his left, the Gulf on his right. He kept an eye on his speed so as not to attract attention.

Suddenly he heard the loud blast of a car horn from a vehicle behind him.

Reznick looked in his rearview mirror and saw a dark blue Lincoln tailgating him, desperate to overtake. Farther back, he noticed a black Suburban. There were no other cars following. He let the Lincoln pass him as the driver shook his head.

Up ahead, Reznick saw a sign for an outdoor seafood restaurant, Mangrove Mama's, and decided to pull over, feeling empty inside. He parked the car and grabbed a crab sandwich and some water.

Fifteen minutes later, he glanced in his mirror and saw the same black Suburban as before. Same plates. Had they stopped in Sugarloaf Key when he did?

Reznick drove on. He looked in his mirror again. The black Suburban had dropped farther back in the traffic that was now building up as he approached Key West.

He drove down North Roosevelt Boulevard, shrouded in tropical foliage and bone-dry palms. The pastel-painted bungalows and wooden-framed mansions, the peaked metal roofs, louvered shutters, covered porches, and wooden lattice screens—the feel of Key West was something that had always appealed to him. And it held such precious memories. Moments of peace.

Reznick followed the signs for a parking garage at the corner of Grinnell and Caroline. He drove to the upper level, where he parked the car and switched off the engine. Then he got out, popped open the trunk, and lifted out a backpack containing a couple of pistols, a scope rifle, an electric stun gun, and a selection of knives.

Reznick strapped on the backpack, locked the car, and strode toward the sign for the stairs. Out of the corner of his eye, he saw a dark car edge toward him. He stole a quick glance and saw the black Suburban again.

He sensed the car was slowing behind him. It pulled up and the car door opened. Reznick reached for his gun.

"You're a long way from home, Jon," a woman's voice said.

Reznick stopped in his tracks. He was surprised to hear a female voice. He turned around and saw a strikingly attractive woman who looked in her late thirties, wavy dark hair, standing beside the Suburban. She wore a navy suit, a pale pink blouse underneath.

"I think you got the wrong guy, sorry," he said, turning to walk away.

"We can help each other, Jon."

Reznick turned back and moved toward her. Immediately, four dark-suited guys stepped out of the Suburban in a casual manner and stared at him. He stared back at each one before looking at the woman. "Look, you must've got me mixed up with some other guy. I get that a lot."

The woman took a few steps toward him until they were standing face to face. She was a few inches shorter than him. Her eyes were cobalt blue and her makeup was subtle and soft. "FBI, Jon. I'm Assistant Director Martha Meyerstein."

Reznick said nothing.

She reached into her jacket and held up a picture of Reznick and Elisabeth, arms wrapped around Lauren. The image seared into his head. His most prized possession—the last picture he had of her alive. The last picture he had of them as a family. Two weeks later, *she* was dead.

He looked at his smiling wife's eyes. He felt an emptiness inside.

"If you're wondering, we got it from your screensaver. So let's cut the bullshit. We know everything about you, Jon. We know about your wife, Elisabeth. We know about your father. We know he served his country, as have you. And we also know he brought you up after your mother died. You want me to go on?"

Reznick stared back at her.

"Don't make a dumb move, Jon. There's a fair chance you'll be shot dead before you reach for that gun. But if you're smart, we can talk things over."

"Look, this is all very interesting, but I've got things to do."

She looked him over with a steely gaze. "We know why you're here in Key West, Jon. We know what you've been up to since you drove down from Washington. And I've got a proposition for you."

"What kind of proposition?"

"I want you to get your daughter back. But in return, you've got to help us out."

———

Reznick and Meyerstein took a walk beside the marina, scores of yachts and boats bobbing about in the swell. Country music was playing loud, and dozens of people were drinking in and around the bar, knocking back mid-morning margaritas, beers, and mojitos.

Meyerstein stared straight ahead. "OK, before we can get down to business, I need to get some answers," she said, tucking her hair behind her ear.

Reznick stayed silent.

"Jon, you need to help us."

"Let's cut to the chase. Say what you've got to say."

"I want to help you get your daughter back. But we've got to trust each other, at least a little."

"I'm listening."

"Someone took your daughter. Why? Because you should have killed a government scientist. Now, I'm going to level with you. Someone wants this scientist dead, real bad. But we need him, Jon. And it's no word of a lie to say this man is vital to America's national-security interests."

Reznick listened as he wondered who he could trust— Meyerstein or Maddox. He'd never met this woman, but she didn't seem like a bullshitter, much less a liar. He assumed she could lie if she had to. But something about her told him that she was giving it to him straight.

"Where is he, Jon? Where's Luntz?"

"He's safe."

Meyerstein exhaled a sigh of relief. "We've also got a big problem, Jon. An additional problem. We have a trail of bodies. Some I don't care about, but one of them was a special agent. We found him in a closet. We saw the signs that he'd been neutralized."

"Listen to me and listen good. That wasn't me."

"I want to believe you, Jon. But my colleagues—"

"This is bullshit."

A long silence opened up before Meyerstein spoke again. He smelled a light, citrus perfume.

"No, this is not bullshit, Jon. This is as real as it gets."

Reznick grabbed Meyerstein's wrist, jabbing his thumb into his chest. "I want my daughter back. She is a child. She's out there. And she'll be frightened out of her mind. On a fucking boat. Now, are you gonna stop fucking me around or what?"

"I need answers, Jon. Did you kill Agent Connelly?"

"No."

"Your prints are all over the place."

"Aren't you listening? I didn't kill him. Got that?"

"So who did?"

"Probably the same people who took my daughter."

"OK, let's say for a moment that I believe this. Let's move on to Luntz. Where is he?"

"I told you he's safe."

"Jon, here's what we have. We're up against the clock. You're up against the clock. But what I'm going to propose can help us both. But you must trust me, like I want to trust you."

Reznick released his grip and stared out again over the marina. "Can you help me get my daughter back? That's all I'm interested in."

"Yes—I can."

———

They walked down the boardwalk past a line of shops, restaurants, and bars. On the other side were yachts, catamarans, ferries, and dive boats, all vying for business. Then over to Mallory Square, and the huge plaza on the waterfront. A cruise ship was heading out of the port.

Reznick was aware of the Feds in suits walking about twenty yards behind them. Meyerstein led them over to a big red building—the Key West Museum of Art and History—and sat down on an empty bench.

Satisfied there was no one within earshot, Reznick leaned forward and spoke first. "You mentioned a national security threat to America. What kind of threat?"

"We're talking mass casualties. A possible bioterrorist attack. Do you understand what I'm saying?"

Reznick took a few moments for the information to sink in. This was totally at odds with what Maddox had told him. He wondered if he shouldn't just turn and walk away. But something deep within him sensed not only that she was telling the truth, but that she could be trusted. "That's not the information I have."

"Trust me, this guy is a scientist. I don't know if your handler, or whatever you call him, is in control of this situation. He won't save you or your daughter. Only we can."

"Let's say for a minute that what you're saying is correct. How does the scientist fit in to this?"

It was Meyerstein's turn to go quiet.

"Listen, we're either going to level with each other, or you better speak to someone else."

Meyerstein cleared her throat. "You've not got clearance for this."

"Fuck clearance. You either deal me in or I walk."

Meyerstein pinched the bridge of her nose for a moment. "We believe—we're not one hundred percent sure—but we believe that Luntz had concerns over a fellow scientist. That scientist has disappeared. Bottom line? Luntz is America's leading authority on this threat, and is close to coming up with ways to neutralize it."

Reznick held his head in his hands.

"Jon, we need this scientist. Just like you need your daughter."

"So what do you propose?"

"Before I run this by you, I need to know why you didn't kill Luntz."

Reznick didn't want to elaborate.

"Look, if I'm putting my cards on the table, I want you to do the same. Don't shut me out."

"Let's just say there was a discrepancy."

Meyerstein sat in silence, waiting for him to speak.

He sighed. "I'd been given another name. The scientist was wearing an Israeli dog tag."

"What?"

"Exactly my response. The tag was his son's. He was in the IDF. It showed the name Luntz. He also had a picture of his son around his neck. But there was no ID to corroborate. It had already been cleared out."

"Who by?"

"I don't know. Perhaps by the crew who did your colleague?"

Meyerstein blew out her cheeks and shook her head. "Are you saying this might have been compartmentalized into two separate jobs?"

"Think about it. Everything's compartmentalized in the military. Same with the government. You're given an order and that order—whatever it is—is carried out. It's operational level. But you don't know the big picture. What's really happening? This is how it's done on major jobs. You only know one piece of the jigsaw. The people higher up the chain know how it all fits together. Need to know and all that jazz. The person or people who did the job on your colleague were possibly staying in the same hotel as me, who knows?"

"OK, let's assume that what you're saying is correct. Then what?"

"I received instructions . . ."

"From whom?"

"I'm not going there."

"Why not?"

Reznick just shrugged, eyes dead.

"Oh . . . you got instructions. To do what?"

Reznick told her everything that had happened and how he had got down to Miami via Fort Lauderdale. Meyerstein listened before turning and stealing a quick glance at the agents nearby. Then she faced Reznick. "OK, this is how it's gonna work . . . You've opened up to me, just like I've opened up to you. We both want different things, though. Now, listen closely. Do you know where your daughter is being held?"

"I've got a fair idea."

"But do you know whose yacht it is?"

Reznick nodded. "Wife of a Haitian diplomat."

"As you can imagine, that poses a problem for us."

"So what are you saying?"

"I'm saying this is tricky."

"Listen, am I wasting my time? Are you or are you not going to help me get my daughter back? She's an American in American waters."

Meyerstein sighed. "We can help you, but not directly."

"Why the hell not?"

"Diplomatic immunity. Under the Vienna Convention, the diplomat and his immediate family are accorded full protection under international law. They're out of bounds."

"You're not gonna pull that bullshit, are you?"

"It's not bullshit. It's the law. Whether we like it or not."

"Don't throw that crap at me. International law? This is America. I don't give a shit about international law."

"Well, I do. And here's what I propose. You tell me where the scientist is, and I'll give you free rein to get your daughter. And provide any assistance required. No questions asked."

Reznick wondered if he could really trust her. He knew it would be the easiest thing in the world for the FBI to promise something but then renege on that. It was only business.

He tried to size her up. She wasn't flustered or blustering or blabbering on. She was serious and direct. But he also got the impression that she wasn't fazed by him or what he did.

"And then what?"

"We can deal with that obstacle later. As of now, you either play ball, or it becomes a lose-lose situation."

"OK, let's say I agree to this. What guarantees are there?"

"There are no guarantees."

"So if I manage to make it out of there and get my daughter, then what?"

Meyerstein sighed. "Jon, I've got two children of my own. I miss them like crazy every day I'm away from them. I know what I'd do for them. And I'd probably do what I think you're going to do. If you're smart, you'll take this offer. What I can say is that my number-one priority is getting the scientist back."

"If I agree, I need your word that my friend watching over Luntz won't be charged or anything. He was doing me a favor by looking after him. Can that be done?"

Meyerstein nodded.

Reznick called Tiny and explained that Luntz was going to be taken off his hands. Tiny seemed relieved. "I owe you big time, Tiny."

"You don't owe me nothing, man."

Reznick ended the call and gave Meyerstein the Delray Beach location where Luntz was being held. He clenched his fists, stomach knotted. "I've kept my side of the deal."

"Jon, you've put your trust in me. Now I'm going to put my trust in you."

Reznick stared at her. "How?"

"You're free to get your daughter. However you see fit. But this is between us. You and me, Jon. Do you understand?"

Reznick nodded. "Now, if that's everything, I got stuff to do."

Twenty-One

Six miles out on the Straits of Florida, the sky was pitch black. Reznick saw a faint light in the distance and cut the outboard engine. He anchored the dive boat eight hundred yards away from his target.

He checked the luminous display on his watch, which showed it was 6:28 p.m. He picked up the night-vision binoculars and peered through the darkness in the direction of the light. A luxury yacht was bobbing in the choppy waters. He scanned the yacht and could just make out the name: *Pòtoprens.*

Reznick did a slow sweep across the yacht and saw a man sitting on the deck drinking from a can, feet up on the stern side of the boat. For the next five minutes, he just watched. No sign of Lauren.

Reznick quickly assembled his M24 sniper rifle, aligning the night sights and securely attaching it to a mobile tripod. He crouched down and pointed the rifle in the general direction of the yacht. Then he pressed his left eye up to the rubber eyepiece and peered through the electronic green sights. Using the scope's crosshairs, he zeroed in on the man's chest. But the heavy swell meant he only had the target in sight for a couple of seconds.

The rifle had an optimum range of eight hundred yards. He recalled being on a patrol with a British unit in Afghanistan, and their sniper had killed two Taliban machine gunners from one and a half miles away. The time it took for the bullet to leave the rifle and kill the target was three seconds. Reznick could factor in around two seconds, maybe a fraction less.

One man in range, but what if there was another out of sight? If he fired now, it would alert the other man and spell the end for his daughter.

The sniper option was too risky.

He watched the man on deck finish his drink before crushing the empty can with one hand. The man was oblivious to being watched in the middle of the sea, darkness all around.

Reznick kept on staring through the rifle's night sights. The man got up as a second man, holding a bottle, came up onto the deck and took his place.

A long-distance rifle shot would hit the guy. But he knew that the sound would give the subject a couple of seconds to hit the deck, and the other guy a chance to prepare or to harm Lauren.

The second option was almost kamikaze. Take the boat right up to their yacht, shoot the guy on the deck, then clamber on board and take down the other guy.

The bottom line was that he was clean out of good options. He had to take a risk if he wanted to get his daughter back.

Reznick loaded up the backpack. The last thing he checked was the Beretta. He pulled the magazine from the gun, and cleaned and oiled the barrel. He lubed the slide rails and around the barrel, then the top of the disconnector in front of the breech face. He eased the slide forward until it was almost into battery, and applied lube to the barrel head. Last of all, he ran a bore brush through the barrel, content that it was good to go.

Then he racked the slide, dry firing to make sure it was working before wiping off the excess lube with a rag. Then he pushed the magazine into the butt of the gun.

He attached the suppressor, screwing it securely into place.

Reznick took in a deep breath of the night air, strapped the gun to his left leg, and put on the backpack. Then he started up the boat and headed straight for the target. The boat skimmed across the water in no time, its engine spluttering too loudly for comfort, closer and closer to the lights of the yacht. He slowed down as he got within the last couple of hundred yards, and he switched on the deck lights so they could see him.

He maneuvered the boat to within twenty yards of the starboard side. He could hear hip-hop music blasting out. Then ten yards, as the man on deck stood up and stared down at him.

Reznick smiled up at the guy. The guy didn't smile back. Reznick pulled out the Beretta and fired two muffled shots, straight through the man's forehead. Blood spilled down the man's face as he dropped to the deck with a thump.

Heart racing, Reznick edged closer to the rear of the yacht. Closer and closer.

He stepped forward onto a metal railing on the side and pulled himself onto the deck. He moved quietly and cautiously around to the port side, eyes fixed on the cabin door. Then he crouched down low behind a pile of ropes.

He trained his gun on the door that led to the galley. The music was booming out, the yacht vibrating and reverberating with the sound of the deep bass. But still no movement.

Then the door opened and a man emerged onto the deck, rubbing his eyes.

Reznick did a double tap. He shot him once in the chest and once in the head before the man could react. Blood splattered over the rigging as the man collapsed in a heap. Somehow he was still breathing, swallowing blood, eyes pleading with Reznick in vain.

Reznick stood above him and stared down at him for a moment. The man's dark brown eyes were filled with tears. Reznick pressed the gun to the man's forehead and drilled two more shots into him. Blood poured down his sweaty skin.

Reznick stepped over the body and pushed open the galley door. The smell of hash and spilled beer filled the fetid air. He climbed down four steps. A table with cards, strewn with empty beer cans. He rummaged in closets and opened doors.

More stairs, down into the sleeping quarters. Polished woods, crumpled duvets. Where the hell was she?

A glint of silver in his peripheral vision caught his eye. Reznick turned and saw what looked like handcuffs below a duvet. He pulled back the covers. Lauren lay prostrate and out of it—face gray, lips blue, eyes closed.

"Oh fuck."

Reznick pulled back her eyelids. His daughter's pupils were pinpricks. Reaching over, he took her pulse. Her skin was cold, but he felt a faint beat. "Oh, Christ no, Lauren!" He shook her to try and rouse her.

Nothing.

He pulled her close, kissing her cold face. "Lauren, talk to me, honey. Lauren, please wake up. Come on, honey. It's Dad here. Do you hear me?"

She was still motionless, her breathing shallow.

"Lauren, let's snap out of this," he said, gently slapping her face. "Come on, Lauren. It's Dad here."

She didn't move. No reaction at all. The sense of helplessness was starting to creep into his psyche like a cancer. But he couldn't let it. He couldn't think like that.

Reznick lifted her up and carried her out to the dive boat. He lay her on the deck, wrapped in a blanket. Then he fired up the engine and headed straight for Key West, praying his daughter would still be alive by the time he got there.

Twenty-Two

It was just before 10 p.m. in the FBI's office in North Miami Beach, and Martha Meyerstein was observing from behind a one-way mirror as Dr. Frank Luntz ate hot chicken soup and cheese sandwiches. He sat hunched at a table in the windowless interview room, and had a noticeable shake. But overall he seemed in good physical health, despite his ordeal with Reznick.

She had trusted Reznick down in Key West and her instincts had paid off. The powers that be within the FBI would say it was wrong to aid him. She knew it was against all the rules and laws she had learned. Her father always stressed the importance of ethics, the sanctity of the law, and of doing things the right way. He might have forged a reputation as a pit bull in court, but he was also a stickler for protocol.

The more she thought about it, the more she realized she had crossed the line and had not acted as an assistant director of the FBI should. She was in muddied waters. Here there was no right and wrong, and there was no law. But there was the growing sense that she would live to regret her deal with Reznick.

She stared at Luntz. The team of doctors who had only finished examining him ten minutes earlier said he showed signs of trauma and anxiety, which wasn't surprising in the circumstances. They cautioned against pressurizing him to speak. But that wasn't going to be her course of action.

She needed to find out exactly what had happened—and what he knew about Caan—before he was handed over to Dr. Max Horowitz and his team of scientists for a full debrief.

Meyerstein felt another yawn coming on and covered her mouth. What she wouldn't give for a good night's sleep. Even a bad night's sleep would be something.

She picked up the file on Luntz and opened it up. A recent photo his wife had taken before Luntz was kidnapped showed the scientist carefree, playing football with his children in a park.

Meyerstein's cell phone vibrated. Her mother's name showed on the caller ID.

"Mom, everything OK?"

"We're fine, honey. Jacob just wanted to take a minute to say hello."

"Better make it quick."

A beat. "Mom? Will you be home for Christmas?"

Meyerstein felt her throat tighten. "I'm sure I will, honey."

"Can you read the book the way Grandma reads? You know, with funny voices."

"Yes, darling, we can do funny voices." Meyerstein sighed. "Tell Cindy I love her. And I love you too, darling. Gotta go."

"Love you, Mom."

"Look after your sister."

"Sure thing, Mom."

Meyerstein took a few moments to reflect on her situation. She cleared her throat.

Suddenly, the door behind her swung open and Roy Stamper marched in with two Styrofoam cups of strong black coffee. He looked dog-tired, top button undone. Too little sleep and too much caffeine—same as her. He handed her a cup and she took a large gulp.

"Darn, that's hot!" she said. A jolt of caffeine hit her system.

"Just got some news from Kate down at the biolab."

"Shoot."

"Four guys from the Pentagon have just turned up. They say Kate has not received—and I quote—*proper security clearance* to be shown details of the work Luntz was involved in."

"You kidding me?"

"Nope."

Meyerstein shook her head. It sounded to her like a special access program. It was the name given to ultra-secretive work or operations known only to a select few in the Pentagon. She knew that to get such a program off the ground, it had to be cleared at the highest level of government.

"Anything else?"

"We've been talking to the staff. They said Luntz and Caan were working together on a secret project, and had been for years. And we found out something."

"What?"

"Three vials have gone missing from the lab's freezers, which was discovered during a recent inventory."

"Unaccounted for?"

"Yup."

"So what did the three vials contain?"

"That's the thing. No one knows a goddamn thing."

Meyerstein ran her hand through her hair. "This just got a helluva lot more interesting. OK, I want Kate and her team and the weapons of mass destruction people to let me know the moment they find out anything else. And let's keep digging some more. We're making progress. Good work."

"What do you propose to do with Luntz?"

"We need to get a handle on exactly what Luntz knows. We need to find out how this all came about. And with that information, we might—and I stress *might*—be able to track down Scott Caan."

"What about the Pentagon?"

Meyerstein gave a wry smile and sipped her coffee. "What about them?"

"You gonna find out what they're trying to keep secret?"

"That's the plan."

Stamper gave her a pained expression. "You're on thin ice making that call, Martha. The shrinks are saying to take it easy with him. Might be worth holding off."

Meyerstein felt herself grinding her teeth. This was something she'd found herself doing more often recently.

"We need answers." She stared through the glass as Luntz wiped some crumbs from his face with a napkin. "We need something—anything—from this guy."

"Shouldn't we just sit tight? Wouldn't that be the smart move at this stage?"

She took a final sip of coffee before throwing the cup in a bin. "Maybe it would. But I think we need to get in there and find out the truth, whether it pisses off the Pentagon or not."

Her cell phone rang and she blew out her cheeks.

"Martha, it's O'Donoghue. You and I need to talk. Right now."

She rolled her eyes at Stamper. "Good evening, sir. I'm just about to interview Frank Luntz."

Stamper nodded in recognition of who was on the line, and left the room.

O'Donoghue sighed. "I want to talk about Reznick."

"What about him?"

"I'm hearing that you cut a deal with him. Is that true?"

Meyerstein closed her eyes for a moment, wondering how he had got to hear. "I got our scientist. I want to find out more about Scott Caan. Did you get the message that three vials are missing?"

"Yes, I just got that from Stamper's team. But answer me this— did you cut a deal, Martha? Because that would not be good. We have ways of doing things."

"Sir, I respect what you're saying. Can we iron out any problems when I get back to Washington?"

"Martha, we cannot have people like Reznick out there, killing and destroying whatever gets in his way. I'm not going to let this lie. And another thing—there will be consequences. Did you know that Claude Merceron was a Haitian diplomat?"

"Yes, I did." She explained how Merceron had links to Norton & Weiss, believed to be a CIA front.

"Martha, we can't go beyond the law to carry out our functions." Meyerstein sighed. "We recovered the scientist. But yes, I admit, we got our hands dirty. That didn't sit well with me."

"Martha, with immediate effect, I want you back in Washington."

"What?"

"I've just been on the phone to the Pentagon, and they're saying they want their people who have special clearance to speak directly to Luntz. This is a classified project. Special access program, apparently. They're flying into Miami first thing in the morning."

"Sir, this is not a good time. I'm about to interview Frank Luntz."

"Are you disobeying an order, Martha?"

"Yes, sir, I most certainly am. Do what you have to do. But I've got a job to do here."

Meyerstein ended the call, heart racing. She was facing an internal investigation into her conduct, that was for sure. She knew that and would have to deal with it. And to compound matters, O'Donoghue was telling her that the Pentagon was to take over.

What a mess.

She stared through the glass at Luntz for a few moments. "Son of a bitch."

Stamper came back into the room. "What was O'Donoghue wanting?"

"Someone on our team told him about the deal with Reznick."

"What?"

Meyerstein nodded.

"You want me to find out who it was?"

She shook her head. "I'll deal with it when I get back to Washington. We have more pressing matters."

Stamper looked through the glass. "Let's get started."

———

Meyerstein entered the interview room and smiled.

"Assistant Director Martha Meyerstein," she said. She pulled up a chair and sat down opposite Luntz, her back to the one-way mirror. The smell of soup was still in the air.

Luntz managed to force a smile.

"How are you feeling?" she asked.

He shrugged. "I've felt better."

"Tired?"

"You could say that, yeah."

"Look, I'm not going to take up much of your time. I think you'll be looking forward to a warm bath, a long sleep, and some time with your family, right?" She didn't mention that a full debrief would be taking place in the next couple of hours with the WMD team, before he got any chance to sleep.

"I want to help the FBI any way I can."

"And we appreciate that, Dr. Luntz, really we do."

"Please, call me Frank."

Meyerstein nodded as she noticed a slight tremor in both his hands. "OK, Frank, so you're quite happy for me to ask you some questions at this juncture?"

"Certainly. I want to help in any way I can."

Meyerstein leaned back in her seat and smiled. "Whenever you like."

Over the next hour, Luntz recalled—in minute detail and chronological order—what had happened to him. His memory was precise. He remembered everything from the moment he'd left his home in Frederick with the FBI agent who was assigned to look after him, to when he was woken at gunpoint. All the details tallied perfectly with their timeline.

Meyerstein knew he could provide the breakthrough they so desperately needed. And she knew that it was important not to convey tension or pressure. She needed to be authoritative, calm, and reassuring. Like a trusted, reliable friend.

"That's great, Frank. You've got a better memory than me," she joked.

Luntz smiled as he picked at the cuticles of his bitten fingernails.

"Now, Frank," Meyerstein said. She shifted in her seat, concentrating on making her voice softer and more empathetic. "Let's think back to why you wanted to see us in the first place. About your concerns on biosafety at your lab. Tell me about your work, first of all. The FBI scientists, specialists in this area, will want to speak to you later. But for now, just fill me in so I'm up to speed."

Luntz shook his head. "I'm real sorry, but that's classified."

She could see how he was going to play it. "What's classified?"

"The work we were doing at the lab."

Meyerstein leaned forward in her seat, a matter of inches from Luntz, sensing his vulnerability. "Now listen to me, and listen good. We're talking a possible terrorist plot, if you hadn't realized that already. And I'm not going to have you hiding behind security clearance or some other bullshit. Do you want me to spell it out for you?"

There was fear in Luntz's eyes.

"Your colleague, the esteemed Lieutenant Colonel Scott Caan, has gone missing. And I'm hearing three vials were taken from the lab you were responsible for. Do you know what that means?"

Luntz looked down at the floor.

"Maybe I'm not making myself clear. That means you'll be facing a near-certain criminal investigation into the lax security systems you had at your lab. You've put the security of the United States at grave risk. Do you understand me?"

Luntz nodded quickly and bowed his head.

"So, I'm going to ask you again, what the hell are we dealing with?"

Luntz stayed quiet.

"It's your choice. You either tell me everything, or you're gonna face a long, long time in jail." Meyerstein leaned back in her seat, knowing she was using a high-risk strategy. "Your choice. What's it gonna be?"

Luntz was silent for nearly a minute, occasionally biting his lower lip. Eventually, he took a deep breath and spoke, voice as quiet as a mouse. "I hear what you're saying. It's just that the project is very, very secret."

Meyerstein smiled. "I'm very discreet. Whenever you're ready."

Luntz spoke in a hushed whisper. "My colleague, Scott Caan, and I have been working for years, trying to learn as much as possible about the origins of the 1918 flu pandemic. It killed at least twenty million people worldwide. I was part of the laboratory team, led by Dr. Jeffrey Taubenberg, who resurrected the killer flu."

Meyerstein nodded, not wanting to hurry him unduly. She fixed her gaze on him for a few moments. "I remember reading about that. Can you describe the broad-brush process to me, just so I've got a better idea what we're talking about?"

"We were developing a new, deadly hybrid strain of Spanish flu."

"You were developing a new *hybrid* strain?"

"This is allowed under the Biological Weapons Convention that was signed in 1972. Article One allows exceptions for medical and defensive purposes in small quantities."

The full magnitude of what she was dealing with hit home. It didn't make any sense. How could it be justified to try to recreate an eradicated strain that could wreak unforeseen havoc if released, either deliberately or accidentally? But she also knew that wasn't her concern.

"Was this hybrid strain as deadly as the original Spanish flu?"

"Fourfold. It was given the highest security classification. The Pentagon was funding the whole thing. We all had to have a higher security clearance to protect the program's highly sensitive information."

Meyerstein knew a security clearance application had to be submitted to the Department of Defense for review and consideration. But she felt a growing mix of anger and disbelief that a killer virus was now out of the laboratory setting.

"I see. Please, go on."

"Three months ago, we finally created this new, more virulent strain. We'd worked for years. In the last few months, we were both working very long hours."

"Was it taking its toll?"

"We were both exhausted, but we had a Pentagon deadline to meet. We were verifying procedures and analyzing all the data. It was coming together perfectly, just as I had envisaged."

"Tell me—if you're working closely with someone for so long, in such tight conditions, there must have been tensions. Did you notice anything out of character?"

"Nothing. The one thing that stuck in my mind was that he hardly showed any discernible signs of stress. He seemed to work well under pressure."

"So there were no behavioral traits to indicate anything adverse, or out of the ordinary, from him or anyone on your team?"

"He was quiet, but he'd always been quiet. I tried to ensure a happy and cohesive working environment, and he was very much part of that. He wasn't the life and soul of the party, but that was just him. He was a scientist."

"OK, just to clarify, Scott Caan was not acting out of character. That was his natural persona, right?"

"Indeed."

"So, what happened to make you want to contact us?"

"If I can just fill you in on the lead-up to my concerns. It was all going swimmingly. A month ago or so, we finally got the preliminary results back, which showed that the new antivirals we had developed were working with the hybrid flu we had created. It was a very satisfying moment. It means that if there is, God forbid, such an outbreak again, we'll be well prepared with effective vaccines and antivirals. And we're now starting to understand how pandemics form and cause disease." There was a bead of perspiration on Luntz's forehead. "But then the Pentagon, in the middle of all this, asked me to conduct a spot check. An inventory."

"Was this unusual?"

"It was usually held at the start of each year, and I'd expected to do it in January, maybe February, so it wasn't ideal. I needed Scott to oversee this inventory, but he'd called in sick. It wasn't like him. Three days later, he was still off. Ironically, some flu or something. I tried to call him, but there was no answer. So as you can imagine, I was wondering where he was. I assumed he was in his bed. But I left numerous messages on his phone. This went on for another couple of days, until I decided to head out to his house. I'd never been there before. No one had—he was very private. But still there was no answer. I thought it was a bit odd, but wondered if he hadn't just gone out for some fresh air. Later that day, back at the lab, I went to study the results from the antiviral test on my computer, and there was nothing there. Every computer file pertaining to our research was gone."

"But this was backed up on secure servers, I imagine."

"It was. But when I checked, it was all gone. Nothing on the backup. I thought I was going mad—it didn't make any sense. I couldn't think straight. This was years of work, straight down the pan. Anyway, I called his landline but it was still ringing out, as was his cell phone. Then I decided to do the inventory myself. If nothing else, as a basic security procedure. We have tens of thousands of items stored in the freezer. It showed a discrepancy."

"What kind of discrepancy?"

"The actual stocks didn't match the numbers we thought we had. So it all had to be counted again, for a second time. It took days. Eventually we found we were missing three vials of the hybrid flu virus we had created, in addition to the antivirals and vaccine."

Meyerstein felt her insides knot.

"Did you speak to anyone else about these concerns?"

"I called my contact at the Pentagon overseeing the project, and he told me to contact Dr. Horowitz."

Meyerstein shifted in her seat. "Horowitz? Why not the Pentagon?"

"They referred me to him because he's head of the WMD section of the FBI and has the highest level of security clearance, as he used to work within the Department of Defense."

"Max Horowitz?"

"Yes. I sent him an encrypted email saying I needed to speak to him urgently in person about a security matter at the lab. He was out of the country and arranged for me to be seen in person by his deputy at FBI Headquarters. And he arranged for a special agent to be assigned to me overnight at the St. Regis, ahead of the early-morning meeting."

Meyerstein shifted in her seat. "So you followed the correct procedure, right?"

"Absolutely."

Meyerstein felt an anger build within her. She hadn't been made aware of any of this by Max Horowitz or his team. Was this because of its special-access status? She gathered her thoughts.

"Are there any circumstances in which Caan or any member of your team would be allowed to take three vials of the virus, and the antivirals and vaccines, out of the lab?"

Luntz bowed his head, as if in shame. "No circumstances at all."

"Would it be stretching things too far to say the specter of bio-terrorism comes to mind?"

"I think that's a fair supposition."

Meyerstein's mind was racing. "So as it stood, all you had was circumstantial evidence that Scott Caan might have been responsible. That's all."

"It doesn't end there. The final piece of the jigsaw fell into place after I discovered another anomaly."

"What was that?"

"A lot of scientists were in and out of the freezers where we kept the new strain of the virus. So it could have been any of them. But what was different about Scott was that I found out he had returned to the lab on two separate occasions, in the middle of the night, in the few days before he went missing. The security guard noted it down and said Scott was finishing some vital work."

"Did you take this up with Scott?"

"I was unaware that he'd even entered the lab in the middle of the night. I only found out when I checked the guard's logs. The guard didn't pass on that information to me at the time, assuming it wasn't important."

"And you're quite convinced Scott Caan is the one?"

"I believe it's him. He knew the rules of the lab. Out of hours was only in the most exceptional of cases. It had to be authorized by me. He had no good reason to be in there. And it categorically wasn't authorized by me to be in that lab in the middle of the night."

"Not at all?"

Luntz shook his head. "No," he said, dabbing his eyes.

"Frank, tell me about Caan. We need to build up a profile of him. What we have so far is very sketchy. I mean, where did he come from? Where did he live? What were his passions? Did you know him well?"

Tears were now running down Luntz's cheeks. "I can't believe this is happening. You know, you think you know somebody. With hindsight, I didn't know him at all. What can I say? He was sponsored by the army throughout his time at MIT and they assigned him to the project. He came on board eighteen months after me."

"Why was that?"

"Well, first he had to get Top Secret clearance, and then when that came through, we had to wait for his Sensitive Compartmented Information clearance before he could begin work in the lab."

"Tell me about him. His work."

"From day one, his work was exceptional. Smartest guy the MIT biological science department had seen for years. And he was one of the brightest guys in the operation. He also worked longer and harder and was more dedicated than anyone. He was always there."

"Did he socialize? What about drinks after work? Bowling?"

"He didn't drink. He kept himself to himself."

"What were his interests?"

Luntz went quiet for a few moments before he answered. "He was a keep-fit guy. Ran every lunchtime. Ran to work. Guy was in good shape. Really good shape."

"Tell me, when he didn't turn up for work, was that out of character?"

"Absolutely. He was meticulous, rarely off sick, but if he was he'd let me or one of his coworkers in the lab know either by phone or email."

Luntz dabbed his eyes and sighed long and hard. She could see he was getting agitated.

"OK, let's just step back for a few moments, if we can, to try and get a handle on where we are. It's important that we establish the facts."

Luntz nodded but said nothing.

"What I'm looking to do is build up a picture of this guy, your colleague. You say he was quiet, kept himself to himself, workaholic, kept fit, I get all that. What I'm missing is what he was like as a person. Did he talk politics? Did he read the newspaper and discuss an article? Something on CNN or Fox get his attention, perhaps?"

"You mean was he political?"

Meyerstein nodded.

"You know, it's interesting, looking back—he never expressed any views on anything."

"No views at all? Why do you think that was?"

"Perhaps he had no views on anything going on in the world . . ."

"Or maybe he wanted to conceal his true views."

Luntz frowned. "I hadn't thought of that."

Meyerstein cleared her throat. "Are there any days you know of where he was visiting friends, taking time off, or stuff like that? Did he have spats with colleagues? Anything that sticks in the memory?"

"Well, no . . . Actually, now that you mention it, he didn't once mention friends or family."

"Did you never ask him about his family?"

"We all live such busy lives I never really took that much of an interest. I know he wasn't married. But I don't think I ever knew anything about his private life. I don't like to pry."

Meyerstein felt irritated at Luntz's lackadaisical approach. "What about spats?"

Luntz leaned back in his seat and pursed his lips, as if deep in thought. "You know, it's interesting, there is one thing that comes to mind. I remember a colleague getting frustrated as he was trying to reach Scott to talk about some lab results. But he wasn't around. Apparently he'd called to say his flight was late."

"Late?"

"Yeah, he was late for work on a Monday morning—he said his flight was delayed. Some technical fault on the plane from New York."

"How long ago was that?"

"I remember that it was November nineteen when he was late. That was the Monday morning, my sixtieth birthday, a few days before he went off sick and then went AWOL."

"How long was he away for? Do you know who he visited?"

"I'm guessing he left on the Saturday—November seventeen—as he was in work on the Friday. But I don't have a clue who he met."

Meyerstein scribbled the details on a pad in front of her. "Tell me, what security measures do you have in place to ensure that the correct people enter the lab?"

"Primarily, it's a retinal scan, as used by select government agencies."

"Frank, I'm going to take a break for two minutes, is that OK with you?"

Luntz nodded.

Meyerstein ripped out the page from the pad and stood up, pushing back her chair. "I'll be right back." She went into the side room, where Stamper was watching through the two-way mirror, and handed over the piece of paper. "I want Caan's retinal scan to be fed into the airport databases. Concentrate on Saturday November seventeen, at Dulles and all the New York airports. Check the cameras at the taxi ranks. Then get our face recognition guys onto this. And run it with the biometric database we have. I want to see some results. Some footage of Caan arriving in New York. Where was he going? Who was he with?"

Stamper read the notes on the paper and nodded. "I'll get on it."

"Caan had the highest security clearance, as had Luntz. I want us to get into Caan's life. Something's not right. Something's missing from all this."

"But if he's been cleared through the Single Scope Background Investigation for Top Secret clearance, and then by a higher clearance through the Pentagon, surely they've gone through his life with a fine-tooth comb—where he lived, went to school, interviews with persons who knew him, criminal records, qualifications, previous employment, and all the rest."

"We're doing it all again. Check to see if Caan ever failed a polygraph test. Foreign travel, assets, character references—I want us to go over this one more time."

"That's going to take up a lot of resources, Martha."

Meyerstein sighed. She had learned from her father the importance of not accepting established facts without scrutinizing them one more time. Her team thought she was obsessive in her attention to detail. And Stamper was no different. "Put my mind at rest, Roy. We can't afford not to be meticulous. That's our job, after all. So, let's do it all again."

Stamper shrugged. "OK, whatever you say. It may take time looking into his background. These security clearances can take up to eighteen months."

"I want it all done in eighteen hours."

"Jesus H. Christ, Martha." He cleared his throat. "We've been looking over Caan's house. He hasn't lived there in weeks—according to neighbors—maybe longer. The house had been cleared out. Not a thing. And the name on the lease was Raymond Baker."

Meyerstein stared through the glass at Luntz. "This is so fucked up it's unreal, Roy. There are more questions than answers."

"How do you think he's holding up?"

Meyerstein sighed. "It'll probably hit him in a week. If he's lucky." She had seen dozens of cases—people kidnapped or who underwent a traumatic event—who later crumbled.

She headed back into the room, took a seat, and fixed her gaze on the government scientist. His eyes were black, dark rings underneath. "Frank, you've been very helpful," she said. "And we appreciate that. But we've got a major problem on our hands. We need to find Scott Caan. We've checked his home in Frederick, the address he gave, and it turns out no one lives there. The rent was paid, but the name on the paperwork is a guy called Raymond Baker. Does that name mean anything to you?"

Luntz shook his head. "I don't understand. If the house was rented by Raymond Baker, then where does Scott live?"

"That's just the problem."

"What do you mean?"

"It means, Frank, that Lieutenant Colonel Scott Caan's been covering his tracks for a while, and now we have no way of tracing him. We don't have cell phone details. We can't find out what was on his laptop. The question is, why has he been living that lie, and who helped him do it? The questions just kinda mount up . . ."

She let her comments hang in the air.

Luntz bit his lower lip. "I'm at a loss. Truly I am. He seemed . . ."

Meyerstein leaned over and held his hands. "Frank, we've got to assume the worst. I need to know if you can recreate the antiviral drugs and vaccines."

Luntz ran his hand through his gray hair. "It would have to be from the notes I kept. I think we could have something in a couple weeks, best-case scenario."

"I'm sorry, but that won't work. We're gonna need something within the next forty-eight hours, max."

"That's not realistic. I must test and retest the possible drugs."

"I appreciate that, Frank. But we need a vaccine and antivirals at the very earliest opportunity. Something that has a good possibility of working. And I want you to work with Dr. Horowitz."

"I'm sorry, it can't be done within that timescale."

"We'll give you whatever resources you want. Money, scientists—that's not an issue."

"I'm sorry, but that's unrealistic."

"Are you going to help us or not?"

Luntz bowed his head. "This is my fault, isn't it?"

"Let's forget recriminations. We need to focus. So, are you going to help us or not?"

"I'll do whatever I can."

Twenty-Three

The clock in the ICU room showed Reznick it was 1:47 a.m. He felt guilty as he sat at his daughter's bedside, knowing she was fighting for her life. The only sounds were her shallow breathing, and the constant beeping of the ventilator keeping her alive.

Reznick leaned forward and squeezed her cold hand. He knew that his daughter should have responded by now. The doctors were also concerned about the fluid in her lungs. The prognosis was bleak.

She showed classic symptoms of an opiate overdose. Eleven breaths a minute and miotic pupils. The machines around Lauren were taking her blood pressure, pulse, and respiration and heart rates. The intravenous fluids were pumping dextrose into her blood. But none of it was making a bit of difference.

He looked at the tubes coming out of her mouth and nose, concealing her flawless, beautiful face. He watched her chest rise and then lower, painfully slow.

Reznick got up and began to pace her room. He looked out of the window at the hospital's parking lot. He punched in Meyerstein's number.

"Is it OK to talk?"

"Jon, sure. How's Lauren?"

"It's too early to say."

"I'm sure the doctors are doing everything they can for her. There's still hope."

Reznick turned and faced his daughter. "I hope you're right. Look, firstly I just wanted to thank you for giving me the chance to get my daughter back. I know you didn't have to do that."

"Jon, I can hear how much you're hurting. I'm so sorry about what's happened. No one deserves what you're experiencing."

"Don't they?"

"No, of course not."

Reznick turned away from his daughter and stared out the window. "You're wrong. I deserve this. This is entirely my fault."

"You can't talk like that, Jon. That won't help her."

Reznick closed his eyes, not wishing to open them again.

"I've got some questions to ask you."

"This ain't the time."

"Maybe not. But I'm still going to ask them."

He stayed silent.

"They relate to national security. Jon, I'm gonna level with you, there's an imminent risk of terrorist attack and many lives could be at risk. Many lives. We talked about that before."

"Go on."

"There are people pulling the strings, behind the scenes. I want to ask you something, Jon. Does the name Brewling mean anything to you?"

"Like I said, not the time."

"Not an option—sorry. Jon, I need to know if the name means anything to you. Was Brewling your handler?"

Reznick sighed. "No."

"You're one hundred percent sure of that?"

"Absolutely."

"Jon, this guy Brewling . . . you can't go after him. Is that what you're thinking?"

"I don't even know who this guy is, so how the hell can I go after him?"

"Listen, you've got to let us deal with this from now on. I can't allow you to head off and shoot people all across Miami. We're drawing a line in the sand. Are you clear?"

"Who is this Brewling?" he said. "What is Norton and Weiss, Inc.? Are they working for the Agency?"

"I can't talk about that."

Reznick blew out his cheeks.

"I'm curious, Jon."

"Curious about what?"

"How you got into your line of work. When you left Delta, I mean."

"I got a call from a man. He knew a lot about me. Then he asked me nicely if I wanted to work for him."

Meyerstein went quiet for a moment. "As simple as that?"

"Pretty much. They pay me a lot of money. And I sure as hell don't get asked dumbass questions."

Meyerstein sighed, but waited for him to fill the silence.

"You still trying to figure out why a guy like me is involved in this?"

"I'm curious."

"Quite simple, really. It's called plausible deniability. No direct link to the American government. That's what this is all about. I don't exist in their eyes. But we all know that's a lie. Everyone and their dog knows that assassination is part and parcel of who we are. It keeps us on top of the bad guys, and to hell with the law."

"Fair enough."

Reznick decided it was time he got to the point. "I've just given you some information. Some intel, if you like. Now I need something in return."

"What?"

"I need to get my daughter out of here."

Meyerstein said nothing.

"This place is wide open. She's a sitting duck."

"She's in the best place possible, Jon."

"Until this is over, I won't be able to relax until I know she's safe. Make it happen. I don't care how you do it, but do it. Whoever is behind this will want to teach me a lesson. They'll be crazy that I have my daughter and you have the scientist."

Meyerstein didn't answer, as if considering his offer.

"I thought we had an agreement, Meyerstein."

"We do."

"I'm asking for help. Right here, right now. I need my daughter to be somewhere they'll never get at her. I'll speak to your guys, whatever you want. But I want my daughter at least to be cared for and protected in a secure environment."

Meyerstein cleared her throat. "Leave this with me. I'll call you back."

She ended the call as Lauren stirred slightly.

Ten minutes later, she called back. "OK, here's what we've got. We're rolling. I've just spoken to the head of emergency medicine at the Naval Hospital in Pensacola. They've agreed to admit your daughter. And I can assure you, security won't be an issue there."

"Thank you. But I need to go with her."

"That's a given."

Reznick took a deep breath and then exhaled slowly. "I owe you."

"There will be two special agents with you there. My guys will want to know the chain of events that brought this about. They'll be babysitting you, just so you don't go walkabout. And you still need to answer for Merceron."

Reznick looked at his daughter. Her face was pasty, breathing still shallow. "I don't care about that now. Get my daughter to Pensacola and get her well."

Meyerstein went quiet for a few moments, as if in contemplation. He sensed her empathy, but it was cloaked in steely professionalism.

"If there's anything else I can do, Jon—for you or your daughter—don't hesitate to contact me."

Twenty-Four

Thomas Wesley was already awake when he heard the sound of cars pulling up outside his home. As his wife slept soundly beside him, he leaned over and checked the luminous dial on his bedside alarm clock. It was 3:03 a.m. *Strange.* It was unusual to hear anything in his quiet cul-de-sac after nightfall.

The most noise was when there were Independence Day barbecues being held on front lawns, or in the days leading up to Halloween, when the kids from around the block would go door to door, trick or treating. Most—if not all—families worked during the day, and by 8 p.m. the oak-lined street was dead.

He got out of bed and peered through the slats of the wooden blinds. Two Suburbans were blocking his driveway. Four men in dark suits walked up his garden path. Then his bell rang.

Who were they? Cops? Feds?

His wife stirred and switched on her bedside light, looking confused, rubbing her eyes. "What's going on, honey?"

Wesley pulled some sweatpants on over his boxer shorts, put on a T-shirt and his slippers. "We've got company."

Three sharp knocks on the front door, followed by the ringing of the bell.

"Thomas, what's going on?" she said, pulling on her robe.

"I don't know."

Wesley headed downstairs, followed by his wife. The chain was on the front door. He turned the key, and slowly cracked open the door a few inches.

An imposing man flashed a Department of Defense special agent badge in his face. "DCIS." Then, through the space in the door, he handed Wesley a typed court order with a red wax seal on it. "Thomas Wesley?"

Wesley scanned the court order. "Yes, that's me. What's this about?"

"We've been issued a warrant to search the premises, Mr. Wesley. Open the door immediately. I believe you know what this is about."

Wesley took the chain off the door, and the man brushed past him as the three other men followed. He shut the door and they fanned out throughout the house. Two downstairs and one upstairs. The lead investigator remained in the hallway with Wesley and his wife.

His wife held her hand to her chest. "Thomas, what's this all about?"

Wesley reached out and held her hand. "I don't know," he said. He turned to the lead investigator, a tall, swarthy man. "Am I under arrest?"

"Sir, we hope you'll come with us and answer some questions."

"Regarding?"

The man sighed. "Regarding the possible mishandling of classified information."

It was a forty-five-minute journey down MD-295. No one spoke to Wesley. No small talk—nothing. He sat and stared out at the headlights of the passing cars. Had Lance alerted them? Surely not.

He wondered if he hadn't miscalculated by going straight to Drake. After all, he was a powerful politician with a growing reputation. Had he passed the information on to the Department of Defense?

Wesley felt isolated in the car. The smell of one of the men's cologne was sticking to the back of his throat, making him nauseous. The tension was palpable, not helped by the silence.

When they drove along Army Navy Drive in Arlington—very close to the Pentagon—Wesley assumed they were taking him to DCIS Headquarters. But, instead, at an underpass they passed a sign for the Army Navy Country Club on the right, and then it was a left and a left again, past some nondescript office buildings and down a ramp into a near-deserted basement garage.

Armed guards with semi-automatic rifles were patrolling the garage. What the hell was this?

The car stopped next to an elevator, and the lead investigator got out and opened Wesley's door.

Wesley stepped out of the car. "Where are we?"

"Don't worry, it's just routine."

The man led Wesley to the elevator as the three men followed close behind. The five of them got in and descended in silence to a sub-basement. Then he was led down a series of narrow corridors, and finally into a windowless room.

There was a mirror on one wall. They were watching him.

"Sit down, Thomas," the lead investigator said. "This is not a court of law. We're just wanting to talk to you, get to know you a bit better, see what we can do to help you."

Wesley sat down.

"You want a coffee, glass of water, Coke—anything?"

"I'm good, thanks." Wesley was trying to show he was relaxed and not frightened.

"My name is Carlos Rodriguez," the lead investigator said, pulling up a chair opposite. "Senior investigator in matters pertaining to the NSA." Rodriguez shifted in his seat. "I've just been reading your file."

"Sorry to interrupt, but I was expecting to be taken to four hundred Army Navy Drive. What's this place?"

"Satellite office. It's crammed where we are."

"And the guys with the guns?"

"Heightened security after a recent internal audit."

Wesley nodded.

"OK, Thomas, I appreciate this must all be very unnerving."

He forced a grin. "You got that right."

"But I want you to know that we're here to help. We don't want to point fingers. We just want to try and understand what's happened. But I'll be honest, we need answers." Rodriguez went quiet for a few moments. "You see, what I can't get my head around is how someone like you, a smart guy, would want to jeopardize American security by stealing and then leaking classified files."

"Hey, let's not get ahead of ourselves. I don't believe I have ever jeopardized American security. I'm a patriot."

"OK, we'll leave that aside just now. Would you like to talk about a conversation you had with Congressman Lance Drake, an old friend of yours from way back?"

Wesley said nothing. So, it was Drake.

Son of a bitch.

"Isn't it true that you passed him an alleged decrypted conversation of a top-secret, military-intelligence nature?" Rodriguez leaned back in his seat as if waiting for an answer.

Wesley sighed. "Do you know why I did that?"

"I was hoping you'd be able to help us with that."

"I had no other choice. I went through the system, and no one wanted to know. I was in their bad books because I decrypted a conversation that linked a White House advisor to the Chinese military. I was sidelined, as the advisor was well connected. No one wanted to listen to me. They thought I was an embarrassment."

Rodriguez frowned. "So you alerted the congressman because you thought, as he was an old friend, he might get something done?"

"Precisely. I wanted someone who had the clout to ask the questions. I didn't want to go to the papers. What the hell was I to do when the established avenues were shut down?"

Rodriguez leaned forward and stared at him. "So you're saying you admit leaking this information, is that right?"

"Only to Lance. I thought I could trust him."

"Have you leaked this to anyone else?"

"Of course I haven't. I understand the seriousness of this. The ramifications."

The agent said nothing.

Wesley asked, "Have you listened to it?"

"Yes, it was intriguing. Our guys are currently working on the embedded message it contains. Did you manage to crack it?"

"Nope, but not for want of trying."

"So let's be clear—you didn't uncover the message, if indeed it does contain some form of data communication?"

"Correct."

Rodriguez cleared his throat and smiled.

Wesley sighed. He was tired and wanted to go home. "Look, can we hurry this along a bit?"

"All in good time, Thomas."

"Have you guys established the identities of those on the tape?"

"We have a very good idea."

Wesley clenched his fist. "Well, thank God. At last, someone gets it. And you guys have passed this on to the Feds and the NSA?"

"It's all in hand, Thomas."

A sense of relief swept over Wesley, glad the right people now knew the threat to the country. "Finally, at long last . . ."

"It's a stunning piece of work, piecing this together, I've got to say."

Wesley felt his cheeks go red. "I started getting goose bumps when I started to unravel this. The raw intercept was just audio of a pop song. The Bangles or some crap from the eighties. But then I stripped all that away and got to an encrypted conversation. It took a long time to decipher, but eventually I got it. I ran the programs to see if it matched anyone on the NSA files, and it brought up a perfect match and a near-perfect match."

The agent shifted in his seat as one of the other men left the room.

"Don't get me wrong, I thought the exact same thing as you guys. But it's a very convincing bit of voice morphing. I'm assuming you got right down to the authentic voices, right?"

"I'll come back to that later. For now, tell me in your own words how you deciphered as much of this message as you did?"

Wesley was about to answer when it suddenly struck him that he'd been the one doing all the talking. The one detailing all his work and the analysis he'd carried out. He looked around at the impassive, cold faces of the men scrutinizing him. He didn't know why, but he started to feel uncomfortable. Not overly uncomfortable. Just a feeling that something wasn't right.

"Look, guys, I've been very open with you, and given it to you straight. I need a break, if that's OK. I'd also like to call my wife. She'll be worried."

"That'll be arranged. But let's talk about the other voice on the recording."

"Listen, I want to speak to my wife."

"She's back at the house. Don't worry about a thing."

Wesley said nothing.

"Thomas, can you tell me just now if you have a definitive version of the conversation of the two original voices? Because I think we need to know about that before we go any further with this."

"I need to speak to my wife."

Rodriguez got up and smiled. "Not a problem. I'll go and speak to my boss. Probably have to wake him up. You can have a break and call your wife."

Wesley sighed in relief. His imagination had begun to get the better of him.

"Can I get you a drink? A water? Soda, perhaps?"

"Black coffee would be great."

"You got it."

The agent disappeared with his colleagues. Wesley turned and looked at his reflection in the mirror. He looked haggard. Bloodshot eyes.

A few minutes later, the door opened and a young female agent walked in. She wore a dark blue suit and a white blouse, and was carrying a mug of coffee. She looked in her mid-thirties and was very attractive. "Cream or sugar?"

"It's good as it is," Wesley said.

She handed him the mug, smiled, and left the room.

Wesley sighed and closed his eyes for a few moments, thinking of his wife. She'd be worried sick. He lifted the mug to his mouth and took a couple of gulps of the strong coffee. He tasted the strong flavor that he enjoyed. Then, all of a sudden, he felt a tingling feeling rush up his arms to his head. The coffee mug fell to the floor.

Then blackness engulfed his world.

Twenty-Five

The sun was edging over the horizon when the twin-engine Cessna air ambulance landed on Runway 3 at Forrest Sherman Field, part of the naval air station in Pensacola. Reznick helped the doctor and two nurses lift the gurney—his daughter strapped to it—from the plane and into a waiting ambulance. He sat beside her and held her hand as they sped off on a seven-mile journey, lights flashing, to the Naval Hospital, and were waved past the armed guards at the back gate's security checkpoint. Two Feds followed in a car close behind.

The ambulance pulled up outside the eight-story hospital and Lauren was rushed straight up to the intensive care unit on the fourth floor. Reznick could only watch as his daughter was hooked up to another ventilator. Nurses and a couple of doctors took her vital signs and talked about the risks involved in giving a higher dose of Naloxone, as if Reznick weren't there.

A doctor pulled back the left eyelid and shone a penlight in Lauren's eyes. "That's interesting. Slight dilation." He did the same for the right eye. And then repeated it. "Dilation confirmed."

Then the doctor checked her arms and legs for track marks. "Lauren, can you hear me?" he said. There was urgency in his voice. "Lauren, wake up."

But she didn't respond.

After what seemed a lifetime, one of the doctors finally approached Reznick. "I'm told you're the father, sir," he said.

Reznick nodded.

"Come with me," the doctor said.

He led Reznick out into the corridor and headed up the stairs to his office. He swiped his ID at the side of a door with the sign "Dr. Jerry Winkelman." A beep. "Please come in," he said as he pushed the door open.

The doctor sat down in the black leather chair behind a paper-strewn desk, and leaned back. "Take a seat," he said.

Reznick sat down opposite.

"Lauren, as you've just seen, is seriously ill. To say otherwise would be misleading and wrong. But she did respond to the light, which might give us a bit of hope."

Reznick nodded.

"But her age is adding to our concern, and the length of time she has been in this heroin coma. We're going to give her an extremely high dosage of an antidote, which we think has to be administered right now if we are to have any hope of bringing her around."

Reznick felt disassociated, as if the doctor weren't talking about his daughter.

"We believe that the marks on her arm were caused by skin-popping, where the needle is sunk into any bit of skin, not directly into the vein. And this may be the thing that will save her, although we can't say for sure. Your daughter's case is very similar to one I dealt with earlier this year. A thirteen-year-old who'd tried shooting up with his friends and had been skin-popping. He recovered, despite slipping into a coma for twenty-four hours."

When they returned to the ICU room, Lauren was again unrecognizable, tubes coming out of her nose and mouth, the machines keeping her alive.

The doctor said, "She's on a ventilator because of the low respiratory rate. And I've been told that the blood gases were shown to be hypoxic. We'll monitor your daughter before, during, and after this treatment process, keeping a close eye on temperature, pulse, urine output, electrocardiography, and oxygen saturation."

Reznick stared down at her.

The sound of the beeping from the ventilator was the only response.

"Sorry, but you're going to have to leave, at least for now," the doctor said. "We need to begin her treatment. Why don't you go to the quiet room and get some sleep. It's for the families of patients. You look as though you need it."

He called a nurse over and asked her to show Reznick to the quiet room.

Reznick took one long, final look at his daughter. She looked as if she were just sleeping. Out in the corridor, the two Feds were waiting. They followed Reznick and the nurse along the corridor without saying a word.

The nurse showed him into a large room with wooden blinds. There was a bed, a sofa, a phone on the wall, and a TV on a stand. "If you need anything, just pick up the phone and this will take you straight through to reception."

Waves of tiredness washed over Reznick. The last few days had been insane. "Thank you."

The nurse turned to leave, and Reznick noticed the two Feds were pulling up chairs outside the room to babysit him. The door slammed shut.

Reznick closed the blinds, took off his shoes, and lay down on the bed. He closed his eyes. But he couldn't get the picture of Lauren—covered in tubes and hooked up to the ventilator—out of his head.

Reznick felt his eyelids becoming heavy. He felt himself falling. Deeper and deeper. Then he was gone.

The sky was a perfect blue. He was standing on a beach. He saw Lauren in the distance, aged around six, paddling in the cold summer ocean. Her cheeks were red and she was laughing and splashing in her pink bathing suit.

He tried to shout and warn her of the breakers crashing onto shore. But his voice was lost in the roar of the water and howl of the wind, as the waves rolled up the sand. He shouted again, but still she didn't hear.

Suddenly he was cloaked in darkness. The smell of acrid smoke filled the air. The sound of sirens. He was running through a tunnel. Heart pounding. Darkness all around. Then he was out of the tunnel. Skyscrapers everywhere. He was in the city—Manhattan. And the sun was shining. A perfect sky. He looked up. A tiny figure, high up in the burning building, waving a handkerchief. One World Trade Center.

"Jon! Jon! Please come and get me! Jon! Jon!" He tried to move, but he was paralyzed. He willed himself to move. But he was frozen. All of a sudden, an ominous thunderous roar, and the tiny figure was swallowed in a cloud of dust and ash as the building descended at speed, the smell of burning fuel thick in the air, the screaming unrelenting.

Reznick sat bolt upright in the bed, bathed in sweat and struggling for breath.

Twenty-Six

The Gulfstream was en route to New York, cruising at thirty-five thousand feet, as Meyerstein held a progress meeting with the senior members of her team.

Her phone rang.

She sighed and picked it up. "Assistant Director Meyerstein."

"Martha, it's Freddie Limonton in Washington." He was the FBI's top computer guy working at HQ. "We've run face recognition scanning and retinal scans into the system for Scott Caan in New York for November seventeen."

"I'm listening."

"We got something. We've picked him up from a scan at JFK."

Martha clenched her fist. Then she felt herself flush at the display of emotion in front of her team. They just shrugged, wondering what she'd been told. "Good work."

"I've just emailed you the three minutes and twenty-five seconds we have of Scott Caan. The first part was filmed in and around Terminal Five. One minute and twenty-two seconds of him walking through the terminal."

"You got his flight details?"

"JetBlue from Dulles. The last two minutes of footage were filmed in Tribeca, Lower Manhattan. Corner of Duane and Greenwich is where he gets out. The file should be with you now."

"Lower Manhattan?" Meyerstein scanned her inbox and saw there was one new message. "OK, Freddie, I got it. But I need another favor."

"You don't ask much."

"I know, I know. Listen. Same guy—I want his image run through every CCTV database we can get our hands on, especially government buildings and trains in New York City in the last month. But also businesses in the Tribeca area. What was he doing there? We need to try and get a handle on his movements. Where did he visit? You know the drill."

"You want footage of every surveillance-camera database to be scanned in the last month? Whoa, Martha, are you serious?"

"Absolutely."

"That's a huge trawl. That could take—"

"Then you better get started. You need extra resources, you got it. He's out there somewhere."

Meyerstein double-clicked the file and a frozen still of Caan appeared on the large screen. He was strikingly handsome—high cheekbones, dark hair, dark eyes, clean-shaven. She pointed to the remote control that was on the table where Stamper was sitting.

"OK, Roy, let's run the footage. This is the first visual of Caan, taken just before he went missing from the lab."

A few murmurs from her team.

Stamper rolled his eyes. "A month ago? That's a lifetime."

"I know, I know. But it's all we've got so far. Let's run it."

Stamper pressed the "Play" button. On the screen, Caan strode past the huge windows of Terminal 5, which overlooked the runway. Then past the Lacoste store. He wore a pair of faded jeans, tan boots, and a dark coat.

Meyerstein said, "Very cute. He doesn't stand out at all. Blends in real nice."

Stamper stared at the screen. "It's no wonder this guy hasn't come up on anyone's radar. He looks like an ordinary Joe just visiting the Big Apple."

They watched as the lean Caan ambled past the shops in the terminal before he stopped to look in the window of the Ron Jon Surf Shop.

Stamper said, "Countersurveillance measure—what do you think, Martha?"

"Well, he sure as hell wouldn't be surfing in New York in November, that's for sure."

The footage, spliced together from numerous cameras around the terminal, switched angles as he meandered past the shops, carefully avoiding the hundreds of other passengers with huge bags and suitcases. He walked past a Japanese restaurant, then a jewelry shop, and out to a long line of yellow cabs outside.

"Freeze that, Roy!" Meyerstein pointed at the screen. "Excellent. Now run the plates of that cab, Roy."

Stamper scribbled down the details and handed it to one of his team.

"OK, Roy, let's roll the footage from Lower Manhattan."

The footage picked up Caan as he got out of the same cab. "This is Caan arriving in Tribeca," Meyerstein said. "Let's pay attention."

The film showed Caan carrying a gym bag as he walked across the street at the corner of Duane and Greenwich. "Freeze that, if you will," she said. She turned to look at her team. "He's carrying a bag. Go back to the airport footage, Roy. I'm sure he wasn't carrying anything."

Roy rewound the footage. It confirmed that Meyerstein was right. No bag.

"Where did the bag come from? Was this placed in the taxi for him? We need to know, people."

Meyerstein faced the freeze-framed screen showing Caan at the airport. "Go back to Tribeca."

They watched again as Caan emerged from the cab in Tribeca. "I want our guys in New York to swamp the area around Duane and Greenwich, and start asking questions. I want every resident within one block of there to be shown a picture of Caan. Do they know him? Have they seen him out and about? Was he staying there? Visiting someone? Check all the hotels within a mile. I want to know the instant we have a breakthrough."

Stamper groaned. "This footage is a month old, Martha."

"It's all we have. It's a start."

Meyerstein wasn't as pessimistic as Stamper. He viewed himself as a realist and a pragmatist. And he was. But sometimes he didn't view small breakthroughs in the same light as she did. To her, this was concrete proof that they were on the right track. She'd learned that as a child, watching her father studying. The forensic way he pieced together the smallest facts, and constructed a rational and plausible case as part of his preparation. Nothing was too small to overlook. Now she was doing the same. The FBI knew Caan had visited New York and when. They had something to work with, even if it was a month old.

Meyerstein sank back in her seat. She was so tired she couldn't sleep. It was pure adrenaline that was keeping her going. She was certain her heart was constantly beating faster these days.

She looked around at her team again. Exhausted faces, all running on empty. "We're getting close now. I want every FBI field office, every police force, and all government agencies to be made aware of Caan and his image. I want every avenue explored, and leads followed up."

Stamper gave a wry smile from his seat in the opposite aisle and got up, then took a seat beside her. He leaned in close. "Martha," he said, his voice low, "you need to ease up. You're gonna give yourself a heart attack."

Meyerstein nodded, knowing he was right. She needed to slow down. Maybe even take time off. But that wasn't a realistic option until the investigation was concluded. Too much was at stake. "The bastard is out there. We'll get him. Make sure the New York field office has the footage. I want to know what the hell he was doing in Manhattan. Was this reconnaissance? Meeting with people who may have conceived a bioterror plot?"

"They know what to do. We're getting there. We'll find the son of a bitch."

The team started firing out instructions via secure email and encrypted phones. Within five minutes, Martha had Tom Callaghan, the special agent in charge of New York City, on the phone.

"Where's this come from?" Callaghan asked.

"We got lucky. It's CCTV footage from Terminal Five at JFK, on November seventeen. Have you watched it?"

"My guys are watching it just now."

"We need to throw everything at this, Tom. He was in Tribeca."

"Leave it with me, Martha. You en route?"

"I'll be with you in under an hour."

Meyerstein and five of her team took the elevator to the FBI's New York field office, located on the twenty-third floor of a monolithic forty-one-story, glass-walled slab in Lower Manhattan.

In a conference room, she joined nine of the Joint Terrorism Task Force—including Tom Callaghan—around the table for an emergency meeting, and hooked up with the high-tech operations room at the National Counterterrorism Center in McLean, Virginia, for a secure videoconference. She brought everyone up to speed. On the plasma screen, she could see four men and a woman at the NCTC.

"OK, folks," she said, "we're all coming at this from a multitude of angles. But we need to focus on not only tracking down Caan and trying to establish where he went in Lower Manhattan, but what the possible targets are."

Callaghan piped up. "My team are swarming all over Lower Manhattan as we speak. But this ain't gonna be easy."

Meyerstein looked up at the screen, which showed the counter-terrorism experts staring back at her. "These images are from a month ago, but I believe that Caan is a serious threat. We need to remember that terrorists don't always originate from outside the US."

On the screen, a middle-aged gray-haired man, Principal Deputy Director Arthur Black, put up his hand to interject. "Can I get a straight answer, Martha? Are we talking an imminent attack?"

Meyerstein cleared her throat. "I don't think anyone could say for sure, Arthur, but if pressed, I would say that Caan was doing reconnaissance, perhaps acquainting himself with a target or targets. As we are all acutely aware, New York City is the number-one target for terrorists. There have been nine known plots involving targets in New York unearthed since 9/11, including a couple in the last three months. They include plans to detonate fuel tanks at JFK, plant explosives in the Holland Tunnel, and several plots to attack subway stations. You can take your pick. If we also factor in that it's the largest city in the United States, not to mention a global financial and media center, you can see why it's a magnet for terrorists."

Black and his NCTC colleagues nodded, as did those around the table in New York.

A sharp knock at the door, and Roy Stamper popped his head around, face drawn. "Excuse me, ma'am. Freddie needs to speak to you. It's urgent."

Martha leaned back in her seat. "Roy, we're in the middle of a videoconference, can't it wait?"

"Afraid not."

Martha looked around the room and then up at the faces on the huge screen. "Sorry," she said, "I'll be back with you in a couple minutes. Take five."

She went outside. "This better be good," she said.

"He says it can't wait."

Stamper handed Meyerstein the phone. "Yeah, talk to me, Freddie."

Limonton was breathing heavily down the phone. "We've been running the software on Caan—face recognition, retinal scans, trying to track his movements over the last month," he said.

"What've you got?"

"You need to get the hell out of there! Now!"

"What in God's name are you talking about?"

"Caan accessed the FBI building, dressed as maintenance. And we reckon he's placed dirty bombs in the air vents, the son of a bitch!"

———

Meyerstein had to move fast. She gave the evacuation order after speaking to O'Donoghue and Callaghan, the head of the New York field office. The reason cited to evacuate and relayed to other government agencies working in the building was that there was a bomb scare. Hundreds streamed out into the plaza.

The White House, the Pentagon, and the Office of the Director of National Intelligence were all briefed.

Then she took a call from the head of the FBI's Counterterrorism Analytical Branch, Simon Bullard, whose team had concluded that Caan was receiving outside help, and wasn't acting alone. When Meyerstein asked if there was any hint of foreign involvement, he said ominously, "It can't be ruled out."

Meyerstein and her team immediately headed to an FBI safe house in a suite of offices on the Upper East Side, and remotely viewed the work of a Hazmat team scouring the air vents of the building in New York, while on another screen they reconvened the secure videoconference with the National Counterterrorism Center.

This time, Director Bill O'Donoghue was sitting in. She hadn't heard anything from him since she flat out refused to obey his order to stand aside.

"Martha," O'Donoghue said, leaning back in his seat, "I'm glad everyone got out safe. What's the latest?"

"Thank you, sir." Meyerstein sighed. "Sir, we're searching an apartment in Tribeca as we speak."

"Is this some anti-government thing? Are we talking militia?"

"We can't rule anything in or out at this stage, sir. We don't know who Caan is working with."

O'Donoghue was nodding.

"Caan has, in effect, wandered into a highly guarded government building and possibly planted biomaterials. It's appalling. We could be talking about worst-case scenarios."

O'Donoghue was writing notes. "Go on, Martha."

"Look, sir, we still don't know what the risks are, as we haven't established what has been planted. Secondly, if this is a real bio-threat, then under current guidelines, we do not instigate panic. Telling the public there are bioweapons would turn New York into anarchy. But, what I would say is that this threat is far too sophisticated to be just one lone nut. I'm not buying that."

"What are Counterterrorism saying on this?"

Meyerstein reiterated what she had been told. "And it raises the specter that he's receiving outside help."

O'Donoghue took off his glasses and pinched the bridge of his nose. "This is a potential nightmare scenario for New York. And I agree, Caan is not working alone."

Meyerstein saw on the big screen that the NCTC people were nodding at their comments. Arthur Black put up his hand to speak.

"Go right ahead, Arthur," she said.

"Thank you. America has many enemies. But I don't think it's helpful to speculate as to who could be behind this at this stage."

Meyerstein nodded. "I agree."

She pressed a button and the screen went black, the video-conference over.

It was strange that there was no more footage of Caan in New York. Why was that?

"Someone is shielding him," she said. "This is not the sort of thing that's dreamed up on the spur of the moment. So where the hell is he?"

"God only knows," came the muted reply from Roy Stamper, staring at the live newsfeed from Lower Manhattan.

Twenty-Seven

Reznick was floating in a sea of darkness, a black sky above. The sound of humming, like a chopper blade, and then an incessant beeping. He opened his eyes and found he was sitting by his daughter's bedside, holding her hand. He sat up and stared at her.

Her eyes were closed, face pained. She didn't look peaceful. She made the occasional moan, as if tormented by nightmares in her deep sleep. He wondered if she would ever wake up. Even if she did, what state would she be in?

The sound of footsteps approaching, out in the corridor. A sharp knock at the door, and a nurse entered the room. "Excuse me. There's a call for you at the nursing station."

"Did they give a name?"

"Said they were calling from Miami. Said you're a friend of his father."

Reznick wondered how Ron Leggett knew where he was. His gut feeling told him something was wrong. Surely the Feds hadn't passed on the information?

"OK," he sighed. He followed the nurse out of the ICU room and headed to the nursing station, halfway down the corridor. The two Feds followed.

A receptionist pointed to the phone on the desk. "There you go, sir," she said, flashing a white smile.

He picked up the phone and turned his back to the woman before he spoke, the two Feds close by, watching him.

"Yeah, who's this?"

A long silence on the line. But he knew someone was there.

"Who's calling?"

A long sigh. "I'm very disappointed, Jon." It was the electronically distorted voice that had instructed Reznick to head down to Miami. "You didn't keep your side of the bargain."

Reznick's insides tightened and his heart beat faster. He turned and snapped his fingers, signaling to the Feds. He covered the mouthpiece of the phone and whispered to one of them, "Do a trace on this call. Right now."

The Fed nodded and took out his cell phone to make the call.

"What do you want?" Reznick said.

"Did you think you could move Lauren without us knowing about it, Jon?"

Reznick felt anger gnawing at his chest. He wondered how they knew where his daughter was.

"All you had to do, Jon, was deliver the scientist, and your daughter wouldn't have been harmed. But, instead, you decided to take matters into your own hands. And now look at Lauren. Do you feel guilty, Jon? Do you wonder if you made the wrong call?"

Reznick said nothing.

"I don't think she's gonna make it, Jon."

Reznick could see it was mind games.

"We're not going to go away, Jon. When this is over, we're coming after your little girl and you."

"You finished?" Reznick said.

"No—quite the contrary, Jon. I'm only beginning. You see, Jon, we have plans in place. Plans like you wouldn't believe. This ungrateful, bloated, filthy country, which you profess to love, is going to feel what real pain is. What real loss is like."

Reznick kept quiet, wanting him to do the talking.

"You disrupted our plans, Jon, I'm afraid to say. Plans which took us years to put into place. You and Lauren will pay for that."

Reznick closed his eyes.

"You see, Jon, America is going to suffer, and it's going to suffer a bit earlier than we planned."

The line went dead.

Reznick looked across at the Feds, who were looking grim-faced, one still on his cell. "Any luck?"

"I don't think so."

Reznick shook his head and walked back into his daughter's room. He stood at the window and looked down at the flower-beds in the hospital grounds, a riot of color just before Christmas. He thought back over the chaotic last few days. He thought of Lauren and the terrible last moments before Beth was killed. His mind flashed to seeing Leggett's crumpled body in the shower. This nightmare had all been caused by his refusal to kill Luntz. He knew Lauren would never get peace.

He had to end this. It was never going to stop until he neutralized the people behind it.

"There you are." The voice of one of the Feds snapped him out of his thoughts. The agent walked across to the window and stood beside Reznick. "We couldn't trace the call. They were bouncing the signal off here, there, and everywhere. Very sophisticated."

"Forget that, I want to speak to Meyerstein."

"Now?"

"Right now."

The Fed let out a long sigh. "I'll see what I can do." He left the room for a couple of minutes. When he came back, he held out his cell phone. "Assistant Director Meyerstein for you."

Reznick took the phone. "How the hell can you guys not get a trace?"

"We're still working on it."

"Bullshit. They're running circles around us. How the hell did they know Lauren was here? Can you answer me that?"

Meyerstein sighed. "I don't know, Jon. Honest to God, I wish I did."

"He knows Lauren was moved and knows her condition. Is there a leak in your team? What the hell is going on?"

"OK, Jon, let's back up for a moment. They, whoever they are, might know where you are, but they can't get to your family."

"I don't think you're listening. These are no ordinary Joes you're dealing with. These guys are serious."

"Trust me, your family is safe."

"You don't know that. Look, I want in."

"I beg your pardon?"

"I want to be part of your investigation team. I want to help you get these bastards."

"That's not gonna happen, Jon."

"You're not listening, Meyerstein. These people are very, very serious. And when I mean serious, I mean they're not gonna go away. I want to help you."

"Jon, you need to leave this to us."

"Listen to me very closely." Reznick lowered his voice. "He said they had plans in place and that America was going to feel what real pain was."

"He said that?"

"What, do you think I'm making this up?"

Meyerstein was quiet.

"He also said they were going to bring their plans forward."

A long silence opened up. Eventually, Meyerstein spoke. "Jon, you need to let this go and leave it with us. Lauren needs you now.

I also want you to know that I'm going to be thinking of you and your daughter, and praying she pulls through this."

Reznick handed the cell phone back to the Fed, who left the room. When he'd shut the door, Reznick went across and sat down at his daughter's bedside. He held her hand and stroked her soft hair. Then he leaned in close and whispered in her ear, "Lauren, I love you so much, honey. But I've got something to attend to. It means I'm gonna be away from you for a little while, honey. The doctors are gonna take good care of you. When I come back, this will all be over, one way or the other, I promise you." He kissed her clammy cheek, visible through all the tubes. "Love you forever."

Twenty-Eight

The FBI's three-story safe house on the Upper East Side fell quiet as they listened to the phone conversation—retrieved minutes earlier by the NSA—between Reznick and the electronically distorted voice.

Meyerstein stood in the briefing room, hands behind her back, and stared out of the window over the houses on East 73rd Street. More than one hundred experts—from the NSA, the CIA, Homeland Security, the National Counterterrorism Center, and, of course, the FBI—were all trying to track down Caan, and the identity and location of Reznick's caller.

She was feeling the pressure like never before. The stakes were impossibly high. But she knew that cold logic instead of raw emotion was required.

She turned around and looked at the eerie real-time images from the cameras of the Hazmat team in Lower Manhattan. The night-vision feed was from a camera fitted to Special Agent Kevin O'Hare's biohazard suit as he headed along an aluminum duct in the building's central air-conditioning system.

Another plasma screen showed seven members of her team at FBI Headquarters in Washington, sat around a small conference table. Meyerstein stared up at the Washington screen. "OK, let's get started. I want to know more about this call. It's exactly half an hour since we got working on this. What are the NSA saying about it?"

Gary Clark, an NSA computer and telecommunications specialist, said, "The GPS shows that the call to Reznick originated from Grand Cayman. But we've done our calculations and it's not possible. It's a false location. Classic GPS spoofing, bouncing off hundreds of locations."

"OK, interesting. What else?"

"We're ninety-two percent certain that the call was made from a moving car. We're still working on cleaning up the voice, though. They're very good."

Meyerstein sighed. "Clearly. Any further details about the phone?"

Clark cleared his throat and leafed through a pile of papers in front of him. "Prepaid serial number, originally part of a consignment for a store in Miami."

"Now we're getting somewhere. What about voice analysis?"

"It's gonna take time. There are so many overlays, it's a highly sophisticated operation we're dealing with."

"What about Caan? Do we have anything on him?"

"He seems to have disappeared off the radar, ma'am."

"Are we scanning all cellular traffic? He must be communicating with someone. This is not a lone wolf. The level of expertise tells us this is something entirely different."

"Fort Meade is scanning telephone, fax, and data traffic, including encrypted emails, across the world."

Meyerstein knew they had a database containing hundreds of billions of records of calls made by US citizens from the four largest phone carriers.

"Our analysts are using the extension Caan used at the lab, his home number, and cell, although all three haven't been used in months."

"It's beginning to sound more and more ominous."

"Look, we're throwing everything at it. We're using link analysis software and neural network software to try and detect patterns, classify and cluster data. We've also got a speech recording he made at a conference last year, and we're using advanced speech-recognition software to find him. But to answer your question, nothing so far."

"OK, Gary. Get back to me as soon as we have something."

Meyerstein cut the link to Washington. Then she opened the communications links to Dr. Max Horowitz at the Weapons of Mass Destruction Directorate, down in Lower Manhattan, and the National Counterterrorism Center in McLean, who were monitoring events as they unfolded. "Max, it's Martha. I'm looking for an update, if that's possible."

A loud groan, as if it were the last thing he needed to hear. "We've located ten aerosol devices, in the air ducts on five different floors. We've managed to disable eight of them by jamming, using extra directional antennas, but two of the devices have still not been deactivated. And that's worrying."

"So what do you surmise is causing the problem?"

"We don't know, is the simple answer. Kevin is in the duct, as you can see. He's going to use another antenna, hoping to bounce off a second and third antenna in the duct, to jam the darn things."

Meyerstein's insides knotted tight. "Look, we're very concerned that this call to Reznick might mean this guy or this group will try and advance the timers on the remaining two devices. They know we're on to them."

"We're working as quickly as we can, Martha."

"I appreciate that, Max. Can you tell how far Kevin is from these devices? He looks real close. Isn't it possible to manually deactivate?"

"This is delicate. We've got to be very, very careful."

"Max, I understand that." Her tone was calm, not wishing to instill anxiety into an already tense situation.

"As it stands, we don't know how this device is set up. We reckon he's eight yards away or so. But he's got to be cautious. A movement sensor may set them off. And to compound matters, the devices are located on opposite sides of the ducts. Twenty, maybe thirty yards apart."

"OK, we'll keep this link open. Best of luck."

Horowitz sighed. "We're gonna need it."

Special Agent Kevin O'Hare could hear the conversation through the earpiece of a two-way radio fitted into his Hazmat suit. Crawling through the air duct, the light on his helmet pierced the darkness. A tiny camera was fitted to the light, beaming back pictures to the FBI safe house. He edged closer to the first of the two aerosol canisters, attached to the side of the aluminum duct.

He felt slightly claustrophobic wearing the fully encapsulating biohazard suit, with its full facepiece, self-contained breathing apparatus, and bacterial spore detector. It offered the highest level of protection against any gases, vapors, mists, particles, or spores. But that didn't make it any less uncomfortable under all the protective layers.

The heat was intense. Each movement was such an effort. He felt sweat beading his forehead. But it was the least of his worries.

He'd known the risks when he volunteered, as the most experienced member of the team, to head down the duct. Severe to fatal, if this was indeed the hybrid version of the Spanish flu. His suit would protect him—at least it would in theory. But what about any bacteria seeping through the vents and into the packed streets of Manhattan outside? His wife worked in a deli only three blocks away. She was four months pregnant.

O'Hare's breathing was getting more labored as he edged closer to the device. He heard the voices of his instructors down the years.

There must be focus. There must be patience. The whole scenario was something he had spent twenty years being trained for. He'd done numerous simulations and been involved in a handful of incidents down the years, mostly involving anthrax spores. But this was major-league stuff.

"OK," he said into the two-way radio. "Located the first of the devices. Looks like they are indeed attached. Magnet."

O'Hare opened up the sealed pack attached to his suit's belt and pulled out a directional high-gain antenna, a handheld LCD display, and a military-grade signal jammer. He screwed the antenna to the iPod-sized jammer, and flicked on the switch to activate the device. It was slow work with his protective gloves on.

The green light came on. He was in business.

The frequencies it covered were beyond ordinary cell phone jammers and were intended to combat all radio frequency threats, not just cellular-activated weapons. The jammer worked by preventing radio signals from reaching the radio receiver used to detonate a device. He knew the jammer he was using broadcast interference on multiple frequencies. In theory, all known threats should be thwarted. But it was sophisticated enough not to affect his two-way radio.

He glanced at his fast-scanning receiver display.

"Yeah, as I thought, they're frequency hopping. Do you copy?"

A voice at the other end said, "Yeah, copy that, Kevin."

O'Hare rechecked the LCD display. The two signals would only appear for a few milliseconds on a particular frequency before hopping onto the next.

What the hell was this?

The system he was using should have detected the frequency hopping. Then it should have jammed the short-duration signals.

So, why the hell wasn't it? This wasn't good. Not good at all.

O'Hare felt hot, and his breathing got faster as the seconds ticked by. Someone must be using state-of-the-art jammers against them and rendering his device ineffective. But only a handful of countries—American allies—had access to the United States' SINCGARS system whose frequency-hopping mode hopped one hundred times a second.

This was no ordinary terrorist group. This was a government.

"Sir, I think we've got a problem," he said, crouching within a few inches of the device.

"Yeah, I'm listening, Kevin," said Dr. Horowitz.

"As you can see, I'm inches from the device. But the jamming isn't working. I repeat—the jamming isn't working."

A beat. "That's impossible."

"I think we've gotta be thinking that this is a military-grade frequency hopper that's evading our jammer."

"We should still be able to jam it, shouldn't we?"

"Ordinarily yes, sir. But a foreign government who has our level of technology may have implemented modifications, neutralizing our efforts."

A long sigh. "That's not possible. Can you get up close and give us a handle on what we're dealing with?"

O'Hare peered closer at the device. Welded to the side of the aerosol was what looked like a small metal box. A piece of whitish plastic covered a Fresnel lens. His blood ran cold. It was a passive infrared sensor triggered by body heat. He knew that inside would be two infrared-sensitive photo diodes or phototransistors. They would be bonded to a piece of metal to ensure that their temperature and sensitivity were about the same.

He knew that passive infrared sensors reacted only to drastic changes in levels of infrared radiation emitted in the surveillance area, usually caused by the movement of a person or persons. The sensors were popular among insurgents in Iraq and Afghanistan, who used them as motion triggers for roadside bombs.

"Sir, we've got another problem," O'Hare said, and then he relayed the bad news.

"Kevin, get back from there, do you hear me? Do you copy?"

O'Hare's heart began to hammer. "Sir, please, someone needs to try and disable this. Let me keep on trying."

"Kevin, get the hell out of there," Horowitz said. "We need to seal this vent up."

Suddenly, there was a flash of white light and an almighty explosion that deafened O'Hare. He was in a world of silence. Then a white, powdery cloud filled his vision.

———

Meyerstein was watching the feed from O'Hare's camera, transfixed. Her team stared in disbelief and shock as events unfolded. Puffs of what looked like fine dust filled the screen.

"Max, speak to me," she said. "What are the readings?"

"Hang on a few moments, Martha . . . the readings from Kevin's bacterial spore detector are just coming in. Now . . . Shit, his alarm's going off! Martha, it's gone off! One of those devices is spraying out the spores right now."

Martha and her team could only look on, aghast. Then phones began ringing.

"We'll need fifteen minutes to confirm if this is indeed the virus."

"I think we've got to assume the worst," Meyerstein said. "We must prevent widespread contamination, Max."

"I'll let you know as soon as we have something."

The line went dead.

———

Fifteen minutes later, the phones were still ringing like crazy. Meyerstein had just ended a terse conversation with the President's National Security Advisor when Horowitz called to say that the substance had tested positive. There had been a confirmed biological attack on New York City. But it had been contained, the air ducts sealed off, the building evacuated.

As she struggled to come to terms with the enormity of what had happened, a live feed from FBI Headquarters came through. The welcome face of Special Agent Stephanie Carlyle was staring back at her, surrounded by the rest of the team on the fifth floor.

"I'm hoping for good news, Stephanie."

"We have something which appears linked to our investigation," Carlyle said. "We're putting this into the system as we speak."

"What have you got, Steph?"

"We've been speaking to the wife of a former NSA contractor, Thomas Wesley. This guy gets a knock at the door in the middle of the night. It's the DCIS and he's asked to go with them for questioning. But this is where it gets interesting. His wife calls the family lawyer to get Wesley representation. When the lawyer calls DCIS, they don't know anything about it. The wife is very concerned, naturally, and contacts the FBI."

Meyerstein sighed. "Steph, what's this got to do with our investigation?"

"Wesley used to have the highest clearance, so had access to all categories of information the NSA gathered, until they sacked him after he made a big faux pas and subsequently lost his security clearance."

Meyerstein rolled her eyes and shook her head. "Enough of the background. Will you please get to the point?"

"We have two of our guys in Maryland speaking to the wife. Wesley recently met with an old friend of his, Congressman Lance Drake, about a decrypted intercept call that had alarmed him, and no one was taking seriously. His wife said he was working on an intercept call shortly before he was dismissed, which apparently he'd decrypted. He continued working on it in secret at home. But here's the kicker—he believed he'd decrypted something about some kind of threat to America."

Meyerstein felt a growing sense of excitement. "What kind of threat?"

"We don't know. But she said it had become an obsession, and he'd bombarded Congressman Drake, imploring him to listen."

"Why didn't we know about this?"

"His wife said he tried to contact the NSA, but no one would listen to him."

"This is a goddamn huge red flag if ever there was one." Meyerstein thought back to all the missing pieces of the jigsaw that could have prevented the 9/11 attacks.

"Wesley's wife said he broke down one night, said he was scared. He wanted people to listen—he was talking about a terrorist attack, but no one wanted to know. Eventually he decided to speak to the congressman."

"What about Wesley's computers? Laptops? Cell phones?"

"They were all taken away last night."

"Goddamn."

Meyerstein considered her options for a few moments before she spoke. "I want the two best computer specialists we have over to Congressman Drake's office. And I want two more at his home. Roy will get this approved. We need to find out if Wesley sent any emails to Drake. And I want everything we can get on Thomas Wesley. Get back to me as soon as you possibly can."

Meyerstein paced the room, and looked out of the window at the skyscrapers on the Upper East Side. The smart apartments, the glass towers—only yards from Central Park, and hundreds of miles away from her family in the Washington suburbs.

Less than an hour later, the link to the Strategic Information Operations Center buzzed into life. The face of computer specialist Special Agent Johnny Lopez was on the screen.

Meyerstein said, "OK, what have your team got?"

"The personal laptop of Congressman Drake has just been analyzed by us. The emails sent by Thomas Wesley I've just forwarded to you. They were heavily encrypted, but we've decrypted them all, hundreds of them."

"Good work." She turned and looked over to one of her colleagues, who gave the thumbs-up sign as he studied Wesley's emails. "How did Congressman Drake react when you guys turned up and said you'd need to scan his computers?"

"Smug pain in the ass, if you must know, talking about infringement of civil liberties—you know the spiel."

Meyerstein looked at the emails on the laptop in front of her. "Gimme a few moments," she said as she speed-read the most recent messages. "Wesley claims the conversation he decrypted is about a threat to national security."

She looked up at the screen and saw Lopez grinning from ear to ear. "You have something else, don't you?"

"I've left the best till last. We have a clean recording of the decrypted conversation Thomas Wesley gave Congressman Drake."

Meyerstein clenched her fist. "That's what I want!"

"It was on an iPod, and our analysis shows that the voices have been demorphed. This Wesley is a genius, stripping it right back."

Meyerstein felt elated. "Get this to me right now."

Lopez nodded. "Look, we're still working our way through the emails, but he doesn't name names. Wesley has simply given the recording of the decrypted conversation to Drake, but doesn't indicate who is talking. We're still working on it ourselves. Freddie Limonton and his team are also involved."

"I want those voices identified. Check and double-check and then check it again before you speak to me. I don't want ninety percent certainties. I want one hundred percent or nothing. Do you hear me?"

"You got it." He paused. "There's something else."

"What?"

"Freddie says there are discrepancies he hadn't spotted earlier."

"What kind of discrepancies?"

"An embedded message."

"Who's working on this?"

"We've got the best steganalysts working on it right now. But it's proving a tough nut to crack."

"I don't want excuses, I want answers."

Meyerstein stood and stared at the eerie pictures beamed back from Lower Manhattan. Clouds of powder still floating in the aluminum duct. Her blood pressure hiked up a notch as she thought of what the embedded message contained. A final target? Was that it?

She looked around at her team. "Where is Thomas Wesley? Who were the guys who took him from his house? I want answers, people."

Twenty-Nine

Thomas Wesley came to in darkness. He was blindfolded. He tried to move his hands, but felt tight leather straps cut into his wrists. He ached all over. He slowly realized he was tied to a chair. Hands behind his back, ankles strapped tight to the legs of the chair. A wave of anxiety swept over him as he wondered what was going to happen to him. He struggled hard to get free, but the straps only cut deeper into his wrists.

His heart was pounding, and he felt as though he was about to hyperventilate. He took deep breaths and tried to control the panic that was spreading through his brain. His lips were parched, and there was a chemical aftertaste in his mouth.

"Thomas," a man's voice echoed from somewhere behind him. It sounded like the man from the DCIS who had interviewed him before. "I'm sorry it's come to this, really I am. All you have to do is tell us who knows about this, and you'll be free to go."

"Who are you? Where am I? Please, I just want to go back home to my wife."

"Thomas, I can only help you so far. We know that you've given details to Congressman Lance Drake. But I can't believe that's the only person you told. That's not a realistic proposition. What I'm saying is that there must be others who know about this. Friends, perhaps. Your wife."

"I swear, it was only myself, the NSA, and Lance. But I didn't tell them the full story. Only the gist of it."

"I find that very hard to believe, Thomas."

The man's voice now had a harder edge. Wesley sensed the man was standing in front of him. He smelled cologne mixed with stale cigarette smoke, and felt sick to the bottom of his stomach. What the hell was going on? Who were these guys?

"Who else in the NSA knows about this?"

Wesley sighed. "The Inspector General. One or two others. But they didn't listen to what I had."

A long silence opened up.

"What about your wife?" the man asked.

"What about her?"

"I can't believe for one minute that she doesn't know about the recording and who's on it."

"Listen to me, she doesn't know."

"Thomas, nothing would make us happier than if you could just go back home. Go back to your wife. But you've got to look at it from our point of view. It doesn't look good. We're talking national security. This is not a fucking game."

Wesley said nothing.

A deep sigh. "Thomas, I'm a regular guy, just like you. I'm a Midwestern boy, too."

"Where you from?"

"Not far from where you grew up, in Galena, Illinois. Small-town boy, same as you. Same good American values. Hard work, honesty. We both love our country, right, Thomas?"

"Absolutely."

"So let's just try and get along, so we can both get back to our families. Now, I feel like I'm repeating myself, but I need to clarify your position, Thomas. Who else knows about this apart from Lance Drake?"

"The NSA and Lance and myself, and that's it. And they don't know who's on the tape. That's the God's honest truth. And it doesn't matter how many times you ask that question, I'll still give you the same reply. I can't say something that isn't true."

"You're not making this easy for yourself. I'm sorry you've not been more forthcoming, Thomas. Really I am. You seem like a decent enough kind of guy. Smart. But there's only so much time I can spare before I have to hand you over."

Wesley smelled the man's sour breath close by, as if he were stooping down beside him.

"What do you mean, hand me over? Who are you? You're not DCIS!"

Wesley struggled against the straps, but after a few seconds he didn't have the energy to continue and his body slumped back in the chair. He broke down and wept, unable to stop the long, deep sobs. "Please, let me go home to my wife."

"I'm sorry, Thomas. We need answers. A colleague of mine is in the next room. He's not an understanding kind of guy like me."

Wesley felt sick. A sense of dread swept over him. He now began to feel what real fear was.

"Our man next door, he likes to be what some just think of as . . . thorough. Do you know what I'm talking about?"

"Who the hell are you? You aren't DCIS."

"I'm going to—"

"I'm an American. A patriot. You can't do this to me!"

A prolonged sigh. "Thomas, do you know how easy it is for people to disappear? To appear to kill themselves for no apparent reason?"

The words were spoken in a gentle manner, as if from a life coach. But to Wesley, they struck terror in his heart. He didn't dare think about what was about to happen. "I've told you what I know. I can't tell you anything else."

"You're in a basement with very thick walls. No one can hear any screams. Nothing. The sound just echoes around the room. It's a little while since we've used this room. Do you know what happened to the last person we brought down here?"

Wesley felt nauseous and light-headed, hot and anxious.

"They tell me he went mad." He let the words hang in the air, as if for effect.

Then the sound of the man's footsteps across the concrete floor, the heavy door opening and then slamming shut before it was locked.

Wesley was alone. A sense of dread and terror entered his soul. Terror of the unknown. He had heard stories about unlisted sites where high-value detainees were taken and tortured until they were broken; where no one knew they were there. Then they disappeared.

His mind was racing. He was an American. Why was this happening? What had all that to do with him? Who were these guys?

A few minutes later, the sound of the door opening and softer, muffled footsteps, as if the person were wearing rubber soles.

He jerked around feebly. "Who's there?"

He felt a sharp jab in the back of his neck.

"What the hell are you giving me?" He struggled again and clenched his teeth, desperate to escape. He inadvertently bit his lip and tasted blood. Suddenly, he felt a tingling run up and down his arm and then up his neck. His heart pounded hard. He felt a surge of adrenaline and struggled wildly against his restraints. But he was trapped.

A moment later, the blindfold was ripped from his face. He was in suffocating darkness. He squinted as his eyes took a few seconds to adjust, and he made out a silhouetted figure in front of him. The figure turned and left the room, and the door slammed shut.

The minutes went by in the still, black basement. Then, suddenly, the fluorescent lights flickered to life, flooding the room with a harsh white glow. Wesley screwed up his eyes. It took him several moments before he could see properly. He looked around. Whitewashed walls in a windowless room. The metal chair he was strapped to had been welded to a metal plate on the floor. The wrist and ankle straps were thick brown leather. The floor was concrete.

He felt completely at their mercy. He waited for the effects of whatever drugs he'd been given to take hold.

Slowly, almost imperceptibly at first, he saw flakes of white paint fall from the wall. Then a pulsing sound emanated from the cracks in the wall. It got louder. And louder. The deep bass sound of hip-hop.

Military-loud. Assailing his senses.

Wesley felt as if his eardrums were going to explode. The hypnotic and terrifying beats were cranked up a notch for several moments. The flakes of white paint became like snow, falling from the wall. Underneath, from the cracks in the bricks, emerged insects.

He watched, transfixed, as dozens of beetles appeared. Then scores. Then hundreds. Swarming out of the bricks.

He shut his eyes tight to block out the image as his heart pounded faster and harder. He felt liquid dripping onto his face. He forced his eyelids open and looked up to the ceiling. Blood was dripping down onto the chair and onto him. He looked down at his feet. Maggots, swarming all over.

He looked at his hands and saw worms emerge from his cuticles.

Wesley started screaming as the lights were switched off. He saw snakes crawling in the bloody darkness, circling him. Heard dark, whispered voices in his head. He felt sick and his insides moved. Dark vomit spewed from his mouth down his front.

The sour smell made him cry. He sobbed as rats squeezed through the cracks in the walls and swarmed all over him. They were chewing his ankles and neck, and he felt their piercing bites sink into his skin. He screamed and screamed as he was swallowed up by the darkness.

Wesley was aware of leaves blowing through the trees as he was walked through a darkened wood. He tried to open his eyes but couldn't. He heard them talking about the canoe. It would be found at the same time. Step by step. Legs heavy, brain woozy.

He tried to open his eyes again. Murky darkness. Blurred rocks and fast-moving water. He wanted to struggle, but nothing happened. He felt a jab in his neck and he collapsed in the mud. He tried to move but he couldn't. Paralyzed.

He thought of his wife and saw her smiling eyes. He was sure he could hear her talking to him.

Hold on, my darling. I won't be long. I'll get you out of there.

Her voice echoed in his head like an angelic whisper. He wanted to see her face, but he couldn't see a thing. Then he forced himself to open his eyes. Standing above him, blurred, was the man who had interviewed him. His face was partially hidden in the shadows from the trees. Then he felt the water lapping around his mouth and into his lungs.

He felt himself floating on the black water. On the far shore, he saw the blurred silhouettes of two men walking back through the woods.

Thirty

The feed from the FBI's New York field office showed WMD agents in Hazmat suits scouring the air ducts for other lethal weapons. It never ceased to amaze Meyerstein how brave and selfless her colleagues could be. The public didn't know the half of it.

Another screen had a Fox News anchorman speculating that the building may have been leaking dangerous asbestos. But she knew that line—or any line—could not stand up indefinitely.

Hundreds of special agents across America were trawling numerous encrypted calls, emails, and security-video footage culled from the NSA. A specialist team was working on Thomas Wesley's recordings. Meyerstein was focused on two objectives: tracking down Scott Caan and identifying the two people talking on the tape.

The face of Freddie Limonton, the bureau's top computer expert in Washington, appeared on one of the huge screens. He looked bug-eyed as he hooked up to the videoconference facility.

Meyerstein had known Limonton since she joined the bureau. At the time, the atmosphere of sexism and racism were still ingrained from the Hoover generation of special agents. It was a world where the Anglo-Saxon male was king. But Limonton was always a loner, didn't enjoy the locker-room atmosphere, and just got on with his job. He was Jewish, like her, and was often the butt of anti-Semitic jokes from a hardcore few of the old school. When caricatures of hook-nosed moneylenders were taped to his desk or computer screen, he just shrugged his shoulders and smiled. Meyerstein fumed, but as the years went by, the culture began to disappear as a new generation of smarter special agents emerged, changing the FBI for good.

On the screen, Limonton cleared his throat.

"Freddie, can you hear and see me?"

"Loud and clear."

"OK, you guys have been working on this a helluva long time, Freddie. This better be good."

Freddie remained stone-faced. "I've had my best guys working on this flat out, Martha, gimme a break."

"What have you got?"

"We've been trying to figure out why we can't get a location trace with our face recognition software. It's the best there is. But we've had nothing. A few close things, but nothing concrete."

Meyerstein looked at her watch, which showed it was 7:09 a.m. "You want to get to the point? I'm due to hook up with the Director in six minutes precisely."

Freddie smiled, panda shadows around his eyes and stubble on his chin. He clicked to open a file, and the profile of what looked like a youthful middle-aged man with longish hair appeared on one of the big screens.

Slowly it dawned on Meyerstein what Freddie Limonton was going on about. "Goddamn son of a bitch." She stared long and hard at the image. "What are we talking about? Some form of facial surgery, is that it?"

"Dead on. Within the last forty-eight hours. But of the non-invasive variety."

"I'm not an expert in that area, although I could probably do with the same sort of work." Her self-deprecating humor made Freddie smile.

"We've talked to two Beverly Hills plastic surgeons and sent them the photos, before and after. They both came back with the same analysis. Caan has had three bits of work done. Firstly, a nose job—non-surgical rhinoplasty, which only takes about an hour. A soft-tissue filler is injected in small amounts under the nasal skin to change the shape and contour of the nose. Typically, it's used to straighten a crooked nose, but the opposite has happened here, and that would throw off the readings in the central region of the face. Secondly, there was a brow lift and eye lift, created by Botox."

Meyerstein nodded, seeing how the changes had affected the contours and profile.

"I'm told it can also remedy a fleshy brow or one that is naturally lined. Compare and contrast." He clicked again. "It shows noticeable differences between the forehead area before and after. The third thing is the cheekbones. Collagen filler. Changes the shape of the face, don't you think?"

Meyerstein walked up to the plasma screen and took a closer look. "Son of a bitch."

"The cumulative effects of all these small changes on Caan's face have, in effect, fooled our best face-recognition systems. I'm telling you, this guy is good."

The conference room door behind her opened and Special Agent Tom Jackson shouted across, "Director's on the feed in the briefing room across the corridor, and wants you now, Martha."

"Tell him I'll be there in a couple minutes."

"I can't say that, Martha."

"I'll speak to him in two minutes." Her tone was cold.

Jackson blushed and nodded before disappearing.

"Now, listen to me, Freddie. Is this a true match? I can't afford any errors at all. I need to be certain that this is Caan."

"It's him. We checked out the changes, and realized immediately why the face recognition wasn't finding him. Then we ran this face." He clicked again. A long-haired man wearing glasses descended the stairs of Penn Station in downtown Manhattan, caught on camera. He froze the image. "This is our guy. One hundred percent match."

Meyerstein's heart was beating harder as she stared at the image. "Train station. You must have his destination."

He opened two more image files: the back of the long-haired man boarding an Acela Express, then the same man emerging from the train onto the concourse of Union Station, Washington, DC.

A few moments later, Meyerstein was in the briefing room across the corridor and flicked a switch to commence an emergency videoconference that included the Directors of the FBI, SIOC, NCTC, the White House Situation Room, and Langley.

"OK, Assistant Director Martha Meyerstein here. I'll lead, if that's OK."

The Director spoke up, his voice gravelly and strained. "You got a development, Martha?"

"We most certainly have, sir. Caan has changed his physical appearance. The still images from Penn Station are being sent to you now."

The Director cleared his throat. He stared at the image that had just appeared on his monitor. "Good God."

"This man, ladies and gentlemen, is Lieutenant Colonel Scott Caan. We have reason to believe he smuggled out three vials of a hybrid virus from the biofacility in Maryland. We believe he is an integral part of a highly sophisticated operation to attack America, and we believe he is in Washington, DC, intent on recreating what has happened in Manhattan."

A silence opened up for a few moments, as if everyone was letting the information sink in.

O'Donoghue spoke first. "So, where do we go from here? Tell me about Thomas Wesley. What the hell was going on there?"

"What indeed?" said Meyerstein. "It's a mess. The NSA claim they know nothing about any decrypted intercept. We have people working on the recording given to Congressman Drake. We hope to identify the two people by the end of the day."

"You hope? Is that what we're relying on?"

"We have our best people on it, sir."

"What about Wesley?"

"DCIS deny taking him out. He's disappeared off the radar."

"What about Luntz?"

"The latest I have from Dr. Horowitz is that Luntz is working on antivirals with every available scientist at our disposal. But this is going to take time, something we don't have."

O'Donoghue shook his head. "So where does the investigation go from here? I assume there's full interagency cooperation?"

"Across the board, sir. The investigation's focus is now on Washington. It makes sense from a terrorist's point of view—the seat of government. We have to assume that Caan didn't use all the virus in New York."

O'Donoghue scribbled on a pad, nodding quickly.

"But we need to keep this very, very tight," Meyerstein continued. "Circulate the photo we have. Working his new image into Washington transport hubs and shopping malls to try and get a position on this guy. He must be staying somewhere. So we have all the hotels, hostels, guest houses, you name it—all their surveillance footage scanned."

O'Donoghue looked up. "We've got to be cautious that we don't alert Caan or cause any panic among the public."

"Absolutely, sir. We're just informing each hotel's head of security, usually someone who is former military, Fed, or police, so there's no problem."

The Director leaned back in his seat. "You got the scientist for us, Martha. That was terrific work. And now we've got a city for Scott Caan. But we're still missing the endgame location. We're playing catch-up."

"I'm well aware of that, sir. Our best analysts are going through everything we have. Email traffic, hidden files, but it's tightly encrypted. We're also scouring all the electronic devices and computers owned by Norton and Weiss in Miami. We're leaving no stone unturned, I can assure you, sir. It's just a matter of time."

"Something we don't have, Martha."

A knock at the door, and Roy Stamper walked in.

Martha turned around and glared at him. "Middle of a video-conference, Roy."

"They've just dragged a body out of the Potomac. A man in his late forties, or early fifties perhaps. Near the Chain Bridge on the Virginia side. He had a suicide note wrapped in cellophane in one of his pockets."

"Who is it?"

"It looks like Thomas Wesley, the missing analyst."

———

The mood among Meyerstein and her team as they were driven to the 34th Street Heliport was of quiet determination. It was important to remain focused.

Via a secure iPad, she monitored the real-time events in downtown Manhattan, and a feed to SIOC on the fifth floor at FBI Headquarters.

The cold realization that a bioterrorist attack might be in the offing in the nation's capital made her think again of her children. Their school was in Bethesda. Her gut instinct was telling her to call the principal and get her children back to the safety of their house. But she knew that would be against all protocols, and would also jeopardize the news blackout, especially if the principal suspected something was amiss.

A few minutes later, two choppers whisked them out to Newark, New Jersey. Then they transferred to the Gulfstream jet that was already waiting for them. Within moments of the plane taking off into the bright winter sunshine, climbing steeply as they headed south to Washington, Meyerstein's phone on her armrest rang.

It was from one of the SIOC team, Reed Steel.

"It's Reznick."

"What about him?"

"He's gone missing."

"What are you talking about? He's in a goddamn naval hospital. Two of our guys are babysitting him, for Chrissakes."

"Calm down, Martha."

"No, I won't calm down. Tell me what the hell happened."

He sighed. "After Reznick spoke to you earlier, he complained of being unwell. Dizzy, nauseous. The doctors examined him. They said he was mentally and physically exhausted. Traumatized by what he'd been through. They prescribed a couple sleeping tablets so he could sleep the rest of the day."

Meyerstein closed her eyes for a moment and groaned.

"It appears Reznick went for a lie down in a quiet room. But when someone went to check on him a short while ago, they found he was gone."

"Well, that's just great. You want to explain how he was gone?"

"I mean he pushed back some ceiling tiles and escaped from the main part of the hospital. A soldier's civilian clothes are missing from a locker, along with his car. We think Reznick just drove out the front gate."

"You better be kidding me, Reed."

"Afraid not. It's a fuck-up, I know."

"I'll deal with this later. Alert the team about Reznick."

"What do you think he's gonna do?"

"I just hope he stays in Florida. I've got enough on my plate to last a lifetime."

She ended the call. Almost immediately, her phone rang again.

"Martha, we got something else." It was Freddie Limonton. "We've cracked it!"

"Give me what you've got."

"It's an embedded message within the audio signal."

Meyerstein felt her stomach tighten. She knew how good Limonton and his team were. "What does it contain?"

"The encrypted conversation is banal. The sort of conversation no one would give a second thought to, right?"

Meyerstein ground her teeth in frustration as she waited for Limonton to get to the point. "Could this have been intended for Caan?"

"You got it. Caan is super bright. If he had a decoder and the cell phone number of the guy who made the call . . . with his knowledge, that's a serious possibility."

"OK, explain."

"This is classic stuff. When we were running the tests for the voices and the conversation, we found that there was a short data message hidden within the conversation Wesley had decrypted. Data-hiding in audio signals is incredibly challenging, as it covers such a wide range."

"I need to know what it contains, Freddie."

"I'm getting to that. Martha, I've just been told you're on your way to Washington, right?"

"That's right."

"The embedded message was hiding a target address in Washington."

"Where?"

Limonton let out a long sigh. "Two South Rotary Road."

"Where the hell is that?"

"It's the postal address for the Pentagon Metro station."

A short while later, as the jet headed south en route to Washington, DC, the most senior officials from each government agency were on the videoconferencing facility. The bank of TV screens in the plane came on, showing the White House Situation Room, which was located on the first floor of the West Wing. It showed the Joint Chiefs of Staff, the CIA Director, and the National Security Advisor, among others. A separate screen showed the members of Meyerstein's team who were in the SIOC command center at FBI Headquarters.

Horowitz kicked off proceedings. "My team has talked through the scenarios until we're blue in the face. Bottom line? We believe Caan may change tack. While he used aerosol devices in the air ducts, I believe that if the Pentagon Metro station is the target, and he's mobile, he'll be carrying the virus in small lightweight containers. I think he'll release the virus on the train tracks, or on an escalator leading to the Pentagon concourse, or perhaps a crowded car. He'll either discreetly smash the containers, or simply open them to release the biomaterial."

A ripple of turbulence shook the plane as Meyerstein said, "The rushing trains would help keep the virus aloft and efficiently spread it around the platform. It would take the virus right into the heart of the Pentagon, unseen by its thousands of employees, right?"

Horowitz nodded. "That's the scenario my analysts and I envisage—"

Meyerstein put up her hand and Horowitz went quiet. "If this virus was allowed to escape in the cars and tunnels of the Metro, and to infect the Pentagon workers riding the Metro—then, unbeknown to them, they are potentially infecting each and every person who works at the Pentagon. Within a matter of days, the Department of Defense could be wiped out. Nearly twenty-three thousand staff."

Richard Blake, the national security advisor, leaned back in his seat and shook his head. "In the name of God."

A few moments later, once the enormity of what they faced had sunk in and everyone had composed themselves, Horowitz answered a few more technical queries about the virus and when the antivirals and vaccine would be ready. Then Meyerstein took questions for another fifteen minutes, mostly focused on the whereabouts of Scott Caan. The tone was businesslike and brisk. No one was panicking or pointing fingers. It was just a matter of "Let's find this guy, let's neutralize his threat, and let's destroy the organization and people behind this attack."

A media blackout was agreed, as no one wanted widespread panic.

"One final thing," Meyerstein said. "We need to shut down the Washington Metro system. We can blame electrical faults. But we've got to close it down until this threat has passed."

Blake shook his head. "That's not gonna happen, Martha. If we close it down, the word will leak out why the whole Metro has ground to a halt. You can guarantee it. And then all hell would break loose."

"I'm sorry, sir, and with respect, but we cannot have people riding the Metro until this threat is over."

"The Pentagon is of the belief that if this gets into the hands of the transport authority, then it will definitely leak. Mass panic guaranteed."

Martha struggled to contain her fury. "Then it should be on a need-to-know basis. We need the cooperation of the Metro Transit Police. But we need to close down this threat."

"Martha, the decision has been made. Fine, let one person at the transit police know. The chief. He'll cooperate, he's ex-army. But the Metro has to stay open or this whole thing will come out."

"You can't think about it like that. The risk of people being infected is huge. And the personnel within the Pentagon . . . You can't risk this."

"Martha, the decision's been made. Let's find this Scott Caan and neutralize him—now."

After the plane landed at Dulles, Meyerstein and her team were taken the short distance to Arlington, and then underground into the Pentagon Metro station. She saw plainclothes FBI Special Weapons and Tactics operatives in evidence as she was taken to an office that overlooked the platform.

A burly man stepped forward. It was Lester Michaels, chief of the Metro Transit Police. "What the hell is going on?" he asked. "I was told you might have answers."

Martha stared back at him. "I've checked your resume. You have classified clearance, you're former army intelligence. You know the drill, right?"

"That's right."

"If this leaks out, you'll be hung out to dry. Do you hear me?"

"Do you mind telling me what the situation is?"

"The situation is we believe a man with bioweapons is planning to release them at this very station. We don't know when. Or even how. Now, have I got your attention and absolute cooperation?"

Michaels just nodded, expression neutral. "Most certainly. What do you want from us?"

"I believe you have Counterterrorism officers on your team?"

"Twenty."

"I want them all assigned to the line through Pentagon Metro. I want them to work alongside the FBI on this very sensitive operation. Can you do that?"

"I can do that."

Meyerstein handed him a printout of Scott Caan, before and after. "This is the guy. He's white. In his thirties. Has had non-invasive surgery in the last forty-eight hours."

"What the hell is that?"

"Botox injections, collagen filler around his cheeks, nose job. Should be noticeable, although he might be wearing a hat, maybe a wig, makeup. We need to neutralize him. He may be carrying containers of biomatter which he intends to release in cars, perhaps on the station concourse."

Michaels looked at the photos and shook his head. "Is this for real? This ain't some dumbass training exercise, is it?"

"Sadly, this is as real as it gets."

Her cell phone rang, interrupting the conversation, and she signaled that she needed to take the call.

"Yeah—Meyerstein speaking."

"How are you?" It was Reznick.

She placed a finger in her ear to block out a train pulling up. "I'm sorry, this isn't a good time." A rumbling sound in the background. "Jon, where are you?"

"In Washington, the same as you."

Meyerstein froze. "What's going on, Jon?"

"Why don't you come out and ask me?"

Meyerstein looked at a monitor showing the platform and gasped. Staring back up at her was Jon Reznick, cell phone pressed to his ear.

Thirty-One

Two Feds, both sporting dark overcoats, walked up to Reznick as a phalanx of officers surrounded Meyerstein. The taller of the two Feds stood in front of Reznick. He had to be at least six foot nine, and over two hundred and fifty pounds.

"We need to search you," he said.

Reznick put his hands on his head. "Go right ahead."

The man frisked Reznick. He produced a miniature GPS receiver and a cell phone. He handed them over to his colleague, who bagged the items. "Now, I'm going to search you once again, for hidden weapons. Are you OK with that?"

Reznick nodded.

Again the man rifled in his jacket pockets, patted around his ankles for knives. And checked his back for hidden guns. But Reznick wasn't packing.

The huge Fed turned around as Meyerstein approached. "He's fine."

Meyerstein brushed past her colleagues and stood staring at Reznick. "I thought we were done."

"So did I."

"You mind explaining why you're here?"

"I want to help."

"Jon, let's quit playing games. How the hell did you find me?"

Reznick said nothing.

Meyerstein stepped forward, her face within a few inches of his. The smell of her fresh, citrus perfume again. "Look, either you tell me how you found us or you'll be hauled away in handcuffs. Your call."

Reznick let out a long sigh. "You have a secure cell phone, right?"

Meyerstein nodded.

"It also has GPS. I know a guy who provides a service to private detectives. If he has a cell phone number, he can pinpoint a cellular call to within a twenty-five- to hundred-yard radius of the caller. He just pings the cell phone. Even secure cell phones. Should try it some day."

Meyerstein stood, face impassive. Nonplussed, big time. He found her very attractive. Her simmering anger was controlled, which he liked. And he could see she wasn't scared of him. He liked that as well. A lot.

"I assume you know that's illegal."

Reznick was silent.

"Look, Jon, I'd have thought you'd want to spend time with Lauren."

"There's nothing more I can do at the hospital. She's coming out of the coma."

"Don't you want to be there for her?"

"It's not a question of wanting to be with her now. It's a question of making sure she has a safe future. You heard the threats against my family. Well, I want to try and help you. In any capacity I can."

"Jon, that's not going to happen. This isn't your fight."

"That's where you're wrong."

Meyerstein stared him down.

"Do you mind if I put my hands down?"

Meyerstein nodded.

Reznick lowered his hands and felt acutely conscious that all eyes were on him.

"Look," she said, "we're dealing with a very serious situation here, but it's all in hand."

"Is it? I'm offering to help in any way I can. Advice, situational awareness, you name it."

"We have our own experts, Jon. Besides, the FBI has rules."

"You know the first rule I ever learned when I joined Special Forces?"

Meyerstein shook her head.

"The first rule is that there are no rules. You've got to use your initiative. Like you did down in Key West. Don't be restricted by some dumbass rules and regulations. Are you serious about finding the people behind all this?"

"Jon, look, I don't have time for this." Meyerstein signaled to the huge Fed to take Reznick away. The guy reached out to grab Reznick's arm, but he easily shrugged him off.

Meyerstein nodded to the Fed to hold off.

Reznick said, "OK, answer me this. Did you manage to trace the guy who called me on the hospital phone?"

Meyerstein shook her head. "We're working on it."

"What about the bioterrorism threat? They're targeting Washington, aren't they? You're trying to track them down, right here and now. Is that it?"

"Look, I can't say any more."

"You don't have to. I can help you."

Meyerstein let out a light sigh.

"I handed over the scientist to you. And you let me get my daughter. But don't shut me out now."

Meyerstein looked at him long and hard, as if trying to figure him out. "Jon, I have specialist FBI units who train for this kind of thing."

"You don't think I know that? You wanna know who trains them? Guys like me. I've trained countless teams at Quantico or the Farm down the years. I've trained SWAT teams—you name it."

Meyerstein's cell phone rang. "Don't move," she said as she walked toward the rest of the Feds on the platform. She put her cell phone into an inside pocket and was handed another cell. She nodded as she listened to whoever was on the line, and glanced around occasionally to check on Reznick. Two minutes later, he heard her say, "Yes, sir, right away."

She handed the cell phone back and approached Reznick, flanked by four Feds.

"I've got work to do. So you need to go with my men to an FBI mobile command center in the parking lot of the adjacent mall, right now."

Reznick said nothing.

"This isn't your fight, Jon."

"Isn't it?"

Meyerstein ran a hand through her hair and he saw the steely expression on her face. "I don't know if you're just nuts or what."

"I aced all my psychological tests. I work better than almost anyone on the planet under extreme stress. Look, any fucking malcontent can kill or pull the trigger. But it takes a certain type of person with real expertise to make sure you get the right target. Can't you see what I'm saying? I can help you."

"Goddamn, what's wrong with you?"

"What's wrong with me? I don't know when to quit, that's what's wrong with me. Never have. And not when my family's involved."

"This is personal now with you, isn't it?"

"Someone has threatened to kill me and my daughter, and you ask if it's personal. What do you think?"

"I'm having a real bad day, Jon. This doesn't help me one iota. It's only given me another headache."

"Look, I didn't come all this way just to kick my heels. So do me a favor. Let me in."

Meyerstein shook her head and smiled. Then she walked away as her team of Feds surrounded Reznick.

Thirty-Two

It was a seventeen-minute drive under leaden December skies from Arlington, across the 14th Street Bridge, to FBI Headquarters in downtown Washington. Meyerstein sat up front in the passenger seat beside the experienced driver, Will Collins, with three of the most senior members of her team, including Stamper, crammed in the back. No one spoke during the short journey, and Meyerstein welcomed the quiet time to think through the fast-moving investigation. She thought of Caan. Then she thought of Reznick.

They were nearing the endgame, and Caan was somewhere in America's capital city. She knew her team were closing in. But Caan was still on the loose.

She noticed her hand, which was resting on her lap, shaking, but maybe that was down to caffeine and lack of sleep.

The traffic was bumper to bumper as they crawled through the downtown traffic. Past sidewalks with people laden with Christmas shopping. Eventually they pulled up at the security booth at the entrance to the FBI's parking garage. She flashed her ID at the armed security officer, who scanned it with a mobile reader. Then the rest of her team did the same. A beep from the reader confirmed their identities, and they were waved through to her designated parking space.

Meyerstein and her team took the elevator straight up to the command center on the fifth floor. The air of tension was palpable. Ninety percent of those inside were on the phone, other phones ringing unanswered. Printers churning out paper, updates shouted across the room, tasks being given, TVs turned onto news channels.

"OK, people," she said, clapping her hands to get their attention. "Let's try and keep it down. We need to focus. First, can we bring up the map of the Washington Metro network on the screens?"

James Handley, a Metro expert who'd been brought in, clicked a computer mouse and it duly appeared.

"OK, James," Meyerstein said, taking her seat. "Give me an overview and we'll take it from there. And keep it broad-brush."

Handley got to his feet and pushed back his chair. "The Metro network includes six lines, ninety-one stations and one hundred and seventeen miles of track. The system makes extensive use of interlining—running more than one service on the same track."

"And we're not just talking about one jurisdiction, right?" Meyerstein interjected.

Handley nodded. "There are forty stations in the District of Columbia, fifteen in Prince George's County, eleven in Montgomery County, eleven in Arlington County, six in Fairfax County, and three in the City of Alexandria. About fifty miles of the Metro is underground."

"How many stations are underground?"

Handley shared more information, which made the monumental task of monitoring the network clear to all.

Meyerstein stood up again. "OK, that's enough, thanks. So, Metro Center is the hub. That may or may not be important." She turned and looked at the screen showing the network layout. "Bring up Metro Center—facts and figures, maps, entrances, whatever."

She scanned the details and something jumped straight out at her. "Hang on, hang on." She focused on the Metro Center layout on the huge screen, in particular an adjacent area of the building's plans showing a hotel. Her years within the FBI had honed her analytical skills. But this was something else. Intuition, perhaps.

Then again, maybe it was just a hunch.

"What is it?" Handley asked.

Meyerstein looked around at the group and pointed at the map. "This is the Grand Hyatt. A rather nice hotel in the Penn Quarter. But it also has lobby access to the Washington Metro system."

Stamper whistled. "Jeez."

Meyerstein pointed across at Freddie Limonton. "Run the face recognition program for the cameras in and around the Hyatt. How long will it take?"

Freddie punched in some commands on his laptop. "If he's been there, a few moments."

The few moments seemed like a lifetime to Meyerstein.

"OK, we got something." He pressed a couple of keys and an image appeared on the screens. A casually dressed man with collar-length blond hair, wearing a button-down pale blue shirt, slacks, and tan shoes, a brown satchel slung over his shoulder, carrying a quilted navy jacket.

Freddie zoomed in for a close-up shot.

"Scott Caan, leaving the Hyatt forty-two minutes ago."

Meyerstein felt herself grinding her teeth. She moved closer to the screens to get a better look. "Shit, he's on the move, people! Get this image out to all our guys. He's probably wearing the navy jacket." She looked across at Freddie. "Get on to the Hyatt. What name has he been signed in under? When did he arrive? We need to search his room. We need a team on the ground at the hotel now. OK, run this image for all stations on this line."

Freddie punched a few keys. A minute later, another image appeared on the screen. "This is Scott Caan getting off the Blue Line train at Crystal City."

Meyerstein stepped within a few feet of the screens, the image of Caan looming large over her. He was still carrying the satchel but now, as she thought, wearing the blue jacket. "Damn. That's two stops farther down the track than the Pentagon Metro. What the hell is he playing at?" She turned and looked around at her team. "Crystal City is home to numerous defense contractors and satellite offices of the Pentagon. Is that what this is about? Is this a stopping-off point? A base camp? Let's open this up, people. I want your take on why Crystal City. Are we missing something?"

Jimmy Murphy, a senior all-source analyst, spoke up. "Well, as you'll know, a lot of Crystal City is underground. They've got a huge underground mall. Look, this guy is going to extraordinary lengths. He's had his face changed. He's got a new look. Maybe he's doing a run-through of the station. Is he checking that there's nothing out of the ordinary en route? This is meticulous detail. Does he suspect a tail?"

"Good points. But why Crystal City?"

Murphy cleared his throat. "I think he's being real cute. Perhaps he wanted to flush out any tail as he passed the Pentagon Metro."

"Definite possibility. I think we've also got to be alive to the possibility that there might be someone else with him. A wingman."

"In case Scott Caan is taken down. That would make perfect sense."

Meyerstein looked around at her team. She could see the focus and resolve on each and every one. "OK, people, get the word out." She turned and pointed to the image of Caan on the screen. "This man must not get on a train under any circumstances. He has to be apprehended, taken down—whatever it takes."

Thirty-Three

Reznick was sitting with three Feds in the back of a Suburban heading for the Crystal City mall, tapping his foot the whole way, his mind racing. He was wired, after discreetly popping his last two Dexedrine pills. He sat in silence, not wishing to engage the Feds in small talk—or any talk. He scanned the Glock 22s that they were packing and felt envious. He felt naked without a gun.

He had been allowed onto the team and had been briefed. He was going to be an "eyes and ears" guy on the ground. It felt good to be involved, even in a peripheral capacity. He had the before and after images of Caan imprinted on his brain. The plethora of small cosmetic changes had radically altered his face. It was bizarre. His face looked more swollen, despite looking younger. But both pictures still showed the same cold, dark eyes.

They parked alongside other government vehicles, next to the entrance of a suite of administration offices within the mall. Then they headed through some doors to an elevator, where they were met by two armed Metro cops who took them to an underground conference room. Meyerstein was already there, as were three other Fed teams. It would be four groups of four.

Meyerstein looked around for a few moments before she spoke, quietly exerting her will over the guys on the ground. She exuded gravitas just by the way she scanned the group. Her gaze stopped at Reznick for a brief moment before she went around the rest of the team.

"OK, this is what we've got. The Crystal City Shops span eight blocks. In effect, it's a network of tunnels and walkways. There are numerous exits and entrances. It's like a warren. But that's just underground. There are shops and offices on the higher floors, too. Three teams will concentrate on the underground level, and in and around the station, and one team will work the upper floors. First thing's first—I want the Red team assigned to the platform with me, and that includes you, Jon, OK?"

"You got it," Reznick said.

"Service frequency just now will be every three minutes. They come thick and fast, and platforms get crowded."

Everyone nodded.

"Any train to the Pentagon goes from this side of the platform. This is the Blue Line. The electronic boards on the platform show when a train is heading for Largo Town Center. Each train will have six cars and can cope with up to twelve hundred people. That's a helluva lot of people. Keep alert. You know what you've got to do. We have the Blue team and Green team heading down the mall from the opposite side. The White team's gonna do a walk-through sweep of the upper levels. Red team, spread out on the platform, no bunching up. This is a big, big area. But if we squeeze from both sides, we'll get him. It's just a matter of time. Any questions?"

Everyone shook their heads.

"OK," Meyerstein said. "Let's do this right. Stay sharp."

As the teams filtered out to the lower-level platform and into the mall, some taking the elevator to the higher floors, Meyerstein pulled Reznick aside. "OK, Jon, here's how it's gonna work. You'll follow my direct orders or Roy Stamper's. I've put my neck on the line for you, do you understand?"

Reznick nodded.

"You *will* respect my authority. If this gets out, your involvement will be denied. You don't exist as far as we're concerned. Do you understand?"

"Is this a shoot-to-kill op?"

"It is. But not for you, Jon. Your job will simply be as an extra pair of eyes and ears."

Reznick nodded again. He wanted a gun bad.

"Look, we don't know for sure, but there may be a wingman. And before you ask, we don't have an ID on him. There might not be one, but you need to be alive to that possibility. Do you understand?"

"Absolutely."

"You'll stay on the platform. Your job is to assist any requests from agents on that platform. It's the last line of defense. We must assume this is the day, and this is not a dry run. He must not get on a train. Instructions will go to and from the operations center at FBI Headquarters to us on the ground."

Reznick nodded.

"Remember your earpiece and microphone. Everything you say will be fed back to HQ. Bear that in mind."

Meyerstein led the way as the Red team—including Reznick—followed. He saw the way she commanded the utmost respect among all the agents. She was in control of her side of the operation.

They took the stairs down to the track level and fanned out along the busy platform. The curved roof was like a concrete honeycomb. Diffused lighting came from recessed lights. On the platform, around fifty or sixty people milled around.

He scanned, looking for the image that had been printed out in the back of the SUV and was now scorched into his brain.

Reznick knew the drill. He kept a neutral expression and began to mingle with the rest of the passengers. Occasionally, he glanced at his watch or the electronic destination board.

The voice of Stamper could be heard in his earpiece. "OK, guys," he said. "The cameras are trained on you. Nice and easy, Jeff, cover the entrance, lean against the wall. Excellent. Jon, you're right in among the throng, just stay there. Scratch your head if you heard that, Jon."

Reznick duly scratched his head.

"Good."

Reznick knew what to look for. He was on the lookout for the brown satchel Caan had walked out of the Grand Hyatt with. But he also knew that it would be easy to switch that to another bag or case.

"Panhandler at three o'clock, Jeff." Stamper's voice was strident, almost aggressive.

Reznick stole a glance at the disheveled old guy rummaging inside a filthy paper bag on the ground. Almost immediately, two burly Metro cops approached the panhandler and got him to his feet.

"OK, stand easy, guys," Stamper said.

The cops hustled the old guy away from the platform as they watched and waited. The seconds became minutes, and the minutes dragged. Slowly, almost imperceptibly, more and more people joined the platform. Reznick felt himself getting pressed up against other bodies.

The rumble of an approaching train got passengers jostling for position before the doors opened. A loudspeaker announcement echoed around the cavernous, enclosed space. Reznick scanned the faces all around him. Some people seemed more stressed than others. But that was natural in a hectic Metro station, packed with men, women, and children, each using up each other's oxygen, getting in each other's space.

Most of the passengers averted their eyes. It was a common and understandable reaction in any large city in the world.

Reznick saw Meyerstein approaching him.

"You OK?" she asked.

"I'm fine. What about you?"

"What about me?"

"Something's bugging you, I can tell."

Meyerstein stared at him, long and hard. "We've got this."

"No, you don't. We haven't had a sniff of Caan or any accomplice. We've got face recognition software scanning all the cameras. What the fuck?"

Meyerstein sighed, waiting for some passengers to walk on by her. "We've got a problem. Six of the cameras in and around this station and mall are either out of action or being repaired."

"So we've lost him?"

"Not necessarily."

"What do you mean?"

"I think he's still here. If he had headed out onto the street, there are numerous cameras that would have detected him. But they haven't. I think he knows the cameras are out of action. He's still here. I know it. And he's waiting for the right moment."

Reznick knew the pressure she would be under from the FBI's Director.

Meyerstein's cell phone rang. She looked at the caller ID and turned her back to Reznick. "Talk to me, Freddie. This better be good." She nodded her head a few times. "Who knows about this?" She nodded again. "Let Roy know, and the command center. Top priority, you hear me?"

She ended the call and stood, shaking her head, her back still to Reznick.

"What is it?" he asked.

Meyerstein turned and faced him. "We may have a handle on who's behind this."

"Who?"

"Get back to work, Jon."

"Who the hell is behind this?"

She held his gaze for a fleeting moment. Then she turned and walked away, heading out of the station.

Thirty-Four

Lieutenant Colonel Scott Caan chewed a codeine tablet to numb the pain of all the Botox and collagen injected into his face, as he headed along one of the climate-controlled underground walkways on the periphery of the Crystal City mall. His quilted jacket was zipped up to the collar and he gripped the brown satchel tightly. He headed along more zigzagging, subterranean passageways and past fashionable boutiques, a modern art gallery, hair salons, gift shops, and a plethora of restaurants. The air was heavy with the smell of pizza and fries.

He couldn't abide the ersatz 1970s architecture. It was like America—soulless, empty, a monolithic creature.

A group of uniformed military with ID badges, easygoing smiles, went by on their break from their Pentagon desk or some other subset of government.

Caan avoided eye contact as he walked on. Up ahead, he saw the huge white clock outside Starbucks. But instead of stopping for a double espresso and granola bar like he sometimes did back at his local coffee shop in Frederick, he took an elevator to the eleventh floor. He stepped out of the elevator and walked past Ruth's Chris Steak House, and on for another fifty yards until he got to a suite of offices. He swiped a card and went in, the door locking softly behind him.

Caan looked around. Beige carpets throughout, rudimentary office furniture, no pictures on the wall. No computers, files, or anything. It was the first time he'd visited the inside of the office. He had scouted out the mall and acquainted himself with the shops and the layout. But they didn't want him to go near the office in case it blew the whole operation.

They were concerned that the one-year lease could be traced to the fake travel agency on Grand Cayman. The cover was in place for a reason.

He pulled down the blinds. A few moments later, his cell phone rang.

"The GPS says you've arrived," an unfamiliar man's voice said.

"This very minute."

"How do you feel?"

"I feel focused. Fresh. I'm ready."

"We know you are. But no doubt you'll be looking forward to your well-deserved vacation."

Well-deserved vacation.

Caan's stomach was churning. He had been given the go-ahead with the operation.

"We're sure it will be most memorable," the voice continued. "Is there anything you still require?"

Caan sighed. "I have everything I need." He felt a lump in his throat. "I'll send you a postcard."

"That would be great. Take care. See you soon."

The call ended.

Caan went to the restroom, stripped off his clothes, removed the blond wig, and took out the blue-colored contact lenses, dropping them on the floor. He scrubbed his face clean and dried it with a small towel. Then he unpacked the fresh clothes from his bag. He pulled on the gray Abercrombie & Fitch sweatshirt, faded jeans, old Nike sneakers, and carefully placed the new tortoiseshell-framed glasses on the bridge of his broken nose. He reapplied some cover cream to his face and neck, concealing the redness from the Botox injections and also lightening his skin tone. Then he brushed back his short, newly dyed brown hair.

Caan closed his eyes for a few moments to compose himself, taking long, deep breaths. He felt sharper and more assured than ever.

Slowly, he opened his eyes.

The man staring back at him in the mirror looked like a complete stranger. That was good. That was very good. He thought he looked like his father had when he'd arrived in America as a young man. He wondered what his father would make of what he was about to do.

Would he understand why he had to do this? The answer was: certainly not. The riches and accolades of America had seduced his father. Caan saw it differently. He saw what America really was. He saw the voracious monster, which polluted, corrupted, and violated peoples and nations. He saw it try to remake them in its own image. No matter the cost.

It was all about spreading liberal democracy. But that was phony. The real reason was resources. Oil, land, people. America's interests were corporate interests. The Pentagon called the shots. The countries they had defiled, the millions they had killed—be it in Vietnam or Central America—had been terrorized into servitude. It wasn't about stopping communism, it was about getting access to resources and cheap labor, so American corporations could stride in and open up sweatshops, and resell products at one thousand percent markups. They would spread the homogenous artificial world of Mickey Mouse and Hollywood to new and emerging markets. But Caan also saw, like millions of others did, the crusade to wipe out *his* people.

His father preferred the easy cynicism and atheism of the metropolitan left. But he hadn't lived to see a new generation emerge.

A generation like his son's. A generation that was about to throw off the shackles of the West. It was 9/11 that had been his wake-up call. He'd seen it for what it was. The call to arms. He began to read about the real "American Dream"—turning countries to ashes. And he realized they were embarking on a crusade to wipe out as many Muslims as they could. He saw it so clearly now.

Caan was from a new generation. He was born in America, but his bloodline was mujahideen. His blood brothers were being slaughtered each and every day by pilotless drones. He had watched the videos, again and again. He saw what American freedom really meant. He saw women and children mown down in cold blood. Screaming all around.

He would avenge them. He would avenge them all. He was going to make his own history. This was their time. Their place. Their future.

Caan snapped out of his thoughts and went through to the kitchen. Inside the top cabinet was a biometric safe. He pressed his thumb against the scanner and, after a couple of beeps, the safe opened. Inside was a black, water-resistant travel bag. He unzipped it and saw a clear plastic box containing two white Christmas baubles adorned by gold glitter.

This was it. This was everything he had prayed for. The time had come.

Caan zipped up the bag and slung it over his shoulder. Then he checked himself in the mirror one last time. His eyes were sparkling, face impassive.

He was ready.

A short while later, his cell phone rang again. This was the final call before his mission was due to commence. It was from a private residence at the foot of the Margalla Hills in Islamabad.

A Pakistani man spoke in Pashto: "Can you remember that verse from your favorite book?"

Every soul shall taste of death, and you should only be paid fully your reward on the resurrection day; then whoever is removed far away from the fire and is made to enter the garden, he indeed has obtained the object; and the life of this world is nothing but a provision of vanities.

Sacred words from the Koran he had been taught to memorize.

Caan spoke in English: "I know the words by heart. They will always be with me."

The Pakistani man sighed. "I'm glad you enjoyed it. Until the next time . . ."

Then the line went dead.

Caan closed his eyes and did his breathing exercises for several minutes. When he opened his eyes, he realized he was smiling.

Until the next time.

Caan walked out of the suite of offices, which automatically locked behind him, and headed toward the elevator. He rode it alone to the underground level, his heart rate quickening as he descended.

The world was going about its business, oblivious to what he was about to unleash. He afforded himself a self-satisfied smile and headed straight for the Metro.

Thirty-Five

The tension in the crammed investigation room within the FBI's Strategic Information Operations Center was palpable as Meyerstein walked in. Stamper was on the phone, hunched behind a paper-strewn desk. She noticed that all the available workspace was being used up by analysts and special agents seconded to the investigation. Six plasma screens were showing real-time feeds. The largest showed the White House Situation Room, and another two screens relayed live pictures from the Metro platform at Crystal City. She caught sight of Reznick and the Red team mingling with the commuters and Christmas shoppers, wondering if she would come to rue the decision to let Reznick join the operation. Two other screens were showing Fox News and CNN. But Meyerstein's gaze was drawn to the sixth feed, showing a fresh-faced white kid with foppish brown hair staring out of the screen.

The kid was a computer genius the FBI had recruited from Brown University after the head of the computer science department—a former military man himself—let his old bosses at the NSA know about the research fellow's ability. A short while later, he was leased out to the FBI.

His name was Brandon Lally, and he was presently in the second-floor office of Congressman Lance Drake, in the nearby Rayburn House Office Building in Washington, DC.

Stamper put down his phone and looked across at her. "Need a couple of minutes, Martha."

She walked up to his desk. "Real quick, Roy."

"You asked us to look into Scott Caan's life."

"So, what've you got?"

"This Scott Caan is something."

"How so?"

"Martha, he's concocted a fantastic cover story."

"Cover story?" Her gaze was drawn again to the plasma screens.

"You gotta listen to this. He was born in Syracuse. That's all been verified. He's an American. His father registered his name four days later. On the surface, all well and good."

"I don't see where this is going, Roy."

"I've not finished. Then we started digging into the father's past. The records we have show his father was also born in Syracuse. But I did some more digging. Turns out his father's name was changed forty-six years ago."

Meyerstein's interest was piqued. "What do you mean *changed*? Changed by who?"

"The father himself. Here's the kicker. You wanna know where he was born?"

"Is he a foreign national?"

"You're gonna love this. Caan's father became a naturalized American, although our records show that he was born here. We don't know how the system shows this, but it's incorrect. The guy was born in Karachi. You believe that?"

"Bullshit."

"I kid you not. You wanna know the father's real name?"

"Spit it out, Roy."

"The real name of Scott Caan's father is Mohammed Khan. Spelled K-H-A-N. How cute is that?"

"How did we miss this?"

Stamper lifted up a copy of the original document from his desk and handed it to Meyerstein. "The father's story reads like something out of the American Dream. He was an immigrant. Came to the country in 1955. He used to work as a political cartoonist. Hence the reason he left. Moved to a small town in upstate New York and became a successful syndicated cartoonist. Winner of the National Press Foundation's Ravelston Award in 1994. Also scooped the 1995 Best American Political Cartoon Competition. Truly bought into the American way of life. So much so that he changed his name. He Americanized it and became Caan. We're still checking, but I'm being told by Freddie that from what they've seen so far, the computer records of Caan's father have been altered by a third party. We're still trying to verify if and when, and by who."

Meyerstein's brain was racing. There were so many strands to the story. She clapped her hands and looked up at the screens. "Brandon, can you hear me?"

"Sure, coming in loud and clear."

"Look, there are a lot of people waiting to hear about a breakthrough. I want to find out if there was anything on Congressman Drake's computer or the Wesley recording. Any progress?"

He nodded. "We're still piecing this together, but we've finally got something."

"Give me what you've got."

"The guy that decrypted the original conversation—Thomas Wesley—is either a genius or a lunatic. He stripped it down to the real voices, but I don't know if he knew who the two guys were."

"I'm listening."

"We've run this through numerous voice analysis tests, checked and rechecked with the NSA—who're freaking out that they seem to have missed this. The problem was that the voice in the conversation Wesley intercepted had been voice morphed. They wanted us to think, if this was uncovered, that it was the Israelis. But it wasn't. We are now one hundred percent certain of the voice. A perfect match."

"Tell me, for Christ's sake," she snapped.

Lally pressed a button on the laptop in front of him, and a grainy color picture came up on one of the screens. The image showed a handsome Asian man with short hair in his late fifties, wearing a military uniform adorned with medals.

Meyerstein's blood ran cold as a ripple of excitement went through the room. She knew the man. They all knew the man.

"Major General Muhammad Kashal. Are you sure? This is the number two in the ISI."

"One hundred percent, ma'am. No doubt about it."

"What about the other guy?"

"No question about it, this is a retired senior CIA officer, Vince Brewling. He works at Norton and Weiss in Miami."

Meyerstein was speechless as she absorbed the information. She couldn't believe how this was playing out, the various strands concealing the true motive: a terrorist attack on America. "Brandon, stay on the line."

Meyerstein took a few moments to compose herself, before turning to face the senior military men and women staring back at her from the largest screen.

"Ladies and gentlemen, Assistant Director Martha Meyerstein, FBI. I've got a critical update you all need to be aware of."

In the White House Situation Room, Richard Blake cleared his throat. "Assistant Director, we're all ears."

"I think we've been blindsided. I have to inform you that we believe this may very well be a renegade Pakistani terrorist operation, currently in progress—as we speak—in the United States, aided and abetted, perhaps unwittingly, by a senior CIA officer."

Audible gasps from the feed.

Meyerstein said, "Within the last few moments, we've just had confirmation that Scott Caan's father's real name was Mohammed Khan. Spelled K-H-A-N."

Blake shook his head. "I always envisaged an Islamist threat to us on home soil from Iran or Syria. Are we absolutely sure this comes through Pakistan?"

Meyerstein composed herself and continued, aware of all the people hanging on to her every word. "One hundred percent. Scott Caan is a sleeper. I repeat, this is a sleeper. Scott Caan is an American. But his background, his deep background, hadn't been checked properly. Someone fucked up many years ago, at the bio-lab. Or maybe immigration, I don't know. There are preliminary indications that immigration files pertaining to Scott Caan's father have been altered to show he was born in the US."

Blake said, "Who's the Agency guy?"

"Vince Brewling. We believe his part was to hire someone to neutralize Frank Luntz. We also believe he hired Reznick. But Brewling was probably kept in the dark about the biothreat to America."

For a few moments, no one talked.

Meyerstein looked up at the screens. "This is a huge breakthrough."

Blake whispered in the ear of the Chairman of the Joint Chiefs of Staff before he spoke. "Martha," he said, "what is your current assessment of where we are?"

"My view would be that there are two separate aspects. The first part was assassinating Dr. Frank Luntz. Jon Reznick got that job through a CIA front organization. We now know Brewling ran this. The law firm and its operations may or may not have had special access program status. We're still checking. The planting of Scott Caan is a long-term plan by the ISI, or factions within the

ISI, to infiltrate the highest echelons of our biosecurity. The proof? An embedded message, which was hidden within a decrypted phone call. This is as serious as it gets. And the ramifications are, of course, profound."

"This is very grave," said Blake. "We have proof that the number two of the ISI, who I know personally, is behind this, and I can say without fear of contradiction, the fallout will be considerable. The fact that the NSA didn't pick this up is also very troubling."

"I must correct you, sir. The NSA did pick this up. Thomas Wesley alerted them. The problem was that no one listened. Sir, what also concerns me is—who were the people who took Thomas Wesley away? Was it the ISI operating with impunity on American soil?"

"Look, I don't think we can assume this was a sanctioned ISI operation."

"With respect, sir, whether this was sanctioned or not their fingerprints are all over this. The number two ordered this. The last briefing I read on Pakistan, which came out only last week, claimed the CIA had an agenda to get the Pakistan military to dismantle the ISI. We're all over the ISI and they don't like it. They don't like what we're doing in the tribal areas of Pakistan and Afghanistan, and they don't like our developing links with India. And they sure as hell don't like the fact that we tracked down Bin Laden in their backyard and took him out."

Blake shifted in his seat. "I can't possibly comment on such talk."

"We can't deny that there are influential people within Pakistan's Inter-Services Intelligence who want America out of their sphere of influence, sir."

Blake stared down from the screen, face reddening. "There is a significant minority within the Pakistani military who are very hostile to any interference in their affairs. They continue to fund the Taliban. And I know Kashal was very involved with helping the Taliban during our proxy war with the Soviet Union. And he is against any American involvement in Pakistan's affairs. Drones and suchlike. We've asked for him to be replaced on at least three occasions. I also believe, just to compound matters, a cousin of his was killed at a wedding by a drone a year or so ago."

Meyerstein said, "We can also point to the killings in Lahore by Raymond Davis, whose diplomatic status was disputed by the Pakistanis. They claim he was a CIA operative."

"I don't want to comment on the Davis case. Besides, the families in Lahore agreed to take the blood money."

"Sir, if that's all, I need to get back to work."

"Most certainly. Look, the President and the National Security Council need to be told right away. But for now, the FBI needs to find and neutralize Scott Caan."

"Very good, sir."

Then the screen went blank.

Thirty-Six

The sound of two chimes echoed around the platform before the station announcement. A woman's voice boomed over the station loudspeaker: "*See it? Say it. The Metro Transit Police would like to remind you, if you see something out of the ordinary please call the Metro Transit Police on 202-962-2121.*"

Reznick watched the passengers thronging the Pentagon Metro platform. The smell from a cheeseburger being eaten by a young woman wafted his way. He felt sick at the odor. His nerves were jangling as he checked his watch. Where the hell was Caan? Had he escaped the Feds' dragnet?

A buzzing noise in his earpiece.

"OK, people," Stamper said. "We're just being told that no man or woman is being allowed onto the platform without ID being checked, body searched, and bags scanned. Just so you know. Keep alert. And let's keep our focus."

The Red team was well spread out across the length of the platform as the rumble and roar of trains came and went. The pale red lights at the platform's edge came on each time a train arrived. The familiar two chimes echoed, as passengers disembarked to the stairs and then the escalators. He could see crowds bunching up as they came down the steps to the platform. The security checks were fraying nerves.

"What the hell's going on?" a passing man asked his partner.

The crowds began to swell, some people squeezed up against the concrete pillars. The numbers kept on rising. Seventy, eighty, one hundred, two hundred, and then well over three hundred.

A guy jostled Reznick from behind. He spun around—a portly man in a suit was showing his hands. "Excuse me," the man said, blushing.

He had to push past a woman with two children in a double stroller as the roar of a train sparked more jostling and pushing.

"Jon, let's just ease up," Stamper said.

Reznick didn't feel like easing up, but he said nothing. He nodded, to show Stamper that he'd heard him. He'd learned from his father that restraint was admirable and it was essential to think of the consequences of your actions.

A train approached the platform and screeched to a halt. The two chimes, and the loudspeaker blared out instructions for people to stand back as the doors opened. Hundreds of passengers streamed out into the large crowd gathered on the platform waiting to board the six-car train. Women in business suits talking into cell phones; a man chewing gum, looking dead in the eyes, his gym bag over his shoulder; a couple of college kids wearing Georgetown sweatshirts, talking and laughing loudly; blue-collar guys, perhaps heading to or from their shift; soccer moms with their kids in tow.

Reznick took in each and every one in a microsecond while keeping one eye on those boarding. He tried to weigh up the way they carried themselves, how they responded to other passengers— all in the blink of an eye.

The person who was attracting most of his attention was the young man wearing a white button-down shirt, jeans, and sneakers, chewing gum and carrying a gym bag, standing at the far end of the platform. He had just gotten off the train and was lingering. Checking his watch once. Twice. Thrice.

"Jeff," Stamper said into his earpiece. "Guy in the white shirt with the gym bag. You got him?"

Reznick saw Jeff nodding.

"We have close-up cameras showing him looking highly agitated. His expression is changing from pained to paranoid, eyes darting real crazy. Escort him off the platform and find out what the hell is wrong with him. Something's not right there."

Jeff replied, "I'm moving in." He stepped toward the young man, who looked around one hundred and eighty pounds, six foot plus, muscular build.

Reznick kept an eye on the guy as he glanced at those still boarding.

Stamper said, "He's got a glazed expression, Jeff, what the hell is wrong with him? Get him out of there."

Suddenly, the man groaned loudly and collapsed in a heap, clutching his chest, convulsing violently on the ground.

"What the hell . . ." Stamper said as Jeff crouched down to tend to the man.

"Call nine one one!" Jeff shouted as he saw a metal dog tag around the young man's neck. "He's epileptic. This man needs an ambulance."

Slowly, a crowd gathered around the man on the ground.

Reznick turned his attention back to the people boarding. It was at that moment he caught sight of something out of the corner of his eye. For a fraction of a second, if that.

A passenger with a black leather travel bag emerged from deep within the crowd, about to embark. The man studiously ignored the throng around the collapsed man and stepped onto the packed waiting train. Dark hair, Nike sneakers, jeans, gray sweatshirt, tortoiseshell glasses. None of it matched the description they'd been given. But the way the man had glided past the concerned crowd without ever looking at the collapsed man had grabbed Reznick's attention.

Instinctively, Reznick pushed through the waiting crowd before his earpiece crackled into life. "Jon! Jon! Guy wearing the gray sweatshirt. Recognition confirmed."

"I got him."

The doors began to close as Reznick shoved through the throng. Anguished shouts of protest. Four foot open, three foot open, two foot open, one foot.

The doors slammed shut.

"Goddamn!" Reznick said. He frantically pressed the button for the doors to open, but they stayed resolutely closed. He pulled out a slim flick-knife on a key ring and jammed it into the doors, working it like he was working a lock. The passengers on the train looked horrified, some trying to get away from the doors.

Reznick clenched his teeth. "Open you fucker!" he said.

He felt some give. A centimeter. Then an inch. He managed to get his hands in the gap and pulled with every fiber of his being until he prized open the doors and stepped onto the train. He closed the knife and put it in his back pocket, as alarmed passengers stared and the doors shut tight behind him.

The train pulled away, and Reznick squeezed his way past the people around the doors and headed toward the next car. But the passengers were packed in like sardines.

He heard the sound of banging on the window and caught sight of Jeff running alongside, hitting the glass as the train departed the station.

"Jon! Jon!" Stamper snapped.

"I'm onboard."

"Jon, you have no authority! I repeat, you have no authority." Stamper's voice was crackling with tension. "Jon, can you eyeball the guy?"

Reznick looked down the rail car and squeezed past the standing passengers. "Negative. I'm in the sixth car, right at the back. I think he's at the front."

"Shit. Did you see him getting on the train?"

"Affirmative."

"Eyes and ears, Jon. Do not approach Caan. We have two guys on this train and we have a reception party at the next stop, Pentagon City."

Reznick ignored the instruction as he squeezed past more passengers and entered the second-last car of the train. He was sure the target had got on near the front of the platform, perhaps the first car.

"Out of my way!" he roared, and he pushed through the throng again, but he wasn't making the progress he needed.

The smell of strong cologne mixed with oil from the tracks lingered in the air as the train hurtled through the tunnel at breakneck speed. Deeper and deeper into the tunnel, closer and closer to its destination.

The seconds were fast disappearing.

Reznick rammed through the passengers into the third car from the rear, pushing and shoving anyone and everyone.

Three more to go.

He was only halfway through the third car when the train began to slow down.

Not going to make it.

He began to push passengers aside as he barged into the next car, the second from the front. Then he was stopped in his tracks. There were a hundred or so people standing in his way. The operator's voice over the loudspeaker announced, "Pentagon City Station. We will shortly be approaching Pentagon City Station."

The train's brakes began to screech.

He pushed past a few archetypal military types wearing ID badges, some holding briefcases. They were going to get off at the Pentagon Metro, the next stop but one.

The darkness of the tunnel seemed to go on forever.

Reznick's mind went into tight-focus mode. He was still in the second car, and once the train stopped at the next station there would only be a minute until the target destination. He wondered if he shouldn't just get out of the emergency doors in the middle of the second car and out onto the platform, and enter the first car from the platform. But the throng inside was too much. Besides, there was no guarantee he would get into the first car, with hundreds of people from the platform possibly trying to get onto the train.

He had to push on through.

"Out of my fucking way!" he said.

A huge guy stood up and blocked his way. Short haircut, smart suit, shiny black shoes. A Pentagon type.

"Hey, buddy, you wanna try and cool it," he said. "There are women and children on this train, if you hadn't noticed."

Reznick barged past but felt himself being pulled back by the collar. He swung around and kicked the guy hard between the legs. The man groaned, and scrunched up his face in agony. Then he crumpled in a heap on the car floor as a couple of women began screaming.

"What the hell was that?" Stamper asked.

Reznick ignored him and brushed past more people. "Out of my fucking way!" he shouted again. Twenty or more passengers were between him and the doors to the first car.

"Jon, what the hell is going on?"

Reznick moved forward. As he made it to the door of the first car, he heard a man shout, "FBI—freeze! Put your hands in the air!"

Reznick stood still. All around, shocked and scared faces. Time seemed to slow.

Then the sound of semi-automatic gunfire and screaming rang out, as mayhem ensued.

Thirty-Seven

Meyerstein and her team stood and listened in horror as the intermittent bursts of gunfire and high-pitched screaming from the Metro train cut the air like a knife. The real-time feed from inside the cars had gone down and the screens were blank.

"OK, talk to me, people. Who's doing the shooting?" she asked, looking around at her team. "I need a visual from the rail cars. All we have is audio. What the hell's happened to the onboard feed?" She pointed across to the IT specialist. "How close are we to getting the onboard video back up and running?"

The FBI's senior computer guy, Gus Shields, punched in commands as he tried to get a connection to the feed.

Meyerstein turned and looked at Roy Stamper. "I'm staring at static and listening to gunshots. Do we still have people on that train? I specifically said I wanted two people per car. And what has happened to Reznick's feed? Goddamn it!"

Stamper pressed his earpiece. "Hold on, Martha." He looked across the room at her as he received an update, shaking his head. "We have only two agents on this train."

"But I asked for two per car. What the hell happened?"

"Christ knows."

"Who are our guys on the train?"

"Special Agents Jacobsen and Meigle. They're relatively inexperienced. ID'd the target shortly before the feed went down."

Meyerstein pointed at a female IT specialist. "Play the last sequence we have of them. I can't believe they gave a verbal warning. What the hell were they thinking?"

Stamper nodded, grim-faced. "They were all given clear instructions to use deadly force."

The young woman tapped on a few keys. Sound boomed out across the conference room.

"Jacobsen here. I got a visual. I repeat, I got a visual. Front car."

Meyerstein began to pace. "Talk to me about the video feed. Do you think the signal is being jammed? Have our guys been taken out?"

Shields shrugged. "Ma'am, we're trying to get an override feed in. Gimme a couple minutes."

"Soon as you can."

"Working on it," he said, frantically tapping away at the keys of his laptop.

The shooting had stopped, but the panicked screams and shouting continued. The sounds from the rail car added to the febrile atmosphere in the conference room. She sensed it, and felt all her team were locked in that moment as the train hurtled through the tunnel. A couple of phones started ringing as Stamper barked out orders for the SWAT team to hold fire.

Meyerstein zoned out the noise and adjusted her headset. "Special Agent Jacobsen and Special Agent Meigle, do you read me? This is Assistant Director Martha Meyerstein, do you copy, over?"

High-pitched screaming from a woman on the train pierced the chatter in the command center.

"Jacobsen and Meigle, do you read me? Respond urgently, what is going on? Jacobsen and Meigle, this is the command center, do you read me, over?"

Meyerstein stood shaking her head, hands on hips. She looked over at the computer guy. "We have an audio feed, so why can't I hear my two special agents in the first car?"

Suddenly, three of the plasma screens came to life. The room fell silent for a few moments. They saw half a dozen men and women and a couple of children, writhing and moaning in agony. A couple of tiny bloody hands moving at the edge of the picture. Blood splatter on the seats and the floor. Abandoned bags, and coats strewn over seats.

Slowly, the camera panned around. The bodies of the two FBI agents slumped on the floor of the car, blood and gray brain-matter all around, some smeared on the windows.

"Oh, my good God," Shields said, wincing in horror. An audible gasp went around the room as some covered their mouths at what they were witnessing.

Meyerstein felt her stomach churn. "Oh shit, Roy, are these our guys?"

"Affirmative, Martha. That's them."

"OK, we need to concentrate, people. We've got a job to do." She pointed to the screens. "Top right, behind the operator's compartment, that's Scott Caan staring out of the window, his back to us. Middle left there is a guy with a gun. Could this be the wingman?"

Stamper nodded. "Has to be."

"Freeze the camera right there!" she shouted. "And run the face recognition software."

"I'm on it," said Shields.

"Roy, alert the three teams on the platform at Pentagon City right away. OK, computer guy, let's pan around the rest of the car."

A few moments later, they saw that around a dozen terrified passengers were huddled—some seriously injured, a couple not moving, some still screaming—in the corner.

"We've got to predict what Caan's next move will be. And we also need to get those people out of there."

Stamper adjusted his headset. "Martha, SWAT team leader is just waiting for the green light to go in."

"This has to be about containment now."

"Martha, we need to get these people off the train!"

"Roy, they're not top priority. We can't risk them releasing biomaterial. We've got to watch and wait. We've got to think of the big picture." She turned around and looked at the SWAT expert—Eric Holden, a former Marine.

Holden nodded. "If we go in, we'll free most of the hostages from the rear of the train. We could set off a flash bomb and stun grenades and recover the passengers, no question. But the situation is all wrong. I say the same—watch and wait."

Meyerstein felt her heart racing. "I also want to know where the hell Reznick is. Where's he while all this is happening?"

Everyone began to talk at once.

Meyerstein held up her hand. "Can we shut down that train? I need an answer."

The Metro specialist, James Handley, shook his head. "The trains are controlled in two separate ways. The cab signals to protect the trains, and a centralized speed-control system."

"Can we get the cab system to pull up a stop signal?" Meyerstein shouted above the rising din.

"No can do. The cab-signal system is not centralized. And the centralized speed control is only about slowing down or braking."

"Right, so we want this train to stay where it is. Can we get a message to the driver? Give me a simple yes or no!"

"Yes."

Meyerstein pointed at Shields. "You've got access. Get a message to the operator. Tell him this is an emergency. Stop the train!"

A few moments later, Shields shouted, "Done!"

"OK, we don't know what's gonna go down. Let's try and solve this problem."

Stamper said, "What if these guys try and flee this train, here and now? What if they decide to pull the plug and release the contents down in the Metro?"

"It's a possibility. But I think as they're so close to the target area, they'll want to do everything in their power to release it at the target destination, to cause maximum impact to the American military and those working inside the Pentagon."

A WMD expert, Dr. Lorna Renwick, interjected, "If the material is released a station early, our computer modeling shows that we might only be talking a few hundred casualties. The next stop down, and there's a significant risk it would spread inside the Pentagon. We don't believe they want to give us a metaphorical bloody nose—they want to bring us to our knees."

Meyerstein nodded. "OK, let's pull up the map and find possible exits out of Pentagon City Metro. I repeat, Pentagon City Metro. And Roy, I want a lockdown on the Pentagon, right now! Have you got that?"

"The whole Pentagon?"

"Yes, the whole Pentagon. This train is still more than one stop away. But no one gets in or out of the Pentagon complex. I don't give a damn if it's a four-star general or a cleaner—no one gets in or out until I say, got it?"

Stamper punched in a secret Pentagon number and relayed the message.

"Also, I want the air con shut down until further notice."

Stamper nodded.

A few moments later, a detailed Metro map appeared on one of the screens.

"OK, let's figure this out. Firstly, how many exits are we talking about from the Pentagon City station?" Meyerstein asked, looking around the room. "And remember the target destination is still one mile away—the Pentagon Metro."

Jimmy Murphy, the all-source analyst who specialized in seeing the big picture, piped up. "The way I see it, they have one obvious route when the train pulls up. Namely, getting off the train and out of the Metro. I disagree with Lorna. I reckon they'd release the biomaterial if they felt they were cornered."

Meyerstein strode across to the screen and picked up a pen to point at the Metro map. "What is this? A walkway?"

Murphy nodded. "That's a pedestrian tunnel under I-395, connecting Army Navy Drive to the Pentagon's south parking garage. You get to it from the Hayes Street parking lot, which is directly opposite the parking lot at the Pentagon City Mall. That's doable."

Meyerstein's mind was whirring. "Roy, let the Pentagon know everything. Are they on lockdown yet?"

Stamper had just come off the phone. "As we speak. Team heading down the escalators of Pentagon City Metro right now. Do the SWAT guys have the green light to storm this train when it arrives?"

Meyerstein paced the room again as her options narrowed. "No. It's containment right now. Besides, who would bet that they wouldn't empty any biomaterials out into the tunnel?"

Renwick nodded. "The dispersal pattern of the virus in an enclosed space as a rushing train goes past would be their ideal scenario."

Stamper relayed the instructions into a headset.

"There's something we're forgetting, people," Meyerstein said. "What if they decide to go on foot, direct to the target from Pentagon City?"

"I thought I covered that?" said Murphy.

"I'm not talking about that route. What if they decided to run direct to the target, through the goddamn tunnel?"

Stamper turned and looked at her, ashen-faced. "Shit."

Meyerstein snapped her fingers. "Let's keep them on this train. Make sure they don't get off. No point taking out a wingman if the main man survives and pulls the pin."

Shields stood up and shouted, "I think I've got something." He turned and looked at Meyerstein. "It's Reznick, ma'am. His audio feed is back up and running."

"Are you sure?"

"Damn straight. Reznick's still in play."

Thirty-Eight

In the panic following the gunfire, Reznick had squeezed in among a dozen terrified passengers, sobbing and crying together in the rear left of the front car. A few feet away, three men and two women lay dead. They were spread-eagled on the floor, blood seeping from head wounds.

Reznick's left cheek was pressed to the gray rubber floor, and he saw four bodies farther up the car. Blood-spattered glass by two window seats, ten feet away, on the opposite side of the aisle. A few cell phones, dropped in the panic. Then he saw two crumpled bodies he assumed were Feds, heads blown apart. Brain matter everywhere.

The vibration of the hurtling train was hurting his face. It sounded like a high-pitched scream.

Reznick adjusted his body position and slid a few inches forward, keeping low as he peered farther down the car, toward the operator's cab. Then he turned his head to the right and saw one of the bad guys. A smartly dressed, clean-shaven man, with sunken dark eyes and a pale face, stood pointing a Beretta 9000S. It was a compact semi-automatic. The kind Reznick liked.

Where were the Feds' guns?

Reznick glanced at the man with the gun to make sure he hadn't noticed his movement. The man's eyes were black and highly agitated, and the awkward way he was holding the gun indicated that he was clearly not a military man.

Reznick was straining his neck as he scanned the floor. The passengers around him whimpered and wept, clutching at each other, shaking like mad. He saw pools of blood, discarded coats, and dropped books and newspapers. Then he noticed something sticking out from under a seat, eight feet or more away.

It was the butt of a gun. But it was out of reach.

Reznick adjusted his position slightly and looked to the opposite side of the aisle, where he saw a guy wearing a gray sweatshirt. He had the same clothes on as Scott Caan. But something about the man's posture didn't chime with Reznick. Slightly hunched, not quite the right build or the right height.

Was this another wingman? Was this a move to confuse? He needed to be sure.

The screech of the train's brakes as it slowed.

Suddenly, the earpiece crackled into life.

"Jon, it's Meyerstein. We have the video feed back up and running. Listen, the guy with the gun is Faizan Agha, a Pakistani national studying at Georgetown. He's the wingman. Tap on the earpiece—once for yes and twice for no."

Reznick discreetly tapped once on the earpiece.

"The guy in the gray sweatshirt has to be Caan, but we haven't ID'd him with the face recognition software as his back is to the camera. Can you ID him?"

Reznick tapped the earpiece twice.

The train slowed down and Reznick looked up, out of the window. The lights of a deserted Pentagon City Metro came into view. Reznick knew that although the Feds were out of sight, they would be all around the station, locking the whole thing down.

The deafening sound of two gunshots rang out at the front of the car, near the operator's cab. Suddenly, people were screaming, fighting, and falling over each other as they retreated and scrambled into the second car. Reznick did the same.

A few moments later: "Jon, do you read me?"

The passengers who had escaped the first car ran toward the rear of the train. Only Reznick was left in the second car.

Meyerstein sighed. "Jon, do you read me? The driver has just been shot. Point blank."

Reznick didn't understand that move. Why would they kill the guy who could get the train to their target destination? He craned his neck farther and peered through into the first car, a handful of people still lying on the ground, either dead or too badly injured to move. "I can't see the shooter. Where the hell is he?"

"Jon, the shooter has now entered the operator's compartment. He's at the controls."

It was then that Reznick saw another man in a gray sweat-shirt—spread-eagled on the floor at the edge of the car, talking into a cell phone and clutching a black travel bag.

It was him.

"There's a third man in the first car, do you copy?"

The man with the gray sweatshirt adjusted his position on the ground slightly and Reznick caught sight of his profile. The broken nose, the strange tight look around the eyes and the puffy cheeks.

"Jon, can you repeat that, over?"

"There's a third man. He fits the profile. Gray sweatshirt, brown glasses. He's got a damaged nose, the cosmetic changes, and he's clean-shaven. He's hiding on the goddamn floor. And he's got a black bag."

"Jon, I can't see him. Are you sure?"

"You must have a blind spot. I can see him clear as day. He's talking into a phone."

"Christ," was all she could say.

The man scrambled across the floor to the other end of the car near the operator's compartment, still clutching the bag.

A few moments passed without any chat from Meyerstein. Then, "We got him. Son of a bitch."

"What's our next move?"

"As it stands, it's contained within the train. We've switched the lights to red so it can't move. The train is in automatic mode."

"But can they override it?"

Suddenly, the train jolted forward, giving him his answer.

"They're trying to move the train."

"We can't allow that."

The train jolted forward again for a couple of yards, and Reznick could hear the passengers at the rear of the train scream. "I can see one guy trying to move the lever. But they're all spread out. As it stands, there's a high probability I could take them all out."

"With what?"

Reznick thought about the Fed's gun under the seat.

Meyerstein paused. "I need certainty."

"Then we need to cut the power and put the train into darkness, do you copy?"

"Are you serious?"

"Make it happen, and I'll bring them down. It'll give me the cover I need."

Thirty-Nine

The train lurched forward as it headed into the tunnel, and Reznick was thrown to the floor.

"Jon, you gotta kill them all," Meyerstein said into his earpiece. "Cut the goddamn power!"

"Jon, five seconds till the power goes down. Do you copy?"

"Affirmative. Leave it with me."

A click signaled the conversation was over.

Reznick was on his own. He peered through into the first car. The man with the gun was still shouting instructions. Time slowed as he heard his heart pound.

Suddenly, they were plunged into darkness. Muffled screams from the rear cars, and terrible wails as the train ground to a screeching halt.

Reznick crawled fast toward the front car. Head low, body low—flush with the ground. The military crawl perfected in muddy trenches under barbed wire, battle-hardened Marines screaming abuse. Stay low or get hit.

Closer and closer. Inches.

He now saw three separate silhouettes. Two in the operator's compartment and one on the far right.

He crawled into the first car and felt thick fluid on his hands. Blood.

To his right were the dead FBI men, lying slumped. He felt through the men's clothes in the dark, and took out a handgun magazine from an inside pocket, putting it in his back pocket. Then he groped around on the floor until he felt the cold metal of the gun.

He pulled back the slide, and focused on the guy on the right.

He edged a few inches closer. Then he aimed, and squeezed the trigger. Flashes of fire spewed out of the gun, illuminating the darkness around him. The figure collapsed in a heap. Reznick rolled sideways and aimed at the taller man in the operator's compartment. He fired off two shots and the bullets tore through the glass and into the man's head. The fire from the gun lit up the blood-spattered shards of glass. The smell of cordite and smoke was heavy in the air.

But the third man had disappeared.

Had he hit the ground? Had he been hit by a ricochet?

"I've hit two of them, both down!" he shouted. "Can't see the third."

Reznick crawled forward fast, keeping his head low. He moved past the slumped body of the first man he'd killed. Broken glass crunched as he crawled through on his hands and knees, ignoring the searing pain as the shards cut into his skin.

Then he pointed his gun at the operator's compartment and fired off the rest of the magazine. Glass shattered. The sound was deafening in such an enclosed space. His ears were ringing. In the distance, he heard a scream.

Reznick got up and kicked in the operator's door. Caan's second accomplice—dead—and the slumped body of a man in uniform, drenched in blood, glass covering his corpse.

Then he saw a floor panel had been lifted.

Caan had escaped.

"Our guy has gone! I repeat, he's gone."

"Get after him!"

Reznick ejected the empty magazine and slid the new one in until it locked into place. He pulled back the slide and tucked the gun into his waistband. Then he lowered himself onto the tracks and crawled out from underneath the train.

Farther up the line, in the tunnel, the sound of crunching footsteps on gravel.

"He's on the tracks heading toward Pentagon Metro station!"

"Take him out, for Chrissakes!"

Reznick sprinted along the wooden beams of the tracks and headed deep into the blackness of the tunnel. He reckoned Caan had a hundred-yard start. Maybe more.

His blood was pumping and his heart pounding as he gave chase in pitch darkness, all senses switched on.

He pumped his arms harder as he went deeper into the tunnel. Up ahead on the right, he saw a pale blue light. He knew it was an emergency phone. The smell of dirt and damp and oil pervaded the musky air. But the ghostly light gave Reznick the first glimpse of the running silhouette.

The guy was fit. And he had a bag slung over his shoulder.

"He's got to be stopped. And quick."

Reznick knew a headshot still wasn't possible. His mind raced, scenarios running through his brain. He had to stop him in his tracks, now. But a shot to the back—the best target area—might inadvertently pierce the bag as well, and release the biocontents, releasing them into the tunnel.

Caan weaved and bobbed along the tracks. Reznick was gaining on him. Then he disappeared from sight.

"Jon, talk to me!"

Up ahead, the sound of heavy panting and stones crunching told Reznick that Caan was still on the move. Reznick picked up the pace. He felt sweat sticking to his shirt, beading his forehead.

"Reznick!"

His breathing was getting harder. He didn't need distractions. But he didn't want to pull out the earpiece.

Reznick looked down the pitch-black tunnel and saw two tiny, pale yellow strips in the distance. Reflections from Caan's sneakers.

He locked onto the tiny yellow spots, and began running along the concrete ties that ran down the tracks. Faster and faster, gaze fixed on the yellow strips, which moved up and down like pistons as Caan kept running.

A couple of hundred yards up ahead, a red light. Not a train signal, more like a road sign. Reznick's eyes were getting more accustomed to the dark. The red light bathed the tracks in a soft glow. The silhouette was heading straight for it.

Suddenly, the figure stopped and turned. A glint of metal and a flash, before a deafening bang and what sounded like a ricochet.

A searing pain tore through Reznick's right shoulder as if it were on fire. He gritted his teeth as the pain threatened to overwhelm him. It was like a knife in his flesh. He stared into the suffocating darkness and tried to pinpoint Caan's whereabouts, as sweat dripped from his brow. He tentatively touched the wound.

"What the hell is going on down there?" Meyerstein said. "Jon, I need you to speak to me."

Reznick's mind flashed back to the deranged pain of Delta's vomit-inducing, forty-mile cross-country runs. The sixty-pound backpack and weapons. Staff sergeants looking on—no interaction. They didn't give feedback if you were doing bad or good, or going too slow. It screwed a lot of guys up who couldn't adjust to it. It was all about self-motivation. Who had the will to dig deep without any help? He'd had to push through the pain and psychological barriers himself, time and time again. He'd taught himself to love the pain.

Pain is your friend. Suck it up and see.

The sound of running up ahead on gravel echoed around the tunnel. Caan was on the move.

Reznick willed himself to ignore the pain and head down the tracks into the blackness, with only the palest of red lights for guidance. Up ahead, the sound of a metal door screeching open. A sickly yellow light spilled out, illuminating Caan for the briefest moment.

"Jon, are you all right, copy?"

"I've been grazed. I'm OK, I'll survive."

A long pause, then a sigh. "Take him down with a body shot if need be, Jon. Do you copy?"

"Too risky. I need to get in closer."

Reznick felt sweat running down his face and into his ears as he pounded down the tracks. He felt the earpiece slipping, and before he could stop it the thing had fallen out of his ear. "Goddamn," he said.

He was on his own.

Reznick sprinted onward, toward the red sign. A hundred yards. Then fifty. Then he saw it was a red emergency sign glowing in the dark. Yellow markings on a metallic door.

He yanked at the handle and went inside. He flinched as the harsh, yellowish light burned his eyes. A gray sweatshirt and black bag lay discarded on the ground.

Above him, he heard scuffed footsteps and urgent breathing as Caan climbed the stairs. A surge of raw adrenaline shot through Reznick's veins. He ignored the terrible pain in his shoulder and bounded up the concrete steps two at a time, knowing he was a sitting duck. But he had to catch the bastard.

Suck it up.

That's what Reznick had told himself during the Delta selection process as he'd hit mental and physical walls. *Suck it up. Enjoy the misery. It will not beat you. Nothing will ever beat you. Ever.*

He thought of his father, wearing his medals at the Vietnam memorial. He thought of Lauren in her hospital bed. And he thought of his wife, the split second before the towers collapsed. He imagined the horror and fear that must have engulfed her as she disappeared into the dust and the concrete and twisted metal.

He had to do this. He would do this. And he would catch that fuck, for all of them.

The adrenaline continued to surge through his body, giving him huge amounts of energy. He heard the sound of a metal hatch creaking open. Light from the street leaked in, and the roar of traffic and beeping horns.

Reznick climbed higher and higher, until he emerged blinking onto a busy Arlington street. He was on a sidewalk, the sound of police sirens in the distance. He scanned his unfamiliar surroundings, trying to get a fix on the target. The monolithic monstrosity that was the Pentagon loomed in the distance. But then he got a visual on a running figure in the distance.

Reznick ran across the road toward the Pentagon, as cars screeched to a halt and peeped their horns.

"Hey, buddy, you wanna look where you're goin'?"

Reznick kept focused on the distant figure. Through an underpass and across another road. He saw a sign for South Fern Street, and then a sign for the Pentagon Metro. He was gaining ground.

Reznick ran toward hundreds of people milling around police cars and FBI vehicles, red lights flashing. He saw a cordon and realized the Metro station had been evacuated.

Then he spotted Caan, and what looked like an ID badge dangling from his neck. Reznick fixed his gaze on Caan's jacket as he disappeared into the crowd. The last thing he saw was yellow letters emblazoned on the back—"FBI."

A cold finger of fear ran down Reznick as he ran toward the crowd, but he stayed focused on Caan. He barged through the crowd of people—who parted, some shouting and yelling—until he came face to face with two huge cops who were standing behind some yellow police tape.

"Freeze! Police!" one shouted.

Reznick put up his hands as he slowed down and walked toward the cop. He saw Caan head into the station.

"Easy, fella, keep your hands where I can see them."

Anger gnawed at Reznick's guts. The bastard was getting away.

Reznick put out his hands, as if the officer should cuff him. The cop obligingly pulled his cuffs from his belt, and Reznick kicked the gun out of his hands. Then he smashed him in the side of the face, knocking the cop out cold. The other officer went clumsily for his gun. Reznick moved quicker, and kicked him in the stomach. He fell to his knees and the gun fell from his hands.

Reznick burst through the tape and into the Metro station. He headed down some stairs and then an escalator, catching sight of Caan running past some automated ticket machines to the Pentagon screening area. Heavily armed Pentagon police with dogs blocked the way.

A shot of adrenaline coursed through his body one more time as one of the cops took aim and fired at Reznick. The bullet whizzed past his head and ricocheted off some metal.

He sprinted down an escalator and then ran up another.

Caan was on it. Then he was gone.

But then he caught sight of Caan, running down yet another escalator.

Reznick closed in.

At the bottom, Caan turned around and his black eyes met Reznick's. The face was puffy, the nose broken, the cheekbones high. *It was him.* He grinned and unzipped his jacket.

Reznick didn't hesitate. He pointed his gun straight at Caan's forehead and aimed. Then he squeezed the trigger twice. The shots rang out, and echoed around the station. Caan collapsed as blood streamed from the side of his head.

Reznick ran down the moving escalator, gun trained on Caan. He stepped over the body, then kneeled down beside him. Pressing his index finger to Caan's neck, he felt for a pulse.

Nothing.

He opened up Caan's jacket and ripped open a huge Velcroed inside pocket. Inside were two white Christmas baubles with a glitter pattern.

Reznick carefully closed the pocket, and was about to stand up when a voice behind him shouted, "Don't fucking move. FBI SWAT."

Reznick froze.

"Drop the gun!"

Reznick loosened his grip and dropped the gun, which made a heavy clunking sound as it hit the moving escalator.

"Turn around and take three steps backward onto the concourse, hands on head."

Reznick did as he was told. "Don't touch the Christmas baubles in his pocket, whatever you do! Look, I'm on your side. I've just taken this guy out. He was the target. Speak to Meyerstein of the FBI."

"Shut the fuck up and listen. I want you to strip off. Shirt, jeans, shoes, socks. Right down to your underwear."

Reznick complied, ignoring the burning pain in his shoulder. He stood in his boxer shorts, hands on head, blood dripping onto the stone concourse.

"Now, slowly turn around."

He complied, and stared straight at them. They stood, guns pointing at him, gazes locked onto his muscled torso and the red Delta dagger tattooed on his chest.

"Very slowly—*very slowly*—take three steps toward us, and then kneel down with your hands still on your head."

Reznick walked toward them and kneeled, hands on head. "Listen to me," he said. "Do not move that guy on the ground. Do not touch the Christmas baubles, d'you hear me?"

He could feel himself slipping away. He fought to remain conscious. Then he looked up at the lead SWAT guy. He saw Meyerstein appear from behind. She smiled and walked toward him.

Reznick smiled back. "What the hell took you so long?"

Then everything turned black.

Forty-One

The hours that followed were a bit of a blur as Reznick lapsed in and out of consciousness. He felt cold and was losing blood fast. As he was rushed to the emergency room of George Washington University Hospital, the voices of the paramedics and then the doctors and nurses echoed in his head as if in a dream. His every breath induced searing pain in his shoulder.

"Goddamn," he snarled.

Harsh hospital lights. Blurred faces staring down at him.

He felt himself drift away. Deeper and deeper into a faraway land. Elisabeth's face was looking down at him. He felt her stroking his hair.

"*It's OK, Jon. Everything's gonna be all right.*"

When he came to, a young female doctor was smiling at him as she bandaged his shoulder wound. "Welcome back," she said. "You got lucky. The bullet narrowly missed the brachial artery."

Reznick didn't feel lucky. He took a few moments to get his bearings. "I thought it was only a graze." His throat was dry, and he barely got the words out.

"We've given you strong antibiotics, and that will hopefully keep infection at bay. No serious tissue damage—how, I don't know. However, you'll need to rest up for a few days."

The doctor left the room and Reznick was on his own. He tried to move his shoulder, and winced at the searing pain. He tried to sit up straight but his head felt light.

Damn.

He looked around his room. It was all hospital-fresh, and white. The smell of disinfectant in the air.

His eyes felt heavy and he drifted off to sleep. He dreamed of Lauren. As a baby. As a toddler, walking on the beach, holding his hand. And he dreamed of her as a young woman, talking about college. Talking about her mother, late into the night. He dreamed of his wife on *that* day. It was the same dream. Before the towers fell. Then he was back home alone. The smell of the salt air, and before him the cool blue waters in the cove.

When Reznick came around again, he had been asleep for fourteen hours straight.

He was aware that someone else was in the room. He struggled to open his eyes. In his peripheral vision, he saw Stamper and four unsmiling Feds.

Reznick turned and looked at them. One was holding up an expensive-looking navy single-breasted suit, white shirt, pale blue tie, and black Oxford shoes.

"What's all this?"

Stamper was chewing gum. "You're coming with us."

"Not until you tell me how my daughter is."

Stamper smiled. "She's opened her eyes."

Reznick closed his eyes as relief flooded through his body. He realized how close he'd come to losing her.

"You wanna get ready, Reznick?"

"Are we going on a date, Roy?"

Stamper shook his head and grinned. "You're crazy, you know that?"

Reznick eased himself out of bed and winced. His shoulder was heavily bandaged. His hands were cut from the shards of glass in the Metro car. He put on the shirt, taking an age to button it up. He got on the suit, and tried to tie his shoelaces but couldn't manage it. Stamper kneeled down to help.

Reznick looked in the mirror. It didn't look like him. He looked like a stockbroker. He couldn't remember the last time he'd had to wear a suit.

He was signed out and escorted to the elevator. Inside, Reznick turned to Stamper. "How did you know my size?"

Stamper chewed his gum and tried to stifle a grin. "We measured you up when you were unconscious, tough guy."

Reznick shook his head and smiled. "So, are you going to let me know what this is all about? Where are we going?"

"You'll see."

It was dark when they left the hospital's staff entrance to go to a waiting car in the basement garage. He was strapped into the back seat and they drove off. The Washington traffic was a crawl, despite it being evening. He stared out at the people driving past, going about their business, unaware of what had really happened down in the Metro.

His thoughts were scrambled. He thought of Lauren, way down in Pensacola, safe and alive—and for that, he was truly thankful. But he also thought of Maddox, and wondered what his role was in the whole operation.

A short while later, Reznick caught a glimpse of the Hoover building—FBI Headquarters.

"What's going on, Roy?" Reznick asked.

Stamper shook his head as they drove toward a basement garage and scanned their IDs in an electronic reader. Inside, he was marched into the building and taken up to the seventh floor. They got off the elevator, and he was escorted along a corridor to a large conference room. The FBI's most senior executives—including Meyerstein—clapped him in.

Reznick felt light-headed as he was introduced to the Director and toasted with single malt and mulled wine. A letter was read out from the President, thanking him for his efforts. Reznick felt embarrassed at being the center of attention.

He shrugged off his natural inclination to avoid such gatherings, and knocked back the amber liquid, feeling a warm glow inside. The morphine combined with the whisky took the edge off the pain.

After several minutes of excruciating small talk, and a rambling speech from the Assistant Director about "the American way," Meyerstein asked Reznick to come to her office. "Take some weight off," she said, sitting on the edge of her desk, hands folded demurely.

Reznick slumped down and took a few moments to take in the room. The shiny mahogany desk was uncluttered—on it was a gold-framed, black-and-white photo of Meyerstein and her kids, playing in a park. On the wall to his left, a plasma screen, showing a real-time feed from Lower Manhattan. Opposite was a wall covered in awards, and a few pictures of Meyerstein with the Director and the President.

She shifted slightly and looked at him, face impassive. "How are you feeling?"

"I've felt better."

"Well, for what it's worth, you scrub up well."

"Jon Reznick, style icon. What d'you think? Front cover of *GQ*, right?"

Meyerstein smiled and edged off her desk, sitting down in a black leather seat behind it. "Before I forget, you want to know the latest news on Lauren, as of fifteen minutes ago?"

"How is she?"

"She's now fully conscious and has made a remarkable recovery over the last twenty-four hours. Jon, they've done all the diagnostic tests and they're satisfied your daughter is not damaged in any way."

"Thank God."

"Jon, what I'm going to say now doesn't go beyond these four walls, am I clear?"

"I'm listening."

"This didn't happen. None of it."

"I understand."

"The incident is going to be described as an undercover surveillance operation and a gunman killing a couple of Feds. Then he was cornered and shot. There will never be any reference to biomaterials or any foreign governments or their operatives by you to anyone, ever. This never happened. Are we clear?"

"Whatever you say."

Meyerstein looked at him with her cool blue eyes and smiled. "We're in your debt, Jon. But I think we rode our luck, don't you?"

"Sometimes you make your own luck."

"I can't remember when I had so many hard calls to make. But I guess, sometimes, the rule book is just a guide, right?"

"The first rule is that there are no rules."

Meyerstein smiled. He liked her smile.

"You might be interested to know that preliminary tests show that the two baubles recovered from Caan here in Washington contained the same virus as the batch used in New York City. Our scientists say that the contents of two vials were found in the baubles. It's estimated the aerosol containers in New York contained one vial. But thankfully, unlike New York, there was no release here in Washington. There are no traces. And we've now accounted for all the biomaterial stolen from the lab in Maryland."

"What about the guys behind it?"

"What about them?"

"I assume you know who was responsible?"

Meyerstein steepled her fingers on her desk. "I can't say any more."

"Can't or won't?"

"Let's just say we're dealing with this in our own inimitable way." She shrugged. "Is the inquisition over?"

"What do you know about the three people who visited the small hotel in Washington where I took Luntz? Are you at liberty to say who they were?"

"French contractors who were born in Algeria. We believe they killed our special agent at the St. Regis, and then were ordered to the small hotel to kill you and Luntz. But they've disappeared off the planet. We're using diplomatic channels to try and find out where they are."

Reznick felt his eyes getting heavier.

He looked at Meyerstein. She seemed rested and relaxed.

"What about Luntz?"

"What about him?"

"How is he?"

"He's doing well, thank you. I'm told an antidote and vaccine is being rushed into advanced trials in the next twenty-four hours."

"Pass on my regards."

"I'll say you were asking after him. But I think he'll need counseling for the next ten years after what happened to him."

Reznick laughed.

Meyerstein shifted in her seat. "Do you mind me asking something?"

"Sure."

"Why did you trust me, down in Key West? I mean, I could've double-crossed you, couldn't I? It would've been easy for me not to keep my side of the bargain."

"Gut instinct. You have a face I can trust."

Meyerstein smiled. "Yeah?"

"Oh yeah. I've enjoyed working with you, Meyerstein."

"My name's Martha. Do you think you'll remember that, being so doped up and all?"

"Sure. Martha. I like that."

Meyerstein ran a hand through her hair before she stifled a yawn. "It's been an experience, that's for sure."

Reznick felt a burning twinge in his shoulder and winced at the pain.

"You OK?"

"It's nothing. Tell me, what about the guy down in Miami pulling the strings? Brewling."

"We believe he has been professionally disappeared."

"Meaning?"

"Meaning he's being protected by some of those behind this plot. But we'll find him. I personally think he was being played as well."

Reznick said nothing.

"But we have had some progress. We've already intercepted and decrypted a conversation he had with the president of a Swiss bank where he holds five separate accounts, via an NSA operation. We believe the call was made onboard a private jet flying over the Mediterranean."

"You mind if I hear it?"

Meyerstein arched her eyebrow. "And why, may I ask, would you want to know the sound of his voice? I can't allow any spillover from this, do you understand?"

Reznick nodded. "Just curious."

She picked up a remote control and pressed a couple of buttons. The speakers on the huge TV came to life. Then the voice of Brewling.

"Are all my assets liquid or will I have to wait to transfer them to the Caymans? I need this situation to be resolved right away."

The glass of whisky and the morphine had dulled Reznick's brain. His exhausted mind was trying to process the voice. Something about it seemed vaguely familiar.

The voice spoke again. It was cold. Chilling. Mechanistic in its delivery.

The voice was familiar. Eerily familiar. Slowly, it dawned on him.

"You OK?" Meyerstein said. "You look as if you've seen a ghost."

Reznick forced a smile.

It was a ghost. The voice was of the man he knew only as Maddox. He'd been played from the moment the call was made to his cell phone at home in Maine.

"You OK?"

"That voice, are you sure that's Brewling?"

"One hundred percent."

"Well, I'm not an expert in voice analysis, but that sounds a helluva lot like my handler. But I knew him as Maddox."

Meyerstein leaned back in her seat, face impassive. "Maddox. Thanks for that, I'll pass that on. We'll find him, don't worry."

Reznick got up from his seat and reached over to shake Meyerstein's hand. She stood up, and smiled as he gripped her soft hand tight.

"Nice working with you," she said. Her hand felt warm. "Look, we can move you to a safe house until this is resolved."

"Don't worry about me. My only concern is Lauren, and she's safe. I owe you one."

"You don't owe me anything."

He let out a long sigh. "Look, I gotta go."

"Now? Where?"

Reznick smiled. "I'm going to see my daughter."

Epilogue

Six months later, Reznick was sitting alone on his deck—the house to himself—nursing his second bottle of beer on a balmy, early-summer evening in Mid Coast Maine. The last remnants of the sun had turned the ocean a pale red, the tops of the old oaks on fire. He felt at peace, for the first time in months.

His daughter, Lauren, had moved to a new school in upstate New York. She emailed every day with boundless optimism, talking about walks with her friends in the rolling hills.

He was missing her, but the dark days of last winter had passed.

Reznick didn't venture far. He had hung around the Rockland area most of the time. He walked past the abandoned sardine-packing plant his father used to work in. He tried to imagine how hard it must have been for his dad to do a job he loathed, with memories of Vietnam burned into his mind. Reznick took long walks on the beach, did the garden, and took time to watch the flowers grow. He occasionally sat on the beach in the cove and thought of his wife and daughter, playing on the same sand all those years earlier, laughing and joking. He imagined what his life would have been like if his wife had survived. He wondered if they'd have had more children. When he closed his eyes and listened to the water rush up the sand, he thought he heard their laughter and voices hanging in the breeze.

The rest of the time, he tended the trees his father had planted. This was his home. The clapboard colonial his father had built with his own hands. The oak floors, the crafted shutters, the beige and ocean-blue walls.

When his phone rang, he saw an unfamiliar number on the caller ID. He let it ring and ring. Eventually, he picked up.

"Yeah?" he answered.

"Sorry to bother you, Jon." It was the soft voice of Meyerstein.

Reznick sat up straight, rubbing his eyes. "Hi. Long time no hear."

"Indeed. How are you, Jon?"

"I'm fine. What about you?"

She let out a long sigh. "Working. You know how it is."

"Do you guys ever take a vacation?"

"Not as often as I'd like. Look, I'm just calling to check on how Lauren is. I believe she's moved to a new school."

"She has. And she's good. And for that, I'm truly grateful."

"Look, Jon, I have some news."

"What kind of news?"

"Jon, I think from this moment on, Lauren can sleep securely in her bed. It's all over. The job is done."

"I'm sorry, what do you mean?"

"Turn on the TV. CNN."

"Why?"

"Just do it."

A long silence opened up on the line.

Reznick went inside, still holding his bottle of beer in one hand, the cell in the other. He put down the beer, picked up the remote, and switched on the TV to CNN.

"*And the breaking news this hour,*" the male anchor in Atlanta said, "*is that the second-in-command of Pakistan's intelligence agency, the ISI, has been blown up by a car bomb in Islamabad.*"

Reznick stared, transfixed, at the screen.

The anchor continued: "*Pakistani military sources tell us that Major General Muhammad Kashal's car may have been followed by two men on motorbikes from his heavily guarded compound before the remote detonation took place. Pentagon sources say that Kashal's loss was a blow in the fight against the Taliban, both in and outside Pakistan.*"

A picture of a smiling general in full military regalia appeared in the top-right corner of the screen.

Reznick stared at the photo and realized what Meyerstein was saying. This was the mastermind. They had got him—and someone else was getting the blame. A black flag operation, if ever there was one.

"*And in a bizarre twist to this story, a former American military advisor was in the car with Kashal and also died in the explosion. Sources say Vince Brewling had previously served as the CIA station chief in Islamabad in the 1980s, and is believed to have been good friends with General Kashal when they worked together to oust the Soviet Union from Afghanistan. Sources are reporting that Mr. Brewling was paying a private visit to Kashal, and was not on government business.*"

A picture of a whey-faced man with mottled skin and rheumy blue eyes was shown in the top-left of the screen. So this was the man he knew only as Maddox.

Cold justice had been served.

Reznick drank the rest of his beer, switched off the TV, and went outside.

"It's finished, Jon," Meyerstein said. "But I've got a proposition."

"And what's that?"

"I'd like you to work with us."

"For the FBI?"

"On a consultancy basis, so to speak. Certain situations might arise where a man of your talents—"

Reznick sighed. "I'll think about it."

"How about I call you in the morning?"

Reznick stared up at the billions of stars in the inky black sky, as the roar of the ocean echoed deep down in the cove.

"I said I'll think about it," he said.

Acknowledgments

With deepest gratitude, I would like to thank the following people for their help and support:

Many thanks to my editor, Jane Snelgrove, and everyone at Thomas & Mercer for their hard work, enthusiasm, and belief in this book.

Special mention must go to Angela D. Bell, FBI, in Washington, DC, who assisted my numerous questions with good grace and impeccable professionalism. Many thanks also to the FBI field office in Miami.

I was very fortunate that Larry Vickers, formerly of 1st Special Forces Operational Detachment–Delta, commonly referred to as Delta Force, was another who gave his time and expert technical knowledge freely.

During research, I found *Delta Force: The Army's Elite Counterterrorist Unit* (Avon Books) by Charlie Beckwith and *Inside Delta Force* (Bantam Dell) by Eric L Haney really useful books.

I would also like to thank Ash Swanson in Miami Beach for helping out with South Beach research.

Lastly, my family and friends for their encouragement and support. And, most of all, my wife Susan, who was with me every step of the way as each draft developed, offering brilliant advice, coupled with no small amount of patience.

About the Author

J. B. Turner is the author of the Jon Reznick trilogy of conspiracy action thrillers (*Hard Road*, *Hard Kill*, and *Hard Wired*), as well as the Deborah Jones political thrillers (*Miami Requiem* and *Dark Waters*). He loves music, from Beethoven to the Beatles, and watching good films, from *Manhattan* to *The Deer Hunter*. He has a keen interest in geopolitics. He lives in Scotland with his wife and two children.

Made in the USA
Columbia, SC
22 April 2021